BUT NOT FORGOTTEN

A CLINT WOLF NOVEL
(BOOK 1)

BY

BJ BOURG

WWW.BJBOURG.COM

TITLES BY BJ BOURG

LONDON CARTER MYSTERY SERIES

James 516

Proving Grounds

Silent Trigger

Bullet Drop

Elevation

Blood Rise

CLINT WOLF MYSTERY SERIES

But Not Forgotten

But Not Forgiven

But Not Forsaken

But Not Forever

But Not For Naught

But Not Forbidden

But Not Forlorn

But Not Formidable

BUT NOT FORGOTTEN
A Clint Wolf Novel by BJ Bourg
Originally published by Amber Quill Press
December 6, 2015

This book is a work of fiction.
All names, characters, locations, and incidents are products of the
author's imagination, or have been used fictitiously.
Any resemblance to actual persons living or dead, locales, or events
is entirely coincidental.

Cover design by Christine Savoie of Bayou Cover Designs

PUBLISHED IN THE UNITED STATES OF AMERICA

For Amanda...you lit this fire.

I want to thank Sheriff Craig Webre for his support throughout my law enforcement career. While I'd always wanted to be a writer, I never knew what genre to pursue, and it wasn't until I'd worked as a detective for six years that I read a book suggesting I write what I know. Thanks to Sheriff Webre approving all of my training requests, transfers, and promotions over the years, I was fully equipped to write mysteries. I want to thank Shelly Ourso and Christie Pepper for their thoughts on the first draft, and Ben Harang for letting me bounce ideas off of him. I owe a great debt of gratitude to EJ Gilmer, managing editor of Amber Quill Press, for "discovering" me and for all of her editorial services. It's always a pleasure to work with her. To Brandon and Grace: as always, thanks for giving me the best job ever...DAD!

CHAPTER 1

Wednesday, June 13

I stepped out of my truck, walked to the passenger's door and opened it for Michele. She leaned her right leg out first, the slit in her dress pushing upward to reveal a slender sculpture of porcelain perfection. I planted my hand firmly on her exposed thigh, leaned forward and kissed her fully on the lips.

Michele pulled away and turned her head. "Don't, Clint! Not while Abigail's in the truck."

"How many times do I have to tell you there's nothing wrong with a kid seeing her mom and dad kiss?"

Michele planted both feet on the pavement and straightened her dress. "How many times do I have to tell you it makes me uncomfortable?"

I grunted, pushing her door shut. "Whatever."

I started to walk toward the back of the truck to open the door for Abigail, but Michele grabbed me by the arm and leaned into me. She looked up, her green eyes sparkling with moisture. "You know what I love about you?"

"Stop trying to make up for rejecting me."

"I'm not." Michele puckered her lips. "Seriously...do you know what I love about you?"

"My manly gait?"

She laughed, shook her head.

"My money?"

She cocked her head sideways. "You're a homicide detective, not a doctor. Guess again."

"Um, let me see…" I stared upward. I had to squint against the setting Louisiana sun that was taking a lazy dive behind the skyscrapers to the west. I suddenly dropped my mouth open and stared in feigned disbelief at my wife. "You naughty girl! You love me for my large—"

"Clint Wolf, don't you say that!" Michele shot a glance toward the truck. "Abigail can hear you."

I turned and saw Abigail drawing on the opposite window with washable markers. "She can't hear me, and she certainly didn't know I was trying to kiss you earlier. Look at her—she doesn't even remember she's got parents. Watch this…Abigail, sweetie, Santa Claus isn't real. Mommy is the one who leaves—"

"Stop it!" Michele grabbed my shoulders again, yanking me around to face her. Her grin pushed the dimples deeper into her face. "No…while I love all of you, that's not what I was getting at. What I love about you is that—after nearly seven years of marriage—you still open my door for me."

I shrugged. "Force of habit. I've done it for all my wives."

She laughed, poked my stomach playfully, then suddenly glanced down, felt along my waistband and frowned. "Your gun. You forgot it's on."

"I'm not taking it off."

"You can't carry it in private businesses anymore. You know that."

"It's a stupid law."

"But it *is* the law."

"No one will know. It'll be fine."

Michele folded her arms across her chest. "Clint, you know how I feel about breaking rules. What kind of example would that be setting for Abigail?"

"Baby, the protesters have been getting more and more belligerent. Three restaurants got robbed just—"

Michele moved forward and cupped my face in her warm hands. "Sweetheart, you said yourself the riots have been reduced to the inner city. We'll be fine. Just please do this for me. No gun. Okay?"

"Every time we go out now you do this."

"And you always see it my way." Michele smiled. "Why don't you just put it up so we can go inside and enjoy dinner like a normal family?"

I sighed, blowing out forcefully. "One of these days I'm going to stop letting you win all of our arguments."

"You know what they say, Happy wife—"

"No more life." I jerked my concealed-carry holster from under my shirt and locked it in the glove compartment, while Michele grabbed Abigail from the backseat. We then walked the two blocks to the restaurant, me holding one of Abigail's hands and Michele holding the other. Abigail jumped into the air intermittently, and we hoisted her upward each time.

"I can fly," she yelled.

We laughed all the way to the restaurant. I held the door for Michele and Abigail, then followed them into the dim interior. The hostess recognized us. "Table for three, booth in the corner; am I right?"

I smiled. "You've got it."

When we reached the booth, I sat where I could see the door and scanned the room before reading the menu. There were about a dozen tables occupied, mostly couples. I looked across the table at Michele and smiled. "Your eyes look really green tonight."

"And yours look really brown."

"That's because they are—"

"Everyone get down!"

I shifted my eyes to the front door, which had burst open. Four masked men stormed into the restaurant waving guns around. I instinctively reached for my waistband, but cursed out loud when I felt an empty belt.

The men spread out across the restaurant quickly, taking over the room in seconds. The guy who looked to be the leader grabbed the hostess and shoved his pistol in her face. "Open the register now!"

The other three men made everyone put their faces into the table. Michele reached out with one hand and dug her nails into my wrist. She clutched Abigail with her other arm. Her eyes were wide. Abigail buried her face into Michele's torso, crying softly.

One of the men was heavier than the others and he made his way to our booth. He pointed his pistol—a cheap black semi-automatic—down at Michele and opened his mouth to speak. Without thought, I grabbed the barrel with my left hand and twisted it upward. At the same time, I lunged out of my seat, driving my right shoulder into his paunchy gut.

The gun went off as I pumped my legs forward and sent him reeling. Paunchy crashed into a table and fell backward. I landed on top of him, maintaining my death grip on the barrel of his pistol. I punched down at him, striking his rough face repeatedly. He grunted. The rancid odor of stale cigarettes and coffee spewed from his mouth. I turned my head, nearly gagging.

I felt Paunchy's grip on the pistol weaken with each strike. I lifted my hand to punch down at him again when a gunshot went off behind me, and Michele screamed. I twisted around, gasping when I saw Abigail in the hairy arms of the ringleader.

"Get off of him or the girl dies!" Ringleader bellowed.

I slowly released my hold on the pistol and raised my hands. "Okay, it's over. You win. I'm getting off of him."

I eased to a standing position, keeping my eyes focused on the jagged slits of the dirty mask that covered Ringleader's face. Greasy black hair with streaks of silver extended from the bottom of the mask. "Please, sir...put the girl down."

Michele had apparently made a move on Ringleader when he grabbed Abigail because one of the other thugs had her pinned to the wall by her throat. She stifled her sobs, as she spoke softly to Abigail.

Ringleader scanned the restaurant. His front tooth on the left side was missing and he pushed the tip of his tongue through the gap, then scowled. "When I give an order, I expect it to be followed. When it's not, there are consequences!"

"Sir, you're right. I disobeyed your order—"

"I know I'm right!" Ringleader jerked Abigail around in front of him as he stepped forward. She screeched in terror, tears pouring down her pale face.

"Abbie, it's okay," I said calmly. "Just look at Daddy. I promise you, everything's going to be—"

"Shut the hell up!" Ringleader pointed the pistol at me. "Are you a pig? You're acting like a pig right now." He sniffed the air. "You smell like a damn pig!"

There was too much distance between us for me to disarm him. I shifted my eyes from him to the other three men. I could see Paunchy dragging himself to his feet in my peripheral vision. The pistol was on the floor in front of him, but was too far from me.

Ringleader shoved the pistol roughly into the side of Abigail's temple, making her cry even louder. He glared at me. "Are you a pig?"

"No, I'm not a cop. I'm just a guy who took his wife and daughter out to dinner. Please, I'm begging you not to hurt her."

"Begging, eh? Get on your knees and beg me like you mean it."

I dropped to my knees, folded my hands in front of my face. "Please, sir, I beg you not to hurt Abigail. She's six years old. She just recently graduated from kindergarten and—"

"Cops," one of the other robbers called. "The cops are coming!"

"You should've stayed in your seat." Ringleader smiled and pulled the trigger.

CHAPTER 2

Two Years Later
Monday, June 23

I stared down at the pool of blood in the thick grass, then cursed my foolishness when sweat dripped from my face and splattered amidst the crimson puddle. I rubbed the sleeve of my tan uniform shirt against my forehead and pointed to the spot. "Is this where it happened?"

Mrs. DuPont nodded. Tears spilled from her eyes and traveled the deep wrinkles etched into her weathered face. "That gator came all the way out the water to get Buddy."

I followed the blood trail to the bank of the bayou, where it disappeared into the dark green water. The grass had been smashed down and deep divots torn into the ground from the pool of blood all the way to the bayou. It had been a wild struggle. I squatted at the water's edge and scanned the surface of Bayou Tail, looking for any sign of the killer alligator. The smothering sun had already started its westward slide and the thick trees on the opposite side of the bayou made it look even later than it was. "So, the alligator dragged him into the water and that was the last you saw of him?"

"That was the biggest gator I've ever seen." Mrs. DuPont wiped her face on the front of her plaid shirt. "Had to be fifteen feet."

I frowned. "Are you sure? That would be extremely big for an alligator."

"If there's one thing I know, it's gators." Mrs. DuPont nodded her head for emphasis. "I hunted gators with my daddy for thirty years."

Not convinced, I stood and turned to face her. "How tall do you think I am?"

"You don't think I realize you're trying to test me?" Mrs. DuPont scoffed. "You ain't an inch over five-feet-ten in them boots."

I nodded my approval. "Okay, Mrs. DuPont, I'm impressed. Fifteen feet it is." I grabbed the radio off my gun belt, but paused with it in front of my face. *What's her name again?* It was my first day on the job, and I'd only briefly met the four officers and the daytime dispatcher before heading out here. Maybe I should have written— *Lindsay! That's her name!*

"Lindsay, do we have someone who kills alligators or do I do that?"

"The trapper should be there any minute," Lindsay called back over the radio. "I called him as soon as I received the complaint. His name's Dexter Boudreaux."

"Thanks." I clipped the radio back on my belt and walked to where my Tahoe was parked in the front yard of Mrs. DuPont's house. I grabbed my shotgun from the back seat and slung it over my shoulder. My radio scratched to life, and Lindsay's voice blared through.

"Chief, I just got a call from Mr. Boudreaux. He's pulling up behind the DuPont residence right now."

Leaving the radio on my belt, I pressed the button and leaned my head. "*Behind* her house?"

"Ten-four—he's in his boat."

I locked my Tahoe and walked around Mrs. DuPont's house, where I found Dexter Boudreaux on his hands and knees examining the bloody scene. I nodded when he looked up and stuck out my hand. "How are you, sir? I'm Clint Wolf, chief of police here in Mechant Loup."

"Dexter Boudreaux." The old man took my hand and squeezed— harder than I expected. He pushed his weathered baseball cap back to expose a balding crown with scattered tufts of white strands. "So, you're the new chief, eh?"

"Yep, that's me."

Dexter stood and looked me up and down, measuring me. "You ever hunted a gator before?"

I felt my face flush a little. "To be honest, I've never really seen one up close. I did see that show on television a couple of times where they hunt alligators and—"

"That stuff's bullshit." Dexter shook his head after he spat a stream of tobacco juice to the side. "Don't believe anything you see on reality TV." He then turned to Mrs. DuPont. "How big was your German shepherd?"

"Buddy was over a hundred pounds," Mrs. DuPont said. "He was strong—and fast. I just don't understand how that gator could get him. I should've kept him inside."

Dexter's leather face seemed to soften a bit. "You had no way of knowing that gator was into dogs. Don't beat yourself up over it."

"Well, I hope you can get Buddy back. I'd like to give him a proper burial." Mrs. DuPont started to turn away, but stopped and waved her hand to indicate up and down the bayou. "There's kids playing all along this bayou and it would be easy for him to get one of them, so make sure y'all catch that gator before he does something horrible."

I put a hand on her shoulder. "We'll get it, don't you worry."

Dexter turned and stepped into his boat, deftly walking along the length of it as it rocked to and fro. He cranked the outboard motor, took his seat, and grabbed the tiller. I hesitated. The aluminum boat had to be a mere fourteen feet long and the sides were only about twelve inches above the water.

"We're going in that?" I pointed to the tiny craft.

"Unless you'd rather swim." Dexter smiled, exposing a row of tobacco-stained teeth. "I'd vote against swimming—considering the size of that gator."

I stepped into the boat and nearly lost my balance as it dipped under my weight. I leaned over quickly and grabbed the sides of the boat. My shotgun slipped off my shoulder and clanked loudly against the metal frame. Cursing silently, I fumbled with it and, when I'd gained control over it, placed it on the floor. I then sat on the front seat and held on.

Dexter chuckled. "You'll get used to the rocking."

I didn't respond. Dexter revved the engine and the boat backed slowly away from the shore and the front end swung toward the right. We then headed down the bayou. Cool droplets sprayed my face as the boat cut through the water. Enjoying the relief from the heat, I scanned the banks on either side of us, searching for any sign of an alligator. We had only gone a dozen or so yards when I spotted an alligator's head protruding from the water. I pointed. "There's one."

"Too small," Dexter called over the hum of the motor. "The one we're looking for is a monster."

I nodded, kept looking. As we glided along the calm water, I saw a dozen more alligators, but none were big enough to be the killer.

After what had to be a mile or two, we passed a number of camps that were perched along the shadowy banks of the bayou. Many of the cabins looked to have been thrown together with scrap wood and were topped with tin roofs. There were even a couple of houseboats in the mix and one of them had a satellite dish. I pointed to it. "They get satellite television out here?"

Dexter nodded.

I scratched my head. "But where are the electric poles? How do they get power?"

"Generators." Dexter sounded annoyed.

We rode in silence for a few minutes and then I asked, "People actually live this far out?"

"A few families do."

"How do they get back and forth to the store? Like, if they're sitting down to eat cookies at night and they realize their kid drank the last of the milk, what do they do? They clearly can't jump in the car and drive down the highway."

"They go by boat."

I pondered this as we continued on...thankful I lived just down the road from the grocery store. We rode by a thick wooded area and then came upon a small clearing where a weathered gray house squatted on short creosote poles. A covered screened-in porch extended from the front of the structure. It seemed to hang precariously from the front of the house, as though a hard sneeze could blow it directly into the bayou.

"Hey, Dexter," I called over my shoulder, "do you think they're in danger?" I pointed to two small boys—clad only in faded jeans shorts—who sat at the very edge of the wharf that lined the front of the house. The tips of their toes dangled just above the water. One of the boys looked to be about eight and the other had to be five or six.

Before the question fully left my lips, Dexter had pointed the boat toward the wharf. "That gator could snatch them off the wharf before they could blink twice," he said.

When we reached the dock, Dexter pushed the boat up against a tire that hung from one of the pilings, and I stood and grabbed onto it to maintain my balance. I turned to the boys. "Hey, little men, how are y'all?"

The older one squinted and pointed at my right hip. "What kind of gun you got?"

I glanced down at my holster. "It's a Glock, forty caliber."

The boy whistled and said, "Awesome."

The younger boy was disinterested. He stared absently at us and kicked his dangling legs back and forth as he held his fishing pole in his hands. Water sprayed up and onto my pant legs, but the boy didn't seem to mind.

I pointed to the blue-and-white ice chest on the wharf near them. "What are y'all catching?"

"A couple of catfish," the older one said.

"Cool." I studied the calm bayou water. A warm breeze gently brushed the leaves of the surrounding trees and caressed my face. Had I not known better, I'd think this was a safe place to go for a lazy swim to cool off. "Look, y'all might want to head inside for today. An alligator killed a German shepherd just up the bayou from here, so it might not be safe for y'all—"

"Hey," called a masculine voice from the back door of the house. "What's going on?"

I looked up and saw a man stomping across the porch. He pushed his way through the storm door that looked oddly out of place attached to the dilapidated porch front. He was the right age to be the boys' father.

"How's it going?" I asked.

"Okay, I think. Is there a problem?" The man stopped at the edge of the wharf.

"An alligator killed a German shepherd up the bayou," I explained. "I was telling the boys it might not be safe out here."

The man's eyes widened. "Really?"

"Yeah, it was a big German shepherd, too," I said.

"Wow." The man glanced at the badge pinned to my shirt. "So, you're the new chief of police?"

"Yes, sir, that's me."

The man turned to his boys. "Go inside and get cleaned up for supper." He turned back to us. "Name's Red McKenzie. Thanks for looking out."

"No problem," I said.

Dexter continued down the bayou, hugging the bank, and I had to duck under some of the low-lying oak tree branches.

"Do you see any bubbles in the water?" Dexter asked.

I shook my head. "You think he could've come this far?"

"It's been over an hour since I got the call—he could've gone twenty miles in that time."

Dexter kept the boat at a steady pace and, just as the shadows grew longer, turned right into a small canal that intersected Bayou Tail. The narrow waterway snaked through the center of a thick forest, where the underbrush smothered the trees lining the banks.

The water seemed dirtier and logs could be seen just under the surface. I began to fidget on the front seat of the boat. "Sun's going down quick."

"Good," Dexter called. "We'll have a better chance catching him at night. That gator didn't get that big by being dumb."

Dexter revved the motor as the canal broke out into a lake, then he stabbed the front of the boat directly ahead and began crossing to the opposite side, where tall grass lined the shore. Although angry clouds had gathered ahead of us, it was much brighter on the lake and I felt better about being out there. "What's the name of this—"

"Look! Over there!"

CHAPTER 3

I turned to see Dexter pointing to the right side of the lake. My gaze followed his finger. I gasped. A giant alligator was floating near the bank about fifty yards from us, a limp and saturated German shepherd clamped in his jaws. I quickly jumped to my feet and jerked my shotgun to my shoulder. The boat swayed beneath me, and I tried to steady the front bead on the alligator's head.

"Don't you shoot that gator." Dexter's voice was stern.

Keeping my cheek pressed to the stock, I shifted my eyes to stare at Dexter. "Why on earth not? He killed Mrs. DuPont's dog."

"He did what came natural," Dexter said calmly. "That don't rate a death sentence."

I slowly lowered my shotgun. "Then what are we doing out here? I thought we were coming to kill it."

"I'm a trapper, not a hunter." Dexter pointed to a pole that had a dart on one end and a hole in the middle of it. A rope was attached to the dart and extended through the hole in the pole and was tied to some sort of floating device. "We're going to catch it and relocate it. Take it miles away where it can live in peace. Where there're no dogs and where no kids will be in danger."

I could feel my jaw hanging. "You're going to catch that gigantic beast?"

Dexter shook his head. "Not just me"—he wriggled his finger between us—"both of us."

I let out a nervous chuckle. "I'd rather get in a gunfight without body armor than mess with that giant dinosaur."

"It'll be fine," Dexter said. "I've done this a million times. I'll do the fun stuff. I just need you to drive the boat. Once I latch onto him,

he'll try to take us for a ride, so I'll need you to use the boat to fight him like you would if you were shark fishing. We'll take him in when he tires out."

"I've never been shark fishing," I mumbled.

Dexter moved the boat slowly toward the alligator. "Keep an eye on the exact spot where he goes down."

I reluctantly put my shotgun down and dropped to my knees. I held onto the front of the boat as we glided smoothly across the water. We drew nearer and nearer, but the alligator didn't move. He looked even bigger up close, and I felt my heart start to beat a little faster. I could see the rest of his body outlined just under the water and gasped. He was longer than the boat. He seemed to be staring at us through his left eye.

"Close enough," Dexter called as he eased the boat to a stop. It rocked gently as Dexter grabbed his harpoon pole and stepped over the backseat and moved to where I knelt. "Get to the back and take hold of the tiller."

I did as I was told, holding my arms out to my side to keep my balance as I moved to the back of the aluminum hull. Once I was seated and had my right hand on the tiller, Dexter nodded, turned, and took aim with the harpoon. As though sensing something was amiss, the alligator released the German shepherd and the dog slowly disappeared beneath the surface of the water. With a deft swish of its tail, the alligator turned to face us.

"Get ready," Dexter warned. The alligator moved closer. Dexter spread his feet, steadied himself. He took a deep breath and held it. Letting out a grunt, he pulled the trigger and launched the harpoon into the air.

I sat frozen. The harpoon seemed to move through the air in slow motion. My hand gripped the tiller, ready to spring into action. I gasped out loud as the harpoon smacked against the alligator's armored back and glanced off of it, flying harmlessly into the water. Dexter snatched up the rope and began pulling the harpoon back toward him. The alligator dropped out of sight under the water.

"Shit," Dexter said. When he had the harpoon in hand again, he inspected the dart. It was still in place. He leaned over the edge of the boat and scanned the lake. He pointed to a series of bubbles that had floated to the surface of the water. "There he is. Move the boat toward—"

The water exploded in action. The monster alligator lunged out of the water, its mouth wide open, exposing two rows of ominous teeth. I instinctively lurched backward and fell against the opposite side of the boat. Dexter's reaction was slower than mine. He lifted his left arm to shield his face, but he didn't jump back in time. While still airborne, the alligator's jaws clamped down on Dexter's arm like a bear trap. Dexter yelled in disbelief. The forward momentum of the thousand-pound alligator slammed Dexter backward. As the full force of the alligator came to bear on Dexter and the boat, the aluminum hull dipped violently under its weight. My shotgun was flung into the air and water rushed over the side of the boat.

The dip had tossed me forward and my shoulder smashed into the side of the alligator. My uniform was instantly saturated. I pushed off the floor of the boat, but my hands slipped and I fell headfirst over the side. My thighs caught the wall of the boat, and it was all that stopped me from slipping into the lake. I tried to push myself up, but my hands grasped nothing but water. Somewhere behind me, Dexter screamed in agony. I reached out and grabbed the back of the alligator to pull my torso out of the water.

Kneeling in the sinking boat, with water up to my waist, I drew my pistol and turned toward the alligator. It was stretched across the width of the boat and it had a death grip on Dexter's left arm. Blood was everywhere. Dexter struck out at the alligator with his right fist, but it didn't affect the alligator at all. The alligator began rolling to its right. Dexter screamed in agony. The movement from the alligator rocked the boat. Water splashed in all directions. Afraid to hit Dexter with my pistol, I aimed it at the side of the large beast. Jerking violently with the motion of the alligator, I pulled the trigger. The gun exploded in my hand. The bullet didn't seem to have a noticeable impact. I fired again and again. Between my fifteen-round magazine and the bullet in the chamber, I had sixteen bullets—I didn't stop firing until the slide locked back on an empty pistol.

Dexter's screams grew weaker as the alligator's teeth ripped at his flesh. Blood spilled from his gaping wounds. Unfazed by the gunshots, the alligator gave a final roll and slid free of the boat. In a last-ditch effort to save Dexter, I stood so I could throw my Glock at the alligator, but the boat sank out from under me. I fell forward. Muddy water rushed into my throat and the Glock flew from my hand. I slipped under the water.

CHAPTER 4

I thrashed about in the murky darkness. My boots had filled with water. That and the weight of my clothes and gun belt threatened to pull me to the bottom of the lake. My lungs screamed as I strained to hold my breath. I struggled to reach the surface. My feet felt like lead as I kicked and paddled with my hands. After what seemed like forever, my head pushed through and I was able to suck in a mouthful of air. I stared wildly about. My breathing came in labored gasps. The boat was gone, Dexter was gone, and so was the alligator. The only signs they had been there were the millions of tiny white bubbles exploding all around me. I knew they had to be somewhere beneath me.

I treaded water, snatched my expandable side-handle baton from my gun belt, and extended it. Without thinking, I took a deep breath and plunged under the water. Desperate to find Dexter, I headed straight for the bottom of the lake, opening my eyes as I swam. I could see nothing but blurry darkness. By the time I reached the muddy floor of the lake, I'd nearly reached the limit of my breath-holding abilities. I strained through the pain and made a frantic search with my left hand and my baton. For all my grasping, all I got was slush and weeds. After dozens of seconds, and unable to hold my breath any longer, I twisted my body so my head was facing upward and lunged off the bottom. Instead of propelling me upward, I sank to my ankles in the mud.

I struggled, pulling and pushing on my legs, but they wouldn't break free from the clutches of the sucking mud. And then I became very calm. I opened my eyes. I'd heard of diving in black water and how dark and utterly lonely it was down there, but at that moment, I felt peace and I could see.

I could see Michele's blonde hair waving in the wind as she walked toward me holding Abigail. I smiled, reached out for them. I wondered why Abigail wouldn't turn toward me. I called out to her. Told her Daddy was here. Michele looked down at Abigail, and I thought I saw tears in her eyes. Abigail lifted her head and turned to me—

I recoiled in horror when Abigail's distorted face came into view and looked all around. Everything was black.

I remembered where I was and what was at stake. I was Dexter's only hope!

Abigail's face started to float back into view. I shook my head and her image faded into the black wetness that swished about me. I squeezed my burning eyes shut, dropped my baton and bent forward at the waist. Grabbing my pant legs, I pulled myself forward until I reached my bootlaces. As I worked to untie my boots, I swallowed in an effort to buy some time. Once my boots were untied, I wriggled and pulled with my feet—*nothing!* The suction was stronger than I would've imagined. Resisting the urge to panic, I pushed with one foot, pulled with the other, straining until I thought my head would explode. I felt my right foot budge a little and then it was free. My lungs burned. I fought the urge to breathe. I placed my right foot over my empty boot and repeated the slow push-pull method until I felt my left foot start to slide. Once it was also free, I rushed toward the surface, my lungs crying for air. I opened my eyes, looking up. Hope surged through me as I realized the water wasn't as dark. The more I swam, the brighter it became, and I finally saw sunlight approaching. I had made it!

Desperate for air, I opened my mouth and sucked in. Water shot into my mouth and down my throat, as I'd misgauged the distance. I began choking, sucking in more water. When my head made it above the water, I broke into a fit of coughs. Water sprayed from my throat. Between coughs, I was able to suck in tiny bits of much-needed air.

As I struggled to recover, movement to my right caught my eye and I spun to face that direction. It was the monster alligator. It had resurfaced about twenty yards from me and it was swimming away. Heaving from the lack of oxygen and the strain of my struggles, I scanned the lake.

"Dexter!" I screamed. I broke out into a coughing fit again and it took several deep breaths to settle myself. "Dexter!"

No response. No movement other than me and the alligator.

My strength was waning. I screamed for Dexter several more

times, but conceded the obvious—he was gone. Gritting my teeth, I stabbed out at the water, heading for the nearest shoreline fifty yards away. At this point, there was nothing pretty about my swimming technique. I kicked and thrashed with my hands. I swam like I was drowning. I thought each stroke of my hand and each kick of my foot would be my last. I looked back over my shoulder to make sure the monster alligator wasn't bearing down on me, but it had disappeared.

My arms had grown numb by the time I reached the shallow and muddy edge of the lake. I pushed my way through thick seaweed and stumbled through the mud. I pulled myself onto solid ground. I threw myself to my back and groaned as my muscles unwound. While I wanted to remain there forever, I knew I couldn't. I rolled to my knees and ripped my radio from my belt. I pressed the button, but the familiar scratch was absent. Water dripped from the cracks in the radio. I shook it in an attempt to clear it of water and pressed it again. Nothing. I remembered my cell phone, snatched it from my pocket and flipped it open. It was dead, too. I cursed myself for not purchasing the waterproof case the mayor had recommended.

Night was falling fast. I stood to my feet. My drenched uniform clung to my body. I surveyed the area, trying to figure the quickest route back to the canal. The lake was a couple hundred yards across, and I didn't think I could swim it. Even if I thought I could, I didn't want to get in the water with that monster alligator. I peered through the trees, trying to penetrate the deep shadows. I didn't know what was beyond the tree line, but I didn't have time to find out. It appeared the only way to get back to the canal was a long walk around the perimeter of the lake. Not wanting to waste any more time, I set out to my left, walking through the thick grass in my socked feet.

It didn't take long for the mosquitoes to realize I was there and swarm over me. I felt a sharp sting on the back of my neck and slapped at it. More stings followed, and I swatted at them, but it was futile. I would kill one or two and then ten or twelve would replace the dead ones. As I trudged on, I stepped on a cypress knee. The pointy stump pushed into the arch of my right foot, and I stumbled forward, cursing out loud. I flexed the pain out of my foot and moved on, picking my way through the swampy jungle. I couldn't see very well due to the growing darkness and I had to feel with my feet, which made the going slow. The ground was soft in places so I sank to my ankles often.

Before long it was completely black and the swamp came alive with crickets and frogs and other unfamiliar sounds. Unable to see, I stumbled into the shallow water of the lake's edge. Something large splashed in the water nearby and to my right. I froze, reached for my Glock, but cursed when I remembered I'd lost it. Sweat dripped from my forehead. I opened my mouth, turned my head so I could better hear any follow-up movements. The mosquitoes continued their relentless assault and made it difficult to concentrate. I eased back up the bank of the lake and continued onward, trying to put some distance between myself and whatever it was that had made the splash.

When I had gone what I figured was twenty or so yards, I stopped. I had to do something about the swarming mosquitoes. They buzzed in my ears and dove in like kamikaze planes, attacking from all directions. It was a monumental distraction and, in this environment, I had to be sharp. A thought occurred to me, and I dropped to my knees and began grabbing up clumps of soft mud. I smeared the mud on my neck and face, and then on my arms. I caked it on thick, sighing as it cooled my flesh. When I was done, I stood and paused. The mosquitoes continued to buzz around me, but the mud had formed a barrier they could no longer penetrate. I smiled in the dark, continued on.

My saturated socks swished as I reached a patch of solid ground where the walking was easier. The moon had risen above the distant tree line at the opposite side of the lake and it glowed off the water, making it easier to differentiate between the water and the land. I was also able to make out the faint shadows of the trees and bushes, which helped make my travels easier. I had walked about a mile along the rounded perimeter of the lake when I reached the canal that Dexter and I had traveled along.

I studied the bank along my side of the canal. Even in the dim moonlight there was no mistaking the impenetrable wall of green in front of me. I reached out and grabbed a branch to test its strength, but winced as a million pickers embedded themselves in the palm of my left hand. I pulled my hand back and began digging the tiny spears from my flesh. Even after I removed them all, I was left with a burning sensation at the site of the pricks.

Not wanting to spend the night out there, I used my foot to pick my way toward the mouth of the canal so I could weigh my chances of swimming across. If I could reach the other side, I might be able to traverse the opposite bank and make my way back to Bayou Tail. I knew I had reached the water's edge when my foot sank into the damp mud. I paused, studied the water directly in front of me. The canal was alive with movement—a swish here, a croak there, and a violent splash every now and then. I took a step and felt the cool water wrap around my ankle. I took another step and sank to my knee in the mud. The water was up to my waist. As I worked to free my leg, my movement must've spooked something nearby because the water exploded in action. I threw myself to the side and clawed, trying to get back to the shore. Soft mud and underwater weeds squished between my fingers, and my feet slipped on the bottom of the canal. A coarse object brushed against my back, and I propelled myself forward. It took several desperate attempts, but I finally dragged myself to the packed earth of the canal's bank. I continued rushing forward until I had left the mouth of the canal behind and was once again standing along the banks of the lake. I stopped and bent over, resting my hands on my knees to catch my breath.

"How the hell am I supposed to get out of here?" I called out loud. As though they were responding to my question, dozens of mosquitoes stabbed their tiny syringes into my skin all at once. The mud had washed away and I was exposed to their relentless air assault. They swarmed around me, buzzing. I waved my hands like a wild man and searched for another patch of mud. When I found one, I dropped to my knees and clawed chunks of earth from the ground—some of it sticking up under my fingernails—and smeared the cool clay onto my bare skin. I sighed as the layer of mud began to cover large patches of my flesh and kept the mosquitoes at bay.

Once I was done, I rose to my feet. I shook my head. "I'm not going anywhere tonight." I needed to find a place to bed down. I knew if I stayed on the ground I'd become alligator bait. I walked to a tree with a low-lying branch. I scrambled up onto the branch and then continued higher up the tree until I reached a limb that was about eighteen inches across. I stretched out on my new bed and rested my back against the trunk. I was exhausted, wanted to sleep, but knew I couldn't. I dared not.

I tried to occupy my thoughts with plans of escape. Tried to remember every turn Dexter Boudreaux and I had taken on the ride to the lake. When morning came I would have to find a way back to the bayou. *If I can make it there, I should be able to swim to Red McKenzie's camp and call for help.*

I felt my eyelids drooping, but I struggled to keep them open, struggled to keep my mind busy. I stared into the darkness for what seemed like forever. The sun finally started to come up, and I sighed. I'd made it through the night without falling asleep. I relaxed, allowed my eyes to slide shut. Abigail's face suddenly came into view and I recoiled in horror.

CHAPTER 5

Tuesday, June 24

Once the sun was up, I scrambled down from the tree. Just as I reached the bottom, I heard the roar of a jet engine, but it approached from the direction of Bayou Tail. I rushed toward the canal. When I reached the water's edge, I splashed forward until I was waist deep in the muddy soup. I stared toward the bayou, excitement beating a rhythmic tune in my chest as I waited for my rescue craft to arrive. I didn't have to wait long.

A large green hull, backed by an enormous fan, came into view. *An airboat!* The engine was deafening. Water sprayed from the back of the boat like it was being pushed away by a category five hurricane and the trees bent under its force. Perched atop the elevated captain's seat was one of the officers I'd met yesterday. I was almost sure his name was Melvin—Melvin Saltzman.

I waved my hands and immediately drew Melvin's attention. A large smile split his thick face, and he jerked the boat toward my location. I stumbled backward to make room for the wide hull. When it pulled up beside me, I grabbed onto the side and hoisted myself over it. My drenched socks smacked the deck of the boat when I landed and water quickly pooled at my feet. I wondered how ridiculous I looked.

"Damn nice to see you again, Chief! I thought you'd gone off and quit on your first day," Melvin hollered above the noise of the engine. He hit the kill switch and ripped off his earmuffs, then dropped from his elevated position to greet me.

"Dexter's gone," I said. "That alligator—it took out the boat and pulled Dexter in the water with it. I shot at it, but it was no use. I couldn't stop it."

"We figured it was one of y'all."

"What do you mean?"

"Beaver killed a gator in Lake Berg that had an arm in its mouth. We figured it was either you or Dexter."

"Who's Beaver?" I asked.

"Nobody important." Melvin tossed me a set of earmuffs. "He's at the boat launch."

I was thoughtful, then asked, "Did anyone notify Dexter's wife that he was missing?"

"Sergeant Wilson did. She's real good with talking to people. Told Mrs. Boudreaux we were doing all we could and that we would know more as the day progressed."

I nodded, took the earmuffs Melvin handed me, and settled in for the deafening ride. My stomach turned. My mouth was dry. That poor lady, I thought.

The wind felt good against my itchy and bumpy flesh as we rushed toward the boat launch. Melvin handled the airboat like a pro—zipping around logs in the lake at breakneck speed and dodging underwater debris that I couldn't even see. I wondered if I would ever be able to navigate those waters half as well as Melvin, but quickly dismissed the thought. That kind of skill was developed over a lifetime of traversing these waters. I grunted. *You can't teach an old dog new tricks.*

Melvin drove us through the south-side pass and we connected with Bayou Tail. We continued travelling toward town and when we rode by Red McKenzie's weathered gray house, I saw his two boys still fishing on the wharf with their feet dangling in the water. When Melvin slowed as we passed them I could hear myself think again.

"We told them to be careful yesterday, but apparently they don't listen," I yelled over the lower drone of the idling boat. "We even told their dad."

Melvin grunted. "Red McKenzie thinks he's the law out here. Thinks rules don't apply to him. He's always catching over the limit and hunts out of season. I've caught him red-handed a half dozen times, but he keeps getting off on it. Each time he does, he gets more and more arrogant—and his attitude is rubbing off on his boys."

The engine roared to life again, and we resumed our trek up Bayou Tail. After a short time, I recognized where we were and pointed toward Mrs. Dupont's backyard. "Drop me off at Mrs. Dupont's house," I mouthed. "I need to get my Tahoe."

Melvin drove the airboat up against the bank behind Mrs. Dupont's house, where we found her sitting on a backyard swing. I jumped from the airboat and made my way across the yard to her. She stood as I drew near. Concern was etched into her face. She closed the last few feet between us and stared up at me until the roaring from the airboat had faded enough to hear each other talk.

"You poor man," she said. "There's so much pain in your eyes— old pain. I thought I noticed it yesterday, but I wasn't sure. I see it clearly now. What have you seen? What have you done?"

I smiled. "No pain, ma'am. Just a little disappointed that I couldn't do more for Dexter."

"Ah, yes. I heard one of y'all had gotten eaten by that gator. It was like none Dexter had ever encountered. It was too much for him." Mrs. Dupont waved her hand to encompass our entire surrounding. "No one around these parts has seen a gator like that." She stared off into the clouds, and I swore she could see something that wasn't there. "My dad would've welcomed the challenge of capturing that beast."

"Well, we got it. It's over. Some guy named Beaver killed it. He's at the boat launch." I stepped back to walk around her. "I'm heading that way now."

Mrs. Dupont grunted. "Beaver Detiveaux's a coward. Anyone can kill a gator with a gun. That's nothing to brag about."

I started to walk away, but stopped. "Mrs. Dupont, I saw Buddy, but I wasn't able to retrieve him. I'm sorry."

Tears sprang to her eyes. "Did it look like he suffered?"

I hesitated. My instincts told me to say, He didn't feel a thing, but lying was something I only did if I absolutely had to. "I can't be sure."

She pursed her lips. "Thank you for telling the truth." She turned and waved a hand at me. "Come with me before you leave."

I hesitated, looked toward my Tahoe.

"It'll only take a minute, Chief," she called over her shoulder. "Your SUV is not going anywhere without you."

I sighed and followed her across the manicured yard, around a wooden shed, and to a large dog kennel that housed eight whining pups and one quiet pup. The quiet one was solid black with a splash of brown on his front paws and chest. He lay on the ground with his head held high and proud and his eyes alive and alert. I chuckled to myself when I noticed his ears. The left ear drooped over the left side of his head and the right ear leaned toward the left one. They looked too big for his head.

"Which one do you want?" Mrs. Dupont asked.

I jerked my head around to look at her. "Excuse me?" She nodded her head toward the litter of puppies. "Pick one. You risked your life to try and get my Buddy back. The least I can do is give you one of his offspring. He would want it that way."

"That's a very generous offer, Mrs. Dupont, but I can't accept it. It wouldn't be right."

"I want you to have one. I know you'll take good care of it." Mrs. Dupont's eyes softened. "Besides, you need something to love."

I frowned and glanced back at the quiet one. The last time I'd had a dog was when I was twelve. It had been a white German shepherd that had died during a storm when a tree fell on her house. My dad had never bought another dog—he was that upset over losing her— and I'd gone the rest of my boyhood wishing to have another canine companion. I didn't know what Mrs. Dupont saw in me, but she was right that I could use something to love. "Okay," was all I said.

Mrs. Dupont's face beamed. "You'll take it?"

I nodded. "But under one condition."

"Yes?"

"You let me give you your normal asking price."

"No, I couldn't—"

"It's the only way I'll be able to take it."

Mrs. Dupont sighed. "Okay. Which one would you like?"

I pointed to the quiet one, which was also the biggest.

"Good choice," Mrs. Dupont said. She opened the gate and picked her way through the warm bodies until she reached the quiet one. His ears perked up and it was only then that I noticed how huge they were. He gave Mrs. Dupont an inquisitive look as she bent to lift him. "I named this one Achilles."

"Cool name," I said. "I won't mess with it."

"He won't poop or pee where he sleeps, but you've got to remember to take him outside every few hours." Mrs. Dupont cradled him in her arms as though he were a fine piece of fragile china. Achilles looked bored. When she had made her way back to me, she handed me Achilles, and I wrapped an arm under him. He sniffed my chest and chin, trying to decide if he liked me.

"Hey, big man," I said. "I'm Clint—I'm your new buddy."

Mrs. Dupont tried to slip quickly through the gate, but a few of the puppies were right on her heels and she had to stop long enough to shove them back through the opening with her foot. When she'd locked the gate, she grabbed a large animal crate from beside her fence and held it up. "You can use this until he's housebroke."

I waved her off. "He should be fine in my living room. As long as he doesn't pee everywhere."

"Do you have a sofa?"

I nodded.

"Do you want it scattered around your living room?"

I sighed. "How much do I owe you?"

"Five dollars for Achilles. You can bring the crate back when you're done with it. I've got plenty of them."

"No way," I protested. "He has to be worth at least a thousand dollars."

"Not for you."

"Ma'am, I told you I was only taking him if you'd let me give you your normal price."

"It is my normal price—today." Mrs. Dupont nodded her head toward Achilles, who had his head leaning on my shoulder. "You can't very well give him back now, can you? Five dollars and we're even. It's my final offer."

I sighed, and Mrs. Dupont followed me to my Tahoe and tossed the crate in the back. I opened the driver's door and leaned, letting Achilles jump from my arms. He bounded to the passenger's side as though he knew it was where he belonged, sat proudly and waited patiently as I fished a wet five-dollar bill from my wallet and handed it to Mrs. Dupont.

She took the money, shoved it into her bra without a second thought and waved goodbye to Achilles. "Take care of our new chief," she called. "He's a good man."

You don't even know me, I thought, but only smiled and slipped into the driver's seat. It was warm from sitting in the sun and felt nice. Achilles went into high alert when I cranked the engine. He sniffed the air and scanned the interior of the vehicle, as though looking for danger. I reached over and rubbed his pointy ears.

"It's okay, little man. You'll get used to this."

CHAPTER 6

My new puppy and I arrived at the boat landing just in time to see Melvin pull up in the airboat. Other searchers were there and had formed a rugged circle around what had to be Beaver's boat at the edge of the long pier. The boat launch was nothing more than a large shell parking lot with a couple of spots to launch some boats. Having just blown into town, I wasn't sure how much activity the launch saw on a regular day, but the place was crowded today. Townspeople stood at the far end of the pier on the outside of a line of yellow tape that one of my officers must've strung up, and a group of reporters huddled at the edge of the pier near Beaver's boat. Cameras were trained downward at whatever was in Beaver's boat, and the reporters held microphones in Beaver's direction.

I left my Tahoe running and the windows cracked so Achilles could keep cool, made my way through the mess of trucks, cars, and news vans that cluttered the parking lot, wincing as the rough shells stabbed at the bottoms of my socked feet. As I drew nearer, I could hear Beaver's excited voice telling his tale of alligator heroism. I sighed. At least the alligator was dead.

I reached the reporters and started to squeeze my way through them. Melvin looked up from the edge of the pier and motioned news crews back. "Make a hole," he called. "Let the chief through."

The group parted somewhat, and I made my way to Beaver's boat and looked down in it. Beaver was grinning like a schoolboy who'd just scored his first kiss. I nodded my thanks and glanced over at the large alligator. When I took it in, my shoulders drooped. The lifeless alligator took up the entire length of the boat, but was at least two feet shorter than the alligator that killed Dexter.

I turned to Beaver. "It might not look like it in my present condition, but I'm the chief of police here. You said you found an arm?"

Beaver looked me over, turned and spat. Finally, he nodded, flipped open the lid on an ice chest and handed me an old pillowcase. I waved Melvin over to keep the news reporters at bay and then I walked to my left until I was sure no one could see inside the pillowcase. When I opened it and looked inside, my blood ran cold. The arm had been ripped off at the elbow. It was plump and pale— weak-looking. The wound was jagged and the tissue at the tear mark was white. I twisted a knot in the pillowcase, walked back to Beaver's boat.

I lifted the pillowcase. "That's not the alligator that killed Dexter and this isn't his arm. Whoever this arm belongs to was dead before that alligator ripped it off his body. We need to look for two—"

"What are you talking about? There's no way you can know that just by looking at it." Beaver's voice was laced with contempt and skepticism. "This is the gator that killed Dexter and that's Dexter's arm. Period."

Out of the corner of my right eye, I saw the news cameras turn toward me—and I didn't like it. "I appreciate your help, Beaver, but we'll take it from here."

"You're just mad because you got Dexter killed and I had to come clean up your mess. Everyone knows this town would be better off if I'd still be chief. Hell, Dexter would still be alive if I'd still be chief."

So, this is the man I've come to replace. I studied him, thought about pulling him from his boat and beating his ass, but I only nodded. I turned and pushed the pillowcase in Melvin's direction. "Can you take this down to the coroner's office?"

Melvin hesitated, leaning close so only I could hear. "Um...do I have to carry it?"

"Just grab it by the top. It'll be fine."

Melvin licked his lips, grabbed the edges of the pillowcase with the tips of his fingers and walked away holding it at arm's length.

I then turned to Sergeant Susan Wilson, who stood near Beaver's boat. Her brown hair was braided into cornrows and tied off behind her head in twin pigtails. Her uniform fit snuggly and accentuated a body that was in terrific shape. Her tanned arms had the appearance of being smooth, but they were toned, as though she worked out on a regular basis. She reached up to scratch her chin, and I noticed subtle marks on her knuckles and nodded my approval. Either she had a

problem with anger or she was a trained fighter, and I was betting on
the latter. If her courage matched her physique, she would definitely
be able to handle Beaver.

"Sarge, can you see to it that this alligator gets to the vet? I need
him to cut it open so we can see what else is inside. We've got
another dead body out there and we need to learn as much as we can
from that giant lizard."

Susan nodded. She turned immediately to Beaver. "If you're done
crying, get your truck and hitch up your boat. I'll escort you to the
vet."

Beaver's jaw was set, but he climbed out of the boat and stormed
across the parking lot without saying another word. I turned and
walked toward my Tahoe with the group of reporters following in my
wake.

"Chief," called a reporter from directly behind me, "what makes
you say this is not Dexter Boudreaux's arm? What information do
you have to back up your statement?"

"No comment," I mumbled, more to myself.

"Chief, how do you know it's not the alligator that killed Mr.
Boudreaux?" called another reporter.

"Is it true you got Mr. Boudreaux killed?" asked the first reporter.

"Where are your shoes, Chief?" asked yet another.

I continued walking, doing my best to tune out their questions,
when a soft voice asked, "What about you, Chief? Are you okay?"

I froze, before I turned slowly to face the mob of reporters who
had been scrambling on my heels. They all came to an abrupt halt,
some of the ones in the back bumping into the ones in the front. I
scanned the faces, searching for the one who'd asked the question. A
lady in the back of the group bounced up and down on her tiptoes
trying to see above the crowd. She waved her hand. "Here, Chief.
Over here."

Her bright blue eyes met mine and our gazes locked for a brief
moment, then she was lost in the herd of media. I waved the reporters
at the front of the group aside. They reluctantly moved away, and the
woman dropped from her tiptoes and settled into her real height of
about five-feet, three inches. She brushed her long blonde hair out of
her face and moved closer. "Phew, sorry."

"What was your question?" I asked.

Her pale face reddened ever so slightly. "Oh, um…I asked if you
were okay."

I stared down at her for a long moment. No one had ever asked
that question. Sure, there'd been questions—accusations, really—but

they were always about the incident. About the gory details. Never about the feelings of the people involved. When I'd been quiet for so long that it seemed awkward, I finally said, "No one's ever asked me that." Without saying another word, I turned and walked away.

CHAPTER 7

After a quick stop at home to set Achilles up in his crate with a bowl of water, wash what was left of the dried mud from my face, change clothes, and grab some boots, I drove to the coroner's office and found Melvin in the examination room with the coroner. The room was smaller than I was used to—there was only one table at the center of the room—but it was much cleaner and more organized than the coroner's office in the city.

Melvin and the doctor both looked up when I entered, and the doctor flashed a perfect smile, sticking out her hand. "Hello, there. I'm Louise Wong."

I nodded, took her soft hand in mine and gave it a gentle squeeze. "Nice to meet you, ma'am." I suddenly felt very aware of my disheveled hair and the smell of sweat that still lingered beneath my clean clothes. I opened my hand to end the shake.

Doctor Wong turned from us and walked to a row of white cabinets on the far wall. She returned with a box of gloves. "Melvin here tells me you are our new chief of police."

"Guilty as charged." I ran my hands through my brown hair. "Forgive my appearance. I've had a rough first couple of days on the job."

Doctor Wong smiled her understanding. "So I hear." She turned to the white table at the center of the room, pushed her dark hair back into a ponytail and then tugged on a pair of purple latex gloves. "Melvin says you determined the arm was torn from the victim postmortem."

"Yes, ma'am."

"What's postmortem?" Melvin asked.

Ignoring Melvin, Doctor Wong raised an eyebrow and studied my face with eyes that were so dark they looked black. "Not your first rodeo?"

"Not by a long shot."

"Well, you are correct." Doctor Wong looked down at the arm and began probing it with her fingers. "Due to the rate of decomposition, this is definitely not Mr. Boudreaux's arm, as he was alive yesterday at this time."

"Dexter's arm is also thinner, more muscular. His skin is darker. And his palms are rougher." I pointed to the pale hand on the table. "This guy had a desk job."

"Speaking of jobs," Doctor Wong said without looking up. "What did you do for a living before becoming our chief of police?"

"I've done some odd jobs in construction over the last year or two, kind of trying to figure out what I wanted to do with the rest of my life."

Doctor Wong paused to look up at me again. She shook her head. "You did not learn how to recognize postmortem injuries working construction."

I nodded. "That's true. I worked patrol in the city for two years and then transferred to homicide and did that for eight years."

Melvin snapped his fingers. "Damn it!"

I glanced over at him. "What?"

His eyes widened just a little as he realized he'd said that out loud. "Sorry, Chief. Um…we…um, no offense, but we…um, just had a bet going around the office. Susan won."

"A bet?" I asked.

Melvin nodded. "When Mayor Landry announced we were getting a new chief, we all placed bets on what he—um, *you*—did before. I guessed you were in the military, William Tucker thought you were a lawyer who got tired of defending guilty scum, and Jack Jackson said you were the mayor's son and you failed out of college and needed a job."

"What did Susan win?" asked Doctor Wong.

"We put up twenty bucks each—well, except for William. He's always broke. So, she won forty dollars and William owes her twenty."

Doctor Wong took some measurements, snapped a few photographs, and then turned back to me. "I will put this on ice until you can find the rest of it."

"Is it okay if I roll his prints?"

"Of course."

I tuned to Melvin. "Go grab some lunch and then head back out on the water until I can catch up with you. We need to find Dexter."

As I dragged my print kit from the back of the Tahoe, a fully marked police Charger pulled aggressively into the parking lot. Sergeant Susan Wilson jumped out and strode over to where I stood. "Mayor Landry is fit to be tied. He doesn't know what's going on and it's killing him. He wants you to drop what you're doing and go to his office as soon as you can."

"I thought he had a scanner in his office."

"He doesn't want the cliff notes; he wants the full story."

"He can wait. I need to roll the prints from that hand."

"I'll do it, if you want." She looked me up and down. "It looks like you could use a real shower."

I suddenly remembered the alligator. "Hey, did the vet perform the necropsy on the alligator?"

"Yeah, he said it was the most unusual thing he's ever been asked to do." She laughed. "You should've seen him! He's got a small practice that mostly handles household pets—I bring my dog to him once a year—so this was definitely new to him. You'd think a vet would be used to animal guts, but not him."

"Did he find anything in the stomach?"

"He didn't find any human remains, but he did find what looked liked partially digested chicken."

I scowled, staring down at my boots. "We need to find the owner of that arm and we need to find Dexter."

"We will." Susan pointed at the print kit in my hand. "Is that a cadaver print kit?"

"Yeah."

"Cool! I've never actually used one before. I'll go roll the prints right now and meet you back at the office." She stripped the kit from my hand and started to walk away, but I called out to her, and she turned to face me.

I fished twenty bucks from my wallet and approached her. "This is to cover William's bet."

Susan's jaw dropped, but only for a second. She recovered quickly, waving it off. "That's not necessary."

"How'd you know?" I asked.

"Lucky guess." Susan chewed subtly on her lower lip.

I narrowed my eyes. "Right. That might work on Melvin and the others, but I'm not buying it."

"I didn't mean anything by it. I just wanted to know who my new boss would be."

"I'd do the same thing if I were in your shoes." I tucked the twenty back in my wallet, returned it to my back pocket. "Look, I can't tell you what to do, but I'd appreciate it if you kept your research information to yourself. If you don't mind." I slammed the passenger's back door of my Tahoe and started to walk around to the other side.

"Chief Wolf, I'm really sorry about what happened to—"

"Look, we need to get one thing straight if we're going to work together." I fixed Susan with the coldest stare I could muster.

She swallowed hard, but held my gaze.

I smiled. "I don't like titles. Just call me Clint."

Susan exhaled sharply. "You got me! I thought you were really upset."

"It is what it is. It happened, and there's nothing I can do about it but try to move on. And it's definitely no secret."

Susan's eyes were soft. She walked up and put a hand on my chest. "If you ever need someone to talk to, I'm here."

I looked down at her hand and grinned. "From the looks of your knuckles, I should call you if I ever need a sparring partner."

Susan quickly retracted her hand, hiding it behind her back. "I...I dabble in punching stuff for fun. It helps relieve stress."

"I probably need to dabble in some stress relief, myself." I slipped into my Tahoe and drove away.

CHAPTER 8

I had one thing to do before meeting with the mayor. I picked up my radio. "Lindsey, this is Clint. Do you copy?"

"Ten-four, Chief."

"I need the address to Dexter Boudreaux's house."

Within a minute, Lindsey called it out on the radio. After I wrote it down, I stared at the paper. It was at the corner of Coconut Lane and Tenth Street. I scowled. *I can't wait until I know my way around town!* I picked up the radio and asked Lindsey for directions. When she'd provided them, I drove to Dexter's house to meet with his wife.

I swallowed hard when I turned into the driveway and saw an elderly lady sitting on the front porch swing, both hands resting in her lap. She sat up when I shut off the engine, but her shoulders drooped when she realized I was alone.

Mrs. Boudreaux stood to her trembling legs as I made my way up the steps and stopped right in front of her. She was short and frail, with thinning white hair and wrinkles that told the story of a long and rough life. She was holding onto the support chain on the swing with a hand littered with age spots.

"Mrs. Boudreaux," I began. "I'm Clint Wolf, the new chief of police here in—"

"Where's my husband?"

I lowered my head, stared down at my feet. "Ma'am, there was an accident last night."

"Were you with him?"

"Yes, ma'am. We were tracking this alligator and—"

"Where the hell is my husband?" The force of her voice caught me by surprise, but not as much as the stinging slap that landed on my left cheek. My ear rang; my face smarted.

I looked deep into her gray eyes, frowning. "I'm afraid he's missing. The alligator took him under. The last time I saw him, he was struggling with the alligator, but it didn't look good."

Tears streamed down her face, but she held her head up straight. "I know my Dexter. There's no alligator that can take him."

I frowned. "I'm so sorry, ma'am. I feel responsible. I was the one with him and I wasn't able to save him."

Mrs. Boudreaux stepped back from me and eased her way onto the swing. "You can go now, young man. I'll be sitting here when Dexter gets back."

I hesitated.

"Get off my property!" The woman spat the words in my direction.

I turned and made my way back to the Tahoe, wondering how she would survive without Dexter.

I drove to the town hall and found Mayor Malcolm Landry in his office. He was standing behind his desk yelling at someone on the phone. He waved me to a chair in front of his mahogany desk, and I sank into it, my muscles screaming their thanks.

Mayor Landry continued yelling. "I don't give a shit what you have to do, just get it done! No, I won't give you an extension. The ribbon ceremony is next week, and the governor is cutting the ribbon—you don't reschedule the governor!" He slammed the phone to its cradle and turned to me, his plump face ruby-colored. "Those damn architects! They're asking for an extension. They know we can't reschedule this event. The Fourth of July only comes along once a year. Jeez, what idiots!"

I had no clue what he was talking about and knew it was none of my business, but I couldn't help but ask, "The governor is coming here? To Mechant Loup?"

"Yeah. The city council voted unanimously to dedicate the new town hall building to the fallen heroes from Mechant Loup who served in the national guard, and the governor is going to cut the ribbon at the ceremony."

"I hate that prick."

Mayor Landry studied my face and was thoughtful before he spoke. "I understand you and a lot of other cops have taken issue with his policies, but I hope you'll give him the respect his office deserves. After all, he'll be here to honor our fallen heroes, and that's important to a lot of people in this town."

"I know how to be professional."

"Good...now, let's change gears." Mayor Landry took a deep breath and exhaled forcefully, then dropped into his oversized leather chair. "We need to talk about what happened out there so we can get the right story to the press. We don't want to go creating a panic. A lot of tourism dollars flow through here in the summer, and we don't need some wild story about a monster alligator scaring them away."

I frowned. "I hear what you're saying, but I think we need to make a public safety announcement just the same. Not to scare anyone, but to make them aware that they need to take some precautions if they're going out on the water."

"You're right. I'll get my secretary to draw something up to send to the media." He scowled. "Dexter was one of the best trappers around. With him gone, I don't know who we'll call to track that monster, or what we'll do with the nuisance alligator population once things settle down again. He's been doing this so long. I just can't believe he's gone."

"I'm sorry, sir. Everything was so unexpected. That alligator came straight for us and attacked the boat like we were in a damn horror movie. It caught Dexter off guard—definitely surprised me."

Mayor Landry sighed. "The important thing is that you're okay. Nick would never forgive me—or himself—if you got killed your first day on the job."

I frowned at the mention of my father-in-law. "Once people find out the judge is my father-in-law, they're going to think you gave me the job because of him."

"I did."

"Well, maybe you should've picked someone better equipped for this line of work—like Beaver."

Mayor Landry folded his arms across his chest—they seemed to rest naturally on his protruding gut—and leaned back, his chair squeaking in protest. "There's a reason he's no longer chief of police in my town."

"I didn't realize he was the former chief of police until he said so."

Landry sighed. "I guess I should've warned you about him. I just didn't think you'd run into him as soon as you did."

"Why'd you let him go?"

"He was a corrupt cop, and I fired him. It's that simple."

"Nothing's ever that simple. What'd he do?"

Mayor Landry allowed his arms to drift down toward his desk, as he shrugged. "I had gotten some complaints from a few out-of-towners that he was shaking them down during traffic stops. He'd stop them for a simple violation and then tell them he'd let them go if they paid a hefty fine on the spot and in cash."

"Did you investigate the allegations?"

"Well, I didn't have anyone with your background to turn to, so I called him in and asked him if he did it. Of course, he—"

"Came right out and admitted it and you fired him." I shook my head. "You never call suspects in and ask them if they *did it*. They'll deny it every time."

Mayor Landry threw up his hands. "I'm a politician, not a cop. Give me a break." We both laughed, and he continued, "About a week later, this article comes out in the local paper accusing Beaver of shaking down drivers and accusing me of covering it up. I had no choice at that point. It was an election year and my opponent was about to grab it and ride that pony into the ground. I fired Beaver."

I scowled. "Fired? Why wasn't he arrested?"

"Like I said, I didn't have anyone who could investigate it properly. There was no evidence—just a few unsubstantiated complaints."

"How many complaints?"

"I don't know—two, three."

"You know what they say—where there's smoke, there's fire."

Mayor Landry nodded. "I took it to the district attorney, but he said there wasn't enough evidence to pursue criminal charges, so the matter was dropped."

I was thoughtful for a few moments. If those allegations were true, then Beaver was the worst kind of criminal—the kind who wore a badge. "Look, once we find Dexter and the other end of that arm, I can take a look at that file on Beaver if you like. The statute of limitation on malfeasance in office won't expire for several more years."

"Nah, that's all water under the bridge now. Things are back to normal around here and we finally have a real chief of police, so I'd rather just move forward and keep things positive for our little town." Mayor Landry stood and nodded. "What I do want is for you to go home for the night and get some rest—it looks like you need it."

"I need to find Dexter." I started to walk out the mayor's office.

"Oh, Clint…"

I turned back to face him.

"Look, you need to be safe out there. If something ever happened to you, it would kill Nick, then he'd kill me for giving you this job…and I'm too young to die."

"I'm a grown-ass man. I don't need another man worrying about me. I don't like it either."

"Son, you know he can't help himself. You're all he's got left."

CHAPTER 9

I pulled into the sally port of what would be my new place of business. Susan's Charger was already there, and I parked beside it. She must have heard me drive up because she came through the back door and waved at me.

When I stepped out, she hollered, "Get in here. I bought you a burger and some fries. Afterward, I'll show you the prints I lifted. They came out good!"

My stomach growled at the mention of food, and I gratefully followed her through the back door. I had been in the building only twice—Sunday when I rolled into town to meet with Mayor Landry to accept the job and the previous day when I'd received my first call about a dog being eaten by an alligator—and I was a little disoriented when we walked inside. We passed a holding cell to our immediate right and made our way through the processing room. Susan opened the opposite door to the processing center and it led to the patrol room and Lindsey's desk.

"Ah," I said. "Now I know where I am."

Susan pointed to a door located at the far right corner of the room. "Then you should remember that's your office. I ordered a sign to put on the door in case you ever forget where you belong."

I smiled my thanks.

Susan waved me by Lindsey, who gawked at my appearance, and then around the corner to the left and down a corridor. "This first door on your right is the interview room," she explained. "And this next door is the break room."

I followed her inside, and the sweet scent of grilled onions greeted my nostrils and propelled me forward. "Which one's mine?"

Susan shrugged. "They're both the same. Take whichever you like."

I sat down in front of the burger closest to me, ripped the wrapper open, took a giant bite out of it. I groaned when the mixture of beef, onions, tomatoes, and condiments stroked my taste buds. I chewed for a long moment, savoring the flavor. After I swallowed, I turned to Susan, who hadn't even freed her burger from the wrapper yet, and said, "This has to be the best burger I've ever eaten!"

"The little restaurant at the corner of Main and Kate made them." Susan finally made it to her burger and took a bite, her eyes half closing as she nodded her agreement. Neither of us spoke another word as we wolfed down our food.

When we were done, I leaned back in my chair and sighed. "Thanks, Susan. You saved my life."

She wiped her mouth with a napkin, smiling a crooked smile. "You're welcome."

It was at that moment I realized how attractive she was, even with a mixture of mayonnaise and ketchup plastered on her lower lip. The dime-sized purplish scar near the corner of her left eye added character to a face that was perfectly chiseled. Her eyes were the darkest and most mysterious I'd seen. She squinted as she stared back at me. I looked away, embarrassed. "Um...you have a little ketchup on your face."

"Oh!" Susan dabbed at her mouth with the napkin. "Thanks. I would've walked around with that on my face all day."

After cleaning up my mess, I walked back to Lindsey's desk. "Where're William, Melvin, and Jack?"

Lindsey grabbed her dispatcher's log and pointed to some chicken scratch I couldn't read. "Melvin went back out on the water. He said you were going to meet him out there later."

"Who'd he take with him?" I asked.

Lindsey shook her head. "No one."

I scowled. Although he had been alone when he found me, I didn't like him being out there without backup. "What about the others?"

"William and Lieutenant Jackson don't come on duty until six o'clock."

I looked up when Susan entered the room. "Do we have a boat? I mean, other than the airboat?"

"We do. It's parked behind the sally port."

"Can you drive it?"

Susan grinned and a dimple appeared on her upper left cheek.

"Can you breathe air?"

I smiled. "We need to get out there and meet up with Melvin."

"Oh, come see the prints first." Susan led me to her desk, which was situated against the same wall that Lindsey's desk was on. She grabbed two index cards that lay face up on her desk and handed them to me. "I'm not sure if they're dry yet."

The ridge detail was decent for the partially decomposed hand. "Wow, they came out great."

"I took my time with it."

"Does the Chateau Parish Detention Center have an AFIS system?" I asked.

Susan nodded. "They'll run them for us on the spot. I can take them over if you like."

"No, you're coming with me." I placed the prints on Lindsey's desk. "When Jack gets in, can you tell him I said to get these down to the jail as soon as possible and have them run it?"

"Yes, Chief."

Susan shook an index finger in Lindsey's direction. "Don't call him that. He doesn't like it when people call him *Chief.* He practically threatened to fire me when I called him that earlier."

Lindsey sucked her breath. "Oh…I'm sorry."

"I didn't threaten to fire anyone!" I laughed. "I just don't like titles. My first name is still Clint. If it's good enough for my mom, it's good enough for me. I don't need to go changing it now. Oh, and one more thing, Lindsey."

"Yes…um, Clint?"

"You've got it." I smiled, gave her a nod. "Okay, I'm assuming you haven't received a missing person's report in the last few days?"

Lindsey shook her head.

"What about within the last couple of months?"

"I don't think we've ever had a missing person in this town," Susan said.

"Check with the sheriff's office and see if they've had a white male go missing in recent days."

Lindsey nodded and jotted more chicken scratch on a yellow notebook.

"If they don't have any," I continued, "check with surrounding towns and our neighboring parishes."

"Okay. I'll get on this right away."

Susan pointed to the waistband of my jeans. "Do you need a gun?"

"I have plenty, but I forgot to grab one when I changed. I guess I need to get back into the habit of keeping one with me."

"You think?" Susan jerked open the top drawer of her desk and pulled out an old .357 revolver. "This used to be my dad's. You can use it until you get one of your own."

I took the revolver and opened the cylinder. It was fully loaded. I pushed the cylinder closed, twisted it until it locked in place, and shoved it in the front of my waistband. I nodded my thanks to Susan before I headed for the back door. "Let's get out there and see if we can find—"

The front door burst open and Officer William Tucker came running in. I glanced at the clock. He was early for his shift. He was out of breath and his eyes were wide. "Chief! You have to come now! They found him!"

"Found who?" Susan and I asked in unison, but William was already heading back out the door.

CHAPTER 10

I jumped in with Susan, and she sped down Main Street following William. It became almost immediately apparent he was leading us toward the boat launch. Sirens pierced our eardrums. Blue lights flashed. I snatched Susan's radio from its docking station and radioed William to ask who was found. The radio scratched to life, but it wasn't William—it was Melvin. His voice came through in labored gasps, as though he'd been running. "Chief, I'm heading back to the landing...be there in twenty...need an ambulance."

"Come back?" I called. "You need an ambulance?"

"Ten-four! I found Dexter Boudreaux. He's alive, but he's in bad trouble!"

Duck bumps immediately broke out over my skin. "Come back?" Relief flooded over me. My thoughts went to Mrs. Boudreaux sitting there on her porch, waiting for Dexter to come home like he'd done so many other times throughout their long lives. "Did you say Dexter's alive?"

"Ten-four, Chief, but not by much."

I radioed Lindsey and asked her to get an ambulance rolling.

"They're already en route!" Her voice was laced with excitement.

Just then, Susan jerked the steering wheel hard, and I lurched to the left, almost colliding with her. The seatbelt was the only thing keeping me in place as we swerved right onto Grace Street and then made our way onto Bayou Tail Lane. Shells exploded into the air and peppered the undercarriage when she raced into the boat launch parking lot. She zipped between vehicles until she came to a skidding stop inches from the pier. A cloud of dust quickly caught up to us and enveloped the car and members of the news media who were still camped out at the launch.

I could hear people coughing outside and someone cursed. When the air was clear enough to see again, I stepped out and approached the group of reporters standing on the pier. A few of them were waving the air in front of their faces in order to clear it faster.

"Howdy," I said. "I'd like to ask all of you to move back away from the pier. We have an injured man coming in and we need to get an ambulance through here."

"Is it Dexter Boudreaux?" a man at the front of the group asked.

"I'm not at liberty to discuss the case."

The compassionate reporter from earlier pushed her way to the front of the group. "Will the man be okay?"

I looked down at her, and our eyes locked for the second time that day. There was something about her that aroused my curiosity, but I couldn't put a finger on it. Her press badge said her name was Chloe Rushing.

"Chief?" The freckles on her nose seemed to sparkle in the sunlight. "Will the man be okay?"

"I sure hope so," was all I muttered. Shells crunched behind me, and I turned to see William pull up in his marked Charger. When he had dismounted, I moved out of earshot of the reporters and waved him over. "Grab some crime scene tape and mark off an area clear of the pier for the reporters to hang out. I don't want Dexter's wife seeing him torn to shit on the six o'clock news."

"Right away, boss." William ushered the reporters away and set about doing what I'd asked.

I looked over at the reporters one last time and caught another glimpse of Chloe Rushing. She was staring back. I ducked my head, turned away. Sirens moaned in the distance—that long, wailing cry that signaled the approach of the ambulance—and I hurried to the slip where Melvin would be docking the boat soon. Susan was already there, scanning Bayou Tail.

"Do you see anything?" I asked.

"Not yet, but he can't be far. I can hear the hum of the airboat."

As though on cue, Melvin rounded the distant bend in the bayou and shot straight toward us. When he got closer, I could see part of a blanket covering a figure that lay on the floor toward the back of the boat. The sirens grew louder, merging with the increasingly loud roar of the airboat engine.

Susan squeezed the back of my arm and hollered, "I'm going guide the ambulance in!"

I only nodded. My heart was pounding. My eyes were fixed on

what I could see of the blanket. I wiped my sweaty palms on my jeans legs. The last time I'd seen Dexter, his arm was in the jowls of that giant alligator. I couldn't imagine it was still attached. Even if it was, he would have lost so much blood that it might already be too late.

Melvin waved at me to back away as he made his final approach. He gunned the engine and drove the airboat up through the ramp and right onto the parking lot. Shells grated against the hull of the boat. Melvin killed the engine and ripped his earmuffs off, then scrambled to the back of the boat. I jumped over the side of the boat and met him at the back, where we knelt beside the blanketed figure. I paused, straining to see movement from under the blanket—any movement at all.

Melvin knelt on the opposite side of Dexter, looking at me as though waiting for me to make the first move. When he spoke, it was a shaky whisper. "Chief, it ain't good."

I took a deep breath, grabbed the edge of the blanket and pulled back slowly. When the face beneath the blanket finally came into view, I gasped, inadvertently throwing myself back—it looked like Abigail's face.

CHAPTER 11

I shook my head and looked again. It was Dexter Boudreaux, but his face was ghostly. His lips were parched from exposure, but were pale. His clothes were tattered, stained from mud and dried blood. His exposed skin had lost all of its color—he'd been nearly drained of blood. I glanced down at his arm and winced. The lower portion of his arm was precariously attached to the upper arm by several strips of ripped skin. Both jagged ends of the broken bone protruded from the mess of torn flesh. I shook my head. His arm hadn't stood a chance against that monster alligator's death roll.

Inspecting farther up Dexter's arm I saw that his belt was wrapped around the left bicep. It was the only reason he was still alive—although barely. I looked over when I heard Susan yelling commands behind us. She and two paramedics reached the boat and jumped over the side. The paramedics carried a spine board and they all rushed across the hull to where we knelt. I backed away when they arrived to give them room to work.

"Holy shit," one of them exclaimed when they saw Dexter. "What happened?"

"Alligator attack," Melvin said.

Susan helped the paramedics position the spine board beside Dexter, and they began digging tools out of their bags. I walked to the edge of the boat, jumped out. I made my way toward a tree at the end of the parking lot. I needed to sit down. I needed shade. As I walked, news reporters rushed past me, but I didn't even try to stop them. When I reached the tree, I placed it between me and the boat launch. I leaned my back against it, then slid to a seated position. I rested the back of my head against the hard bark and closed my eyes.

Abigail's disfigured face came into view, and I quickly opened my eyes. "Why can't I see you the way you used to be?"

Something touched my shoulder, and I jerked around. It was Chloe, the reporter. I pushed off the tree and stood on uncertain legs. "Hey, um, what's up?"

"Are you okay?" she asked. There was an obvious look of concern on her face.

I waved my hand dismissively. "I'm fine. Why aren't you with the others? You're missing the story."

"I was worried about you." Chloe studied my face. "Do you mind if I sit with you?"

I hesitated, as I looked toward the boat launch. Susan had things well under control. She guided the medics off the boat with Dexter on the spine board and then helped them place him on a gurney. As the medics strapped Dexter down, Susan addressed the media. I couldn't hear what she was saying, but she looked as confident as anyone I'd ever seen. I wondered at that moment why Mayor Landry hadn't named her the chief of police. She was more than capable of handling anything that would—

"Chief, are you sure you're okay?" Chloe's voice brought me back to the there and then near the tree. I stared down at her staring up at me. She smiled, nodding. "It's okay to take a little time out every now and then. I do it often. Some of the stories I cover are gut-wrenching, and it's very saddening. But your work—I can't imagine how stressful and emotionally draining it is." She pointed toward the spot where I'd been sitting. "I'll sit with you if you like. I'm a good listener."

"Thanks, but I have to get back to work." I turned and walked away, leaving her standing there. The paramedics had already loaded Dexter into the ambulance and they sped off, heading for the nearest hospital twenty miles away.

Susan saw me walking toward her and met me halfway. "Hey, Clint, I wondered where you'd disappeared to." Her gaze shifted to a point somewhere behind me and her lips became thin lines. "What were you two doing over by that tree?"

I looked over my shoulder. Chloe was still standing where I'd left her. I turned back to Susan, shrugged. "I needed to clear my head. She just walked over to see if I was okay."

Susan grunted. We walked to the airboat and met with William and Melvin, who were talking softly about Dexter. I slapped Melvin's back. "Good job! How'd you find him?"

"I was traveling the perimeter of the lake near where I found you.

I noticed the marsh grass was smashed and there were large ruts in the mud where I picked you up. So, I continued riding the banks and found track marks where you must've gone into the marsh last night." Melvin shrugged. "For some reason, I decided to keep traveling the edges looking for tracks and found some that were made by Dexter Boudreaux."

"How'd you know they were Dexter's tracks?" asked Susan.

"I didn't. They were just the only other tracks along the lake. I parked the airboat and started following them." Melvin shook his head. "I don't know how he did it, but that old man crawled about half a mile in that condition. I'm not sure when he passed out, but he was unconscious when I found him."

I stared at the orange glow to the west that marked the sunset. "Where'd you think he was going? Or do you think he even knew where he was?"

"He knew," William said. "My dad told me once how Dexter got into a boating accident in the middle of the night with no lights and no stars to guide his way, but he made it across the swamps with nothing but his instincts to guide him."

"That's impressive," Susan said. "Nowadays, kids can't find the mall without a GPS navigational system."

We all nodded our agreement.

Susan turned to William. "How'd you find out about it?"

"I called him," Melvin said. "My radio was fading in and out when I found Dexter, so I hurried and called him on my cell."

"Yeah," William agreed. "I didn't even get dressed for work. I headed straight for the office."

"You can head home now if you want to get ready for work," I offered. "I'll hang around the office until you get back."

William nodded his goodbyes and left.

"Another thing, Chief," Melvin said. "I found a tiny oil slick where the boat went down. If you want, I can redirect the divers to that location tomorrow and see if we can't recover your guns and the boat."

I thought about correcting him for calling me Chief, but didn't. "Are the divers already gone for the day?"

Melvin nodded. "The longest they'll stay underwater in that depth is two hours. They said they'll be back first thing in the morning."

"Okay. Why don't you turn in for the night? You've got to be tired." I paused, then said, "You did a great job, Melvin. You definitely saved Dexter's life."

"If he lives," Melvin said softly.

I couldn't argue and I wasn't about to make any promises. So, all I said was, "Get out of here and get some rest."

Melvin walked away, but called over his shoulder before he was out of earshot, "Welcome to Mechant Loup!"

"Thanks. It was a hell of a first couple of days."

When we were all alone, Susan stood there staring at the ground, quiet.

"What's up with you?" I asked.

"Well, I saw you back there...in the airboat. When you first looked at Dexter."

"What about it?"

Susan looked up at me, and I thought I saw her dark eyes glisten. "Are you okay to be doing this again? So soon after?"

I looked away, not sure how to answer. One thing was certain—I didn't want to talk about it. I finally said, "It's been almost two years. It's time I got back to doing the one thing I'm good at."

I guess she sensed my sour mood because she lightened up the conversation. "You mean there's no future for you in the cabinet-making business?"

"None at all." I glanced sideways at her. "Ready to get back to the office so you can head home?"

She nodded and ambled toward the Charger. I scanned the parking lot before following her. It was nearly empty, except for a few trucks, a red car, and a news van. I caught movement near the red car. Even from that distance and in the waning light, I recognized it to be Chloe. She was placing some things in the passenger's seat and then moved around to the driver's side. Before getting inside, she turned and looked in my direction. It was too far and shadowy to tell if she was looking directly at me, but I felt a tinge of excitement all the same. What was it about her that made me—

"Are you coming? Or do you plan on sleeping out here tonight?"

CHAPTER 12

When Susan and I arrived back at the police department, we found Lieutenant Jack Jackson sitting in my office with his feet up on my desk. He didn't bother moving when we walked in, and I didn't complain. I took a seat in one of the spare chairs, but that didn't sit right with Susan. She stomped around my desk and glared down at Jack, hands on her hips. "Get the hell out of his chair! He's our chief now, and you're going to accept that and respect him!"

"Susan," I said, "it's okay. If I wanted him out of my chair, I'd grab him by the throat and drag him out of it."

Jack's gaze jerked up from the file in his lap and he stared at me with cold, dark eyes. "What did you say?"

"Jack, you heard what I said. You're asking that question so you can buy time to think of your next move." I shook my head. "You don't have to worry about that. Your next move will be to tell me you did a good job figuring out whose arm we found floating in the lake."

I could tell Jack was confused and didn't know what to do next. He tried to hold my stare, but his eyes shifted, and he glanced away. Finally, he dropped his feet to the ground and handed me the file he had been studying. "We got a hit on the prints."

"Good work." I took the file and read the name out loud. "Hays Cain. Do either of you know this man?"

"Everyone knows him," Susan said, still glaring down at Jack. "Hays owns a chain of restaurants throughout the south. In fact, you ate one of his hamburgers earlier today."

I scowled. "And no one reported him missing?"

"No," Jack said. "When I got back here, Lindsey told me she'd called every sheriff's office south of I-10 and every city and town within fifty miles, but no one's reported a white male missing."

I flipped through the file and found some family history, along with his last known address. "Is he still married to Pauline?"

Susan nodded. "And they still live at the end of Kate Drive in a mansion surrounded by dozens of acres of pristine land."

"Does his son still live with them, too?"

"No," Jack said. "Allen was killed while serving in the national guard."

"When was he killed?" I asked.

"A couple of years ago," Jack said.

"Should we notify Pauline Cain?" Susan wanted to know.

"Yeah, we have to let her know what's going on." I closed the file, looked over at Jack. "I'll go make the notification and then turn in for the night. I'll relieve you in the morning."

"I'm coming with you," Susan said.

"Good—you're driving."

*   *   *

When Susan turned down Kate Drive, I whistled. Palm trees and lampposts lined both sides of the mostly bare street. It was bright like the day. The end of the street opened into a large cul-de-sac with an enormous waterfall at its center. The mansion that sprouted from the ground looked out of place in the quaint town of Mechant Loup. "Was this necessary?"

"What's that?" Susan asked.

I pointed. "This house. Did he have to build something so enormous? He could fit a dozen small families in there. It looks like a five-star hotel."

"He's a bit of a showoff." Susan parked in front of a large double gate and pressed the call button.

"Can I assist you?" asked a smooth male voice after a short wait.

"Sergeant Susan Wilson and Chief Clint Wolf here to see Mrs. Cain."

"Do you have an appointment?"

"It's an emergency."

"Let me see if Ms. Pauline will agree to see you."

Susan turned to me. "If he doesn't open that damn gate, I'm crashing right through it."

"He'll open it."

As though on cue, a buzzer sounded and both gates eased open in front of us. Susan didn't wait for it to open completely. As soon as she could squeeze through she did and sped up the cobblestone drive to the front of the house. We both stepped out of the car and were met instantly by a well-groomed man wearing a black tuxedo.

"Please, follow me," the man said.

We did, and he led us up a flight of stone steps and through a set of heavy wooden doors that had to be ten feet tall. We found ourselves in a foyer nearly the size of the police department. A large gold chandelier hung above us, and an entire living room set occupied the foyer. The man pointed to a white leather couch to our right. "If you would wait there, Ms. Pauline will be with you shortly."

Susan and I took a seat, sinking deep into the soft cushion. She slapped the arm of the sofa. "I think your first official act as chief should be to get a sofa like this for the office."

I nodded, figuring Pauline had to get dressed. I was sure she hadn't been expecting company at this late hour. As we waited, I wondered why we hadn't received a missing person's report from Pauline Cain. That arm had been in the water at least three days, so why hadn't anyone noticed he was gone?

After a short wait, a woman appeared atop the twin set of spiral staircases at the end of the foyer. She wore a flowing silk nightgown that was open way too low in the front and had a slit up the leg that exposed entirely too much skin. She smiled as she descended the stairs. Her jet-black hair seemed to float on the air behind her. "Good evening, officers."

I heard Susan groan to herself as we both stood. I tried to keep my eyes focused on Pauline's face, but something in her left hand caught my attention—a wine glass. And it was nearly empty. She extended her right hand when she reached the landing. "How can I help you guys?"

I cleared my throat. "Ma'am, when was the last time you saw your husband?"

Pauline's smile faded. She looked from me to Susan and then back at me. "Is there a problem?"

"Ma'am, I'm afraid we have some bad news..."

"What is it?" Her eyes were wide. "Tell me!"

"Mrs. Cain, we found some remains in Lake Berg."

"Remains? What do you mean?"

"We found an arm—your husband's arm. We don't know your husband's location or what exactly happened to him, but we did verify with fingerprint evidence that it was his arm."

Pauline's mouth opened and closed several times, but no words came out. Her eyes started to slide shut and the glass slipped from her hand and crashed to the floor. Susan and I raced forward and caught her before she landed on top of the wine glass. My hands slipped on the silk nightgown as I worked to secure a hold on her waist and arm.

"She's heavier than she looks," Susan said.

I nodded and helped her guide Pauline to the couch, where we eased her onto it. I called for the man who'd let us in and he came shuffling into the room. His mouth gaped when he saw Pauline Cain slumped on the sofa. "What did you do to her?" he demanded.

"She fainted," Susan explained. "Get me a cool towel."

The man left and returned with a damp white towel with a large, gold-colored *H* embroidered on it. As Susan tended to Pauline, I pulled the man aside. "What's your name, sir?"

The man kept glancing at Pauline. "Um…Stephen. Stephen Butler."

"When was the last time you saw Hays Cain?"

Stephen was thoughtful. "Friday night."

I eyed him skeptically. "You haven't heard from him in four days and no one thought to call it in?"

"It is not unusual for Mr. Hays to leave for days and not even call."

"Where was he headed when he left Friday?"

"He does not share his itinerary with anyone."

"Not even his wife?"

"No, officer. He does not often say to anyone where he is going."

"How does his wife feel about that?"

Stephen sighed. "It is why she consumes so much wine—red wine, the sweet variety."

"I understand that." I scratched my head. It didn't make sense to me that a man would just walk out of the house without telling anyone where he was going. "I understand you don't know where he went, but do you know if he had any business out on Lake Berg?"

Stephen blinked with surprise. "Lake Berg? Mr. Hays does not fish. He does not even own a boat."

"What about friends? Who does he hang out with on a regular basis? Someone who can tell me where he was going Friday?"

Stephen stared up at the chandelier, nodded. "That would be Randall Rupe—the elder. They have been best friends since high school, or so I have been told by Mr. Hays."

"Where can I find him?"

"Everyone knows Mr. Rupe. He is the owner of the only car dealership in Mechant Loup."

"Thanks, Stephen. You've been a big—"

"Who are you?" cried Pauline Cain in a slurred voice.

I hurried to the sofa, where Susan knelt beside Pauline's outstretched body. Pauline was trying to push herself to a seated position.

"Whoa," Pauline said. "The room is spinning."

"Relax, Mrs. Cain," Susan said in a soothing voice, helping her back to a reclining position. "I'm Susan Wilson. Remember?"

The blood seemed to drain from Pauline's face as she remembered why we were there. Tears formed at the corners of her eyes. "Oh, my God! Hays! What happened to my husband?"

Susan placed a hand on Pauline's shoulder and leaned close. "I'm so sorry, ma'am, but we're not real sure yet. We need to ask you a few questions so we can know where to concentrate our efforts."

Pauline settled into the sofa and cried softly. I wanted to tell her I understood, wanted to reach out to her, tell her it would be okay...but those were all lies. The sad fact was it wouldn't be okay. This moment would haunt her for the rest of her life. She would lose a lot—sleep, her appetite, interest in most things. I touched the broken glass and puddle of wine on the black marble floor with the toe of my boot. Apparently, I thought to myself, you've already suffered some sort of loss.

"Mrs. Cain," Susan said, "would you rather it if we came back tomorrow?"

Pauline didn't lift her head. "I just want to sleep."

Susan looked up at me, and I nodded. I turned to Stephen Butler. "We'll be back sometime tomorrow."

Before heading to the office to retire for the night, Susan and I stopped at the hospital to check on Dexter Boudreaux. The double sliding doors swished when they opened, and a gush of cold air rushed out to meet us. The cleanliness of the hospital made me very aware I hadn't taken a shower since crawling out of the swamps earlier in the day.

Mrs. Boudreaux sat alone in a corner of the bright waiting room reading a book. She didn't look up when we walked in.

"I want to visit with her," I told Susan.

Susan nodded. "I'll talk to the doctor and find out how Dexter's doing."

I walked slowly toward Mrs. Boudreaux, but stopped a few feet away. "Mrs. Boudreaux?"

The elderly lady looked up and smiled. "I told you my Dexter was coming home to me. He will always come home to me."

I wanted to tell her to stop living in a fantasy world. Wanted to tell her death was inevitable—that the only thing uncertain about dying was the order in which we would be taken. Instead, I took a seat beside her and nodded. "That Dexter is a tough one."

"He is! Did he tell you about the time he spent over a week in the marsh with no food or water? His boat broke down." Mrs. Boudreaux waved her hand around. "That was before they had those carry-around phones. No matter how long he was gone, I knew he was coming home to me."

Mrs. Boudreaux's eyes lit up when she spoke about her husband and the deep wrinkles that were etched into her face seemed to grow shallower. As her voice droned on, I absently wondered if counting her wrinkles would offer some clue as to just how old she was. She talked nonstop until Susan entered the room.

"Hey, there, young lady," Mrs. Boudreaux said. "Would you like to join us? We have all night because the doctor said I won't be able to see Dexter until the morning."

Susan smiled and cocked her head. "Thank you so much! I'd love to stay, but, actually, I've come to steal my chief away from you. I need him back at the office."

"I understand. You two run off. I'll sit here and read until they let me see Dexter."

I nodded my goodbye and followed Susan out into the parking lot. The warm air felt good on my face. "How is he?"

"Not good. They said he lost a lot of blood." Susan frowned. "He hasn't regained consciousness, and they said it'd be a miracle if he survived the night."

"He's lucky he survived as long as he did."

"That's exactly what the doctor said."

We rode to the office in silence, and after Susan parked her Charger in the sally port, I paused outside the passenger's door. "It's late, so don't feel like you have to be on time in the morning."

"You're not interviewing Randall Rupe without me!"

I shook my head. "I wouldn't think of it. I'll hang around the office until you get here."

"I'll be here early just the same."

I removed the revolver from my waistband and flipped the cylinder open. I turned it backward, holding it by the yoke, and extended the handle toward Susan. "Thanks for loaning it to me. I appreciate it—especially since it was your dad's. That was nice of you."

"Go ahead and hold onto it, just in case you need it."

I shook my head. "It's not necessary, but thanks."

"What if you need it tonight?" she asked.

I smirked. "Um, we're not in the city."

"Bad shit happens here from time to time."

"Not tonight." I placed the revolver on the passenger's seat. "Besides, I have plenty of guns at home."

"Okay, but be careful."

I walked into the office and an elderly lady with snow white hair was sitting at Lindsey's desk completing a crossword puzzle. She smiled. "I'm Marsha. I'm the night dispatcher. And you must be Chief Wolf?"

I nodded, shook her hand. "Just call me Clint."

"Okay, Clint. If you don't mind me saying it, you look like you need a shower and some sleep."

"Is it that bad?"

She wrinkled her nose. "I can smell the marsh rot from here."

I took a step away from Marsha, suddenly self-conscious. "Alright, I'll be back in the morning."

CHAPTER 13

It was nearly midnight when I got home. Achilles gave an excited yelp from his crate and it was then that I remembered having a puppy. I sighed when I saw the mess inside. As soon as I opened the latch, he rushed from the corner of the crate, his over-sized ears flopping up and down as he ran. I dropped to my knees right as he came through the opening and dove headlong into my lap. His soft fur was warm. He wriggled in my arms and licked my face aggressively. I laughed and gently moved him off me and set him onto the floor.

"Whoa there, little man!" I rubbed his neck and muscular shoulders. "I bet you're hungry." I walked into the kitchen, and he followed closely behind me, jumping up on my legs and yapping at me. When I opened the refrigerator, he nosed into it and stood on his hind legs, his front paws resting on the bottom shelf. He sniffed the shelves and then looked up at me with eager eyes. His tongue dangled out of his half open mouth. I rubbed his ears, and he chomped his mouth shut several times, as though telling me he was hungry.

"What about some turkey?" I asked. His mouth clamped shut and his ears perked up. "Yeah, you know what I'm saying." I grabbed the package of turkey I'd purchased upon rolling into town that weekend and coaxed Achilles out of the refrigerator. I put some turkey on a plate and placed it in a corner of the kitchen. He was trampling all over my boots and kicked the plate away in the process. His tail wagged so hard his rear end bounced from side to side. "If I don't do something about you right now," I said, "I'll be dealing with this every time I feed you."

I tossed the turkey on the counter, and Achilles jumped up on his hind legs and tried to reach the food with his front paws.

"Down," I said in a firm voice and pulled him off the cabinet. I led him to the far side of the kitchen and told him to sit. He looked up at me like I was speaking Hebrew. I gently applied pressure on his rump and repeated the command. He was filled with nervous energy, but he sat. I moved my hand from his rump and he popped back up. I repeated the command and pressure on his rump, and only had to do so several times before he caught on. Next, I worked on getting him to stay where he was while I loaded the plate with food, but that was a bit more difficult. I finally gave up and let him break rank as I dumped all of the turkey into the plate.

"Enjoy that while you can," I said. "Tomorrow I'm bringing you some real dog food and then you won't be so happy."

Achilles ignored me as he devoured the soft meat. I grabbed the bowl of water from his crate and set it beside him. He stopped chomping long enough to lap up several gulps of water, but then went right back to eating the turkey.

I cleaned out the dirty crate and then showered and dressed in boxers while Achilles was preoccupied with his food. When I checked on him, he was standing by the back door peering out the lower pane of glass. He looked up when he heard me and bounded toward me. I padded across the wooden floor to let him out—

"Shit," I said when I stepped in a puddle of warm urine. I shook my head, laughing. "I thought you were potty trained."

I walked with him out the back door and let him explore the yard while I leaned against the porch railing and enjoyed the cool breeze blowing through the trees. After a few minutes of roaming around, Achilles finally squatted and did his business. When he was done, he kicked grass over it with his rear legs and loped toward the door. I let him in and locked the door behind him.

"Okay, little man, it's time for bed."

I walked to the only bedroom in the house that my father-in-law had agreed to rent to me. He offered it up free of charge, but I'd insisted on paying rent. I didn't like handouts.

I closed the door so Achilles couldn't tear up the living room furniture and slipped into bed. Achilles tried several times to climb up the side of the bed to get to me, but couldn't. He finally gave up and retired to the corner of the room where I'd laid out a blanket and pillow. He rested his head on his front paws and stared at me with sad eyes, whining his disappointment.

I flipped the switch on the lamp near my bed and—like I'd done every night for over a year—closed my eyes to try to sleep. As soon as I started to doze off, her lifeless and bloodied face came vividly into view, and I jerked to a seated position, fighting to catch my breath. Sweat broke out on my forehead. I felt around in the dark to get my bearings. When I was sure I had been dreaming, I sat in the dark like I'd done every night for two years and tried to talk myself out of it. And, like I'd done every night for two years, I lost the argument and walked to the kitchen.

I heard Achilles padding along behind me in the dark and felt his fur rubbing against my leg. When I reached the cabinet, I opened the narrow door closest to the refrigerator and grabbed one of the half dozen bottles of vodka that was neatly situated on the shelf. I knew without looking that it was unopened—they all were. With hands that shook, I twisted the cap off and took a long drink. I then tossed the cap into the sink and took the bottle with me to my bedroom. I heard Achilles' little body plop to the floor in the corner. He let out a grunt, and I grinned. "It's okay, buddy. You'll get used to sleeping alone— we all do."

I slid into the bed and leaned my back against the headboard, then took another drink from the bottle. A warm feeling started to spread across my chest. I gulped more of the alcohol and my lips began to feel numb. My stomach burned like it usually did when I drank too fast, but I didn't care. I needed to sleep, and this was the only way I knew how.

CHAPTER 14

Wednesday, June 25

The sun bled through cracks in the shade and stirred me from my sleep. I opened my eyes, but shut them when a piercing pain shot through the right side of my head. I eased my feet to the floor and felt for the bottle of painkillers on the night table. I popped two into my mouth and swallowed them dry. Something wet slid up my shins, and I suddenly remembered Achilles. I pried both eyes open and looked down. His tail slapped the floor and he panted excitedly, as though begging me to go outside and play.

"I wish I could go out and play, but one of us has to work so we can buy food and pay the rent."

I let Achilles out to do his business, but he seemed more interested in playing, so I crated him and showered for work. Once I was dressed, I let him out the back door again. I sat on the bottom step nursing my headache, as I watched Achilles sniff his way around the clearing. My backyard measured about fifty feet wide by fifty feet deep and was surrounded by thick woods. While it was a little overcast out, the shadows from the tall trees made it seem darker than it was. Achilles made his way to the far edge of the clearing and stared intently into the dense woods. His ears were on high alert and he let out as threatening a bark as was possible for his puppy voice. I laughed. "Easy, killer. It's probably a rabbit."

Achilles turned at the sound of my voice, but then redirected his attention to the woods. He barked again, and this time I caught a quick movement in the trees. Squinting through the pain in my skull, I watched the movement until a squirrel came into view on the side of a tree. It scrambled higher and paused to grab at a small branch. "You see, buddy, it's just a squirrel. No reason to get all worked up."

I clapped twice, and Achilles turned clumsily and bounded in my direction. I didn't know what was longer, his tongue or his ears, but it was fun to watch them flop up and down as he ran. He wouldn't be winning any races, but he was the cutest puppy I'd ever seen. When he reached me, I leaned over and rubbed his ears. He rolled onto his back and made noises that sounded a lot like an excited kid during Christmas.

Abigail would love Achilles. I frowned and stood. Achilles squirmed until he got to his feet and followed me up the steps. I reloaded his bowl of water and fed him more turkey before returning him to his crate. I then went into my closet and punched in the code on my fireproof gun safe. I grabbed a paddle holster for my Beretta nine-millimeter pistol and clipped it onto my waistband. Next, I pulled my pistol from the gun safe and—out of habit—checked to be sure it was loaded. I shoved it in the holster until it locked in place and walked out the door. When I looked back before pulling it shut, I saw Achilles staring through his prison bars with his head cocked to the side. I could've sworn he was frowning.

When I arrived at the office, Susan and Melvin's cars were already parked in the sally port. Jack was in his office and walked out when he heard me greet Lindsey.

"Hey, Chief—I mean Clint," Jack said. "I stopped by the hospital an hour ago and checked in on Dexter."

"How is he?"

"He's hanging tough. The doctor said he's not out the woods yet—not by a long shot—but they saw a slight improvement overnight that gave them hope."

I knew better than to get excited just yet. "Was Mrs. Boudreaux still at the hospital?"

"No. A nurse said her daughter came from out of town and brought her home." Jack handed me a log sheet. "Nothing to pass on from last night. It was quiet except for a few traffic violators."

I scanned the log. They had made a dozen traffic stops, responded to a complaint of a suspicious man lurking around the gas station, and handled a burglary call. "Anything came of the suspicious subject?"

Jack shook his head. "He was gone by the time William got there."

"What about the burglary?"

"It was an old warehouse for one of the chemical plants on the river. They said they used to store chemicals there, but it had been mostly abandoned since the oil field slump a few years back."

"What company?"

"Blackley and Sons Industries. The family's from Mechant Loup, but their company is in the city."

"What kind of chemicals did they store there?" I asked.

"Ammonium nitrate mostly."

"Ammonium nitrate?" My ears perked up. "Are you shitting me? If criminals with bad intentions get their hands on that, we're in trouble."

"The owner was sure the place had been cleaned out. He said no chemicals had been left on the premises."

"I sure hope not." I handed the log sheet to Lindsey and walked into the break room where Melvin and Susan were talking over coffee. I grabbed a cup of water and sucked it down, grateful my headache was nearly gone. I refilled the cup and sat at the table with Susan and Melvin.

"I'm fixing to head back out on the water," Melvin said. "With any luck, we'll recover Mr. Boudreaux's boat and your guns this morning."

"Is Beaver going back out there with you today?"

Melvin hesitated, nodded. "If that's okay with you."

"It is," I said. "I wanted to ask him to show you the spot where he found Hays Cain's arm. I'd like to get a few more boats out this morning and have them scour that entire area. We need to locate his body so we can find out what happened to him."

"Are we still interviewing Randall Rupe today?" Susan wanted to know.

I nodded. "First thing."

"Okay," Susan said, getting up from the table. "I'll grab the water-boarding kit."

Melvin and I chuckled and watched as she left the room. Melvin pointed after her. "Did you know she was a professional fighter?"

"You're shitting me."

Melvin shook his head. "She's training for a fight right now. In fact, it's this weekend."

"Boxing?" I asked.

"Mixed martial arts. She definitely favors striking and would make a great boxer, but she said there aren't many female boxers around to compete against. She wants to fight men, but the rules don't allow it."

"That's interesting. I've never met a real professional fighter. I mean, I've seen them on television, but never actually came face-to-face with one."

"She's worried you'll try to make her quit."

"Me? Why would she think that?"

"In case you thought it reflected poorly on the police department."

I laughed. "How on earth would her being able to kick ass reflect poorly on the department? If anything, it shows me that she's excellent backup and it'll deter people around here from resisting arrest. And even if I didn't like it, I can't tell her what to do in her personal life."

"Beaver sure tried. She told him she'd quit her job before she'd quit fighting, and he finally backed off."

"I'm not Beaver." I stood, downed the last of my water, and tossed the empty cup in the trashcan. "In fact, I'm going watch her fight. Let me know when and where."

"Saturday night at the bingo hall—eight o'clock."

"I'll be there."

CHAPTER 15

"Why'd you decide to drive?" Susan asked on the way to Randall Rupe's car dealership.

"You drive crazy. I want to make it to my thirtieth birthday."

Susan twisted in her seat to stare at me. "You're only twenty-nine?"

"Do I look that bad?" I asked.

"I'm sorry," Susan said. "I shouldn't have said that. I know you've been through a lot and I can relate a little. If you ever need anyone to talk—"

"I don't, but thanks." I changed the subject. "So, Melvin tells me you're a cage fighter."

Susan nodded slowly. "I hope that isn't a problem."

"Hell, no! I want to come to your fight. Where can I get a ticket?"

"Nonsense! I'll give you one." She was almost bouncing in her seat. "I won't lie. I thought it would be a problem. Beaver threatened to fire me if I wouldn't quit, but when I told him I'd rather fight than be a cop, he finally backed off. Well, he still complained, but he stopped threatening to fire me."

"Wow. Fighting must be real important to you."

"It is. My dad used to box, and I fell in love with the sport while watching him fight." She lifted a hand and tilted her head. "Now, don't get me wrong. I love being a cop, too—almost as much as fighting. It's just that I picked up fighting from my dad and, since he's gone, it's even more meaningful."

I was curious how he died, but dared not ask. I didn't want to be rude and I didn't want her asking me any questions. I was approaching the bridge along Main that connected Mechant Loup with the rest of the world. When Mayor Malcolm Landry first offered me the job, I wasn't sure how I felt about living in a town situated at the southernmost tip of a rural parish that had one road in or out. I also didn't like having to cross a single bridge to get there and had wondered at first what would happen if the bridge broke. Once I was there it didn't seem so bad. "The dealership is over the bridge, right?"

Susan nodded and pointed to the left. "Take the first street. That'll take you directly to the showroom where his office is located."

"Have you been there before?"

"Every five thousand miles. The town buys all of its cars from Randall, and they service them."

"What do you know about him?"

Susan grunted. "He's an asshole. I gave him a ticket once and almost had to arrest him. He refused to sign it; threatened to have me fired. He even called Beaver while I was writing the ticket."

I parked in front of the dealership and we made our way inside, letting the clerk at the window know why we were there. She picked up her phone and spoke for a few seconds, then pressed a buzzer and waved us through a side door. "Last office down the hall."

We walked down the long hallway and passed a dozen other offices. A few were occupied—we nodded as we walked by—but most of them were empty. The door to the office at the end of the hall was open and I stuck my head in. "Mr. Rupe?"

"Come in, officers. Take a seat." Randall watched with squinty blue eyes as we took our seats across from his spacious desk. He rubbed a hand deliberately through his thick gray goatee. "Well, this didn't take long. You haven't been on the job a week yet and you're already knocking on my door. To what do I owe the pleasure, Chief? Did Malcolm send you here to get your new Tahoe?"

I pulled a notebook from my back pocket. "I'm not here about a new car. I'm sorry we have to meet like this, but we're here to talk business."

"What business is that?"

"We're here to talk to you about Hays Cain."

Randall shifted in his seat. "Hays? What about him?"

"Do you know where we can find him?" I asked.

Randall shrugged. "Try the restaurant—or his house."

"When's the last time you saw him?" I asked.

"Um...a few days ago. Why?"

I made some notes, then looked up. "Where were y'all?"

"In town. Why? What's this about?"

"We're just trying to locate him," I said. "If he's not at the restaurant or his house, where else might we find him?"

"How would I know?"

"Stephen Butler said y'all are best friends—that if anyone would know his whereabouts, it would be you." I leaned forward to stare into his shifty eyes. "Did Stephen lie to me?"

"No, he didn't lie to you." Randall glanced down at his desk. "He was my best friend since high school. We'd talk nearly every day and normally he'd tell me where he went, but, like I said, I haven't heard from him in a few days."

"When exactly did you last see him or talk to him?" I pressed.

Randall looked around, only stopping briefly to stare at me. "Wednesday or Thursday, I'd say."

"Do you think it's odd he hasn't called since then?" I asked.

"Not really. As I said, we *usually* talk every day. There've been many times when we went days without talking to each other. No big deal. We're not married, for God's sake."

"How's he handling the loss of his son?" I asked.

Randall shrugged. "He lived day-to-day, like the rest of us do."

"The rest of y'all?" My eyes moved from Randall to the large picture frame that hung behind him on the wall. It was of a young man in a military uniform. He couldn't have been more than eighteen or nineteen years of age.

Randall turned and looked up at the picture himself. "That was my son, Randall, Jr."

"Was he in the army?" I asked.

"National guard." Randall spun back around in his chair and stood. "I have some business to take care of. If that's all…"

I stood and nodded, snatching one of his business cards from the box at the corner of his desk. I held up the card. "We have your number, so we'll be in touch if we need more from you."

Susan followed me out into the hot parking lot, and we slipped into the Tahoe. I cranked the engine, flipped the air conditioner on, and lowered the windows. "So," I began, "what do you think?"

"I think he knows Hays is dead."

I nodded my approval. "You're good."

I backed out of the parking lot, and Susan snapped in her seatbelt. "Where to?"

"We're paying Pauline Cain a visit. She's got to know something about her husband's activities."

"If I were married to a man who'd leave and not tell me where he was going, he'd come home to find a pile of ash on the front yard that used to be his shit."

I chuckled. "That's funny."

CHAPTER 16

Stephen Butler was somber as he led us through the Cain mansion and into the living room. Pauline Cain was a wreck. She sat cross-legged on a white leather sofa. There was a pile of crumpled tissues on the floor in front of where she sat. She was still in the gown from the night before, but had a thick robe draped over her shoulders. She looked up at us with bloodshot eyes. "Did y'all find Hays?"

Susan frowned and sat beside Pauline. "No, ma'am. I'm sorry."

She pursed her lips. "He was having an affair."

My jaw dropped, but Susan's face had remained unchanged—like stone. I inwardly complimented her poker face, but cursed Pauline for not telling us about it last night.

"Who with?" Susan asked, resting her hand on Pauline's shoulder.

"I don't know for sure." Pauline tossed an envelope in Susan's lap. "But that's her number."

I quietly wondered how Pauline didn't know who he was having an affair with, but knew her number.

Susan pulled several folded pages from the envelope and studied them. "It's the highlighted number?"

Pauline nodded. "It's the only one I don't recognize."

Susan handed me the sheets of paper. It was Pauline and Hays Cain's cell phone bill. I skipped over the information on Pauline's phone and went to Hays' details. His last activity was from Friday night. He had sent at least a dozen text messages to the highlighted number and received just as many back. There were a few calls between them, but it seemed they communicated more through text messages. Other than one other number, Hays hadn't had contact with another person at all that Friday. I started to fold the phone bill when that one other number caught my eye and I froze, stared long and hard at it. It looked oddly familiar. I checked the time stamp on the bill. Hays had called the number ten minutes after four in the afternoon. *What is it about this number that—*

"Holy shit!" I fished Randall Rupe's business card from my pocket and glanced at his number. It matched. *Randall, you bastard. You lied to us! What are you up to?*

"What is it?" Susan asked.

"Randall… Hays called Randall Rupe that day."

Pauline Hays shrugged. "There's nothing odd about that. They've been best friends since high school. Served in the military together"—she paused to dab at a tear that had formed—"just like our sons."

We stood quiet for a few moments, and then Susan asked, "Mrs. Cain, do you have any idea at all who she might be? Any suspicions?"

"He just promoted one of the waitresses to head manager at our restaurant here in town." Pauline sighed. "I thought it was odd because the other employees have complained about what a screw-up she is, and we've gotten a lot of complaints from customers. Hays wouldn't promote someone like that under normal circumstances."

"What's her name?" Susan asked.

"Kelly Dykes."

I walked into the foyer and grabbed the police radio from my belt to call Lindsey. "I need you to run a name check on Kelly Dykes. I need address, phone number, and criminal history."

"Ten-four, Chief. Standby."

I paced the width of the spacious foyer and waited for Lindsey to call back. Within five minutes, my radio scratched to life. "Chief, she lives on Walnut. She's got a misdemeanor shoplifting charge from four years ago and a few speeding tickets."

I pulled my notepad from my back pocket and jotted down the information. "Do we have a number on her?"

"Ten-four." Lindsey provided the number, and I compared it to the phone bill. It matched the numbers Pauline had highlighted.

Footsteps echoed on the marble behind me, and I turned to see Susan approaching. "Did you get anything on her?"

I showed Susan my notes. "Pauline was right. The phone numbers match. Can you believe it?"

"Women know." Susan touched the address. "Is that where she

lives?"

"Yeah. Is it far from here?"

"It's across town about ten——"

"Chief, are you on the radio?" It was Melvin.

"Ten-four," I said. "Did you find something?"

"We recovered Dexter's boat and your guns."

"Ten-four. Thanks. Any sign of that alligator or Hays Cain?"

"Negative, but we're still looking."

I clipped the radio on my belt, then followed Susan out of the mansion and to my Tahoe. She told me how to get to Walnut. It was almost lunchtime and traffic was heavy, so it took us about fifteen minutes to reach the street.

"It should be around midway down," Susan guessed.

It was a long street and the house numbers were faded or didn't exist. "I can't even see most of the numbers."

"You'll get used to counting from the last known address around here. Most townspeople don't take the time to hang their house numbers. I guess they figure it'll be harder for the governor to find them when he comes for their guns."

I shot a look at Susan, but it appeared she hadn't meant anything by the comment. I continued down the street, and Susan pointed ahead to a small trailer on the right.

"That should be it," she said.

I pulled to the side of the road in front of the trailer and parked parallel to it. After throwing the gearshift in park, I stepped out and walked around the front of the Tahoe and met Susan near a small ditch. We paused to scan the area. An older model Caprice sat in the muddy driveway. The yard was clean, with the exception of an old dog kennel that lay on its side. "I need one of those for——"

A gunshot suddenly erupted from the area of the trailer and the taillight on my passenger's side exploded into tiny shards.

"Holy shit!" Susan dropped to her face beside the Tahoe and scrambled on all fours around the back of the SUV until she reached the other side and it was between her and the trailer.

Another shot rang out and the headlight on the passenger's side disintegrated. I backed up until I could sidestep behind the hood of the Tahoe. I dropped to my right knee, using the front tire and engine block as cover. My pistol had instinctively appeared in my hand. I leaned out from around the front of the Tahoe and pointed my pistol at the trailer. "Did you see where the shot came from?"

Susan peered around the back of the Tahoe. "The front windows are closed, so I don't think the shot came from inside."

I nodded my agreement. "Cover me."

"Wait...what are you doing? Don't you go out there. It's suicide!"

I bolted from behind the Tahoe and ran toward the left side of the trailer, sweeping the area with my pistol. When I reached the corner of the trailer, I slammed up against it with my right shoulder and glanced back at Susan. She was staring wide-eyed at me, shaking her head. I pointed to let her know I was going around the trailer. She tried to wave at me to stop. I took a deep breath and button-hooked around the corner. I dashed toward the back of the trailer. Trees cloaked the area in shadows. When I rounded the back corner, I came face-to-face with a wooden swing set. Before I could stop, I crashed into it and tumbled forward. As I fell, I caught a glimpse of a human shadow disappearing like a flash into the woods.

The dirt was damp and cool against my cheek and smelled musky. I rolled to my right shoulder and scanned the tree line. Other than the distant sound of snapping branches that grew fainter as the attacker escaped, there was nothing. I jumped to my feet and gave chase, jumping over downed tree trunks and ducking under low-lying branches. Pickers and thick underbrush clawed at my exposed arms, slowing my progress. A twig slapped my face and left a stinging sensation in its wake. Sweat dripped from my forehead. My breath started to come in gasps, as my lungs burned. My legs screamed for me to stop, but I forced them onward. I could no longer hear the suspect due to the noise of my own trampling and my heart beating in my ears. I wondered if the attacker had doubled back to ambush me. I kept a wary eye as I ran, but everything was a blur.

I suddenly broke out into a clearing and stumbled forward when the forest released me of its grip. I stared about. The roaring of a car engine sounded off to my right. I spun around and pointed my pistol in that direction. The sun blinded me. I lifted my left arm to shield out the brilliant light and tried to find the front sight on my pistol. Through the shimmering heat waves in the distance, I saw a large truck kicking up dirt and grass as it sped off. I couldn't tell the make or model of the truck and I hadn't gotten a good look at the suspect. I thought about putting a few bullets into the back of the fleeing vehicle, but I couldn't identify my target and I couldn't be sure what was beyond the truck or if there were any innocent people inside. I dropped my hand and slammed my pistol into its holster. "Shit!"

I dropped to one knee and took several deep breaths to try to calm my racing heart. *I've got to find a way to stop drinking so much.* It occurred to me just then that my knees weren't shaking. I held up my hand—steady as a rock. Much different from the other times I'd been shot at or found myself in a life-threatening situation. *Why does this time feel different? Why am I not experiencing the normal physical responses that go along with high stress situations?* I started to wonder if the doctor had been right about me. I shook my head to dismiss the thought.

I slowly turned and picked my way through the woods. I hadn't realized how far I'd run. After about five minutes, I heard what sounded like a herd of buffalo coming toward me. I reached for my pistol, but relaxed when I saw Susan. She stopped when she saw me, exhaling sharply.

"Are you okay?" she asked in a hushed voice, sweeping the area with her pistol. "Where'd you go?"

I nodded and took a deep breath before answering. "I chased him, but he got away. There was a truck waiting."

"The back door to the trailer is wide open. I didn't clear it yet, so there might still be a threat inside." Susan spun to return to the trailer.

I grabbed her arm. "Hey, are you okay?"

"I'm a little freaked out." Susan wiped sweat off her brow with the back of her hand. "I've never been shot at before. Thought about it—a lot, actually—but never experienced it. I think I shat my pants."

"I've never heard it put that way, but I did, too—shit my pants," I lied, but only to make her feel better. "You never get used to being shot at."

"I felt like I couldn't breathe for a minute there."

"That's normal. Nothing to worry about. It's when you stop feeling it that you have to worry." I looked away because I knew I should be worried, but oddly wasn't.

Susan walked off, and I followed. When we reached the clearing where the trailer was located, she trained her pistol on the back door, and I palmed mine. She nodded to me and I nodded back. We slowly approached the trailer. I kept my eyes on the windows, while she watched the door. When we reached the back steps, we fanned out, each of us moving to opposite sides of the door. I peered inside. All I saw was an empty hallway and a door leading into what looked like a bathroom.

"Can you see anything?" I asked, my voice barely a whisper.

She shook her head, as she craned her neck to see. "I don't hear anything either."

I held up my hand to let her know I would count to three and then we would enter. She nodded. I slowly lifted my index finger, then middle finger, and, finally, my ring finger. We scurried up the stairs and crisscrossed into the trailer. I ran left toward the front of the trailer, and she ran right toward the back. I quickly found myself in a living room/kitchen combination that was well furnished and tidy. There was no sign of life. I relaxed, checked out the living room. A sofa, loveseat, and recliner took up what little space there was in the room. I noticed something on the floor and bent to examine the object. It was a sliver of wood. I glanced up toward the front door, which opened into the living room, and nodded. The door had been secured shut by the deadbolt, but the lock plate for the doorknob hung loose and the doorframe was split.

I strode into the small kitchen. There was a white wooden table with four chairs centered in the tiny area, and one of the chairs had been knocked to the floor. A plate was on the table in front of the downed chair and there was a small amount of scrambled eggs and a half-eaten biscuit on the plate. Something shiny under the table caught my eye. When I bent to look, I saw a fork with a clump of scrambled egg stuck to it. I surveyed the rest of the kitchen, but nothing was out of place. The sink was free of any dishes and the counters were clean. A picture of what had happened here began to form in my mind's eye.

I suddenly realized things were too quiet inside the trailer. I had heard Susan's boots pound the hollow floor when we first entered, but I now heard nothing. "Susan?"

"One second," she called back. I heard a doorknob shake and then the squeak of an opening door. It was followed shortly by a startled gasp.

"Chief!" Susan hollered. "Get in here! We've got a body!"

CHAPTER 17

I hurried down the hallway and through the door of the back bedroom, squeezed by Susan and looked down. The body of what looked like a young woman was prone on the floor between the bed and the far wall. She wore loose pajama pants and a cotton nightshirt. There was no mistaking the four bloody bullet holes in the back of her shirt. One wound was high on her shoulder, another was over the back of her heart, and the last two were at the very center of her back—most likely severed her spinal cord. I scanned the immediate area and spotted two spent shell casings on the floor just inside the door. I picked my way closer to the body and squatted beside it. I leaned forward and placed my index and ring fingers against the inside of her wrist to feel for a pulse. There was none.

"She's dead," I said.

Susan left the room, and I could hear her digging around in the living room. She returned with a driver's license. "This is Kelly Dykes' driver's license. Is that her on the floor?"

I hated to touch her body before documenting the scene, but I needed to know if she was Kelly. Without moving the body's position, I turned her head until I could see her face and frowned. "Yeah, it's her."

"And who else would it be, right?" Susan took a deep breath and blew it out. "What the hell is going on here, Clint?"

I stood, turned to face her. "It's imperative we find out who wanted this girl dead."

"Besides Pauline Cain?"

"We just left Pauline. There's no way she got dressed, armed herself, and then beat us here."

"She could've paid someone to do it."

I frowned, thought it over, but shook my head. "If she wanted Kelly dead, she would've never told us about her. She would've just had her killed and been done with it. She certainly wouldn't send us here to interrupt her hired killer."

"What about Stephen Butler? That dude was creepy."

"He didn't have the opportunity."

"But they're the only two people who knew we were coming here."

"That's true." I walked outside, went to my Tahoe, cursed when I saw the broken taillight and headlight again. I quickly reversed my displeasure. The damage would require a trip to Randall's dealership for a repair job. That would give me another chance to visit with him. I nodded, silently thanking the gunman.

I jerked the rear gate open, removed a crime scene kit and camera bag from the cargo area, and walked back to the trailer. I keyed up my radio and called for Lindsey. When she answered, I said, "Be advised, shots fired on Walnut, one down. I'll need the coroner to respond as soon as possible. No identifiable information on the suspect."

"Shots fired?" Melvin asked over the radio, his voice excited. "Chief, I'm just leaving the boat launch. Do you want me to come to your location?"

"Ten-four." I shoved the radio onto my belt and jogged up the steps of the trailer.

Susan met me just inside the back door and reached for the camera bag dangling from my shoulder. "I'll photograph the scene."

I dipped my shoulder to let her take it. When she had it, I grabbed a flashlight and we began searching every inch of the floor. We were about ten minutes into our search when Susan pointed. "Look in the corner under the sofa flap. Another spent casing."

"Good eyes." I dropped to my knees and looked where she pointed. It had rolled under the sofa, which was positioned against the back wall. I scanned the area from the sofa to the kitchen, but there was nothing. "This was the first shot. Keep moving toward the hallway and you'll find the second casing."

Susan crept along the living room floor toward the hallway and called out when she found another spent casing against the baseboard of the back wall. "That makes four."

"Are they all nine millimeters?" I asked.

"Yeah." Susan's brow furrowed. "How'd you know it would be here?"

I stood and walked to the front door, so I could face the living room and kitchen. "The shooter kicked the door in and interrupted Kelly's breakfast. Kelly jumped up, knocking her chair back, and ran toward her bedroom." I walked to the sofa. "This is where the first round was fired. She continued running"—I walked toward the entrance to the hallway—"and the second round was fired here."

"Not the double spine shots, right?"

"Right. Those shots were fired at close range while she was on the ground—they were too accurate to have been fired while she was running."

Susan grunted. "I think all the shots were pretty accurate. Hell, he fired two rounds to a fast-moving target and hit it both times!"

I nodded, entered the bedroom and stood in the doorway looking down at Kelly. "She collapsed to the ground, and he stood right here and fired rounds three and four." I leaned close to her body, nodding. "Either round one or two penetrated her heart."

"Wouldn't she have been dead instantly with a heart shot? She would've dropped in the hallway."

I shook my head. "Even with a heart shot there would've been enough oxygen in her brain to keep her alive for a short time after, definitely long enough for her to run down the hallway."

"What makes you so sure she was hit in the heart?" Susan turned up an eyebrow. "You some kind of a doctor?"

"I'm no doctor, but I've been around a lot of pathologists in my day." I pointed to the wound highest on her back. "You see this bullet hole to the left of centerline and high on the back?"

Susan nodded.

"That shot didn't hit anything vital, so it's a non-issue. In order for her to eventually collapse, a vital organ had to have been hit." I pointed to the wound directly over the back of her heart. "That one's in the right position—it definitely hit her heart. He pumped two more in her to finish her off when she collapsed."

Susan stood back and stared toward the living room, then back at Kelly's body. "You can tell all of that just by looking at the scene? Like, you didn't even touch anything yet. You just stared at it—and it tells you all of that?"

"I used to be good at my job."

Susan frowned. "Before the incident?"

I stared down at my boots.

"Are you... Do you want to die?" Susan asked softly.

I scowled, looked up at her. "Of course not."

"Out there"—Susan shot a thumb toward the front yard—"when

the first shot was fired, you didn't react. You just stood there. It wasn't until the second shot was fired that you moved, like it was an afterthought. And when you moved, it...it was like you were getting out the way of a kid skateboarding down the street. There was no sense of urgency."

"Look, you can hang up with the crisis line—I'm not suicidal. If I wanted to kill myself, I would've done it."

Susan slowly shook her. "I didn't ask if you were suicidal. I asked if you wanted to die. There's a big difference."

I looked into Susan's eyes. They were piercing, unwavering. I started to tell her to get off my back, but the rear door of the trailer flung open.

CHAPTER 18

"Am I too late?" Melvin asked.

"You're just in time to help us move the body." I moved all of the crime scene equipment into the hallway, slipped on a fresh pair of latex gloves and tossed a pair to Melvin. When we were gloved up, I nodded to the camera hanging from Susan's neck. "Can you document the moving of her body?"

Susan flipped the camera switch to the *on* position.

"Help me drag this bed away from her," I said to Melvin. He grabbed one end, while I grabbed the other, and we slid it away from Kelly Dykes. When there was enough room for us to work, we both moved to a position beside her body—me at her head and Melvin at her feet. I gently gripped her right shoulder and hip and Melvin grabbed her right knee and ankle. I glanced up at Susan. "You ready?"

The camera poised against her eye, Susan nodded. Melvin and I gently pulled Kelly's body and rolled her onto her back. Her right arm flopped across her stomach and something fell from her limp hand. The camera clicked multiple times as Susan captured the entire process. I glanced at Kelly's face. Her eyes were wide and unseeing and her mouth was open. Poor girl knew what was happening and she was terrified. I had to look away as images of Abigail flashed through my mind. I glanced down at the object that had fallen from her right hand.

"It's a smart phone," Melvin said.

"It's not that smart," I mused, "otherwise it would've autodialed nine-one-one." After Susan shot a few photographs of it, I carefully picked it up, turned it to face me. I sighed and handed it to Susan.

"You need to do this."

Susan grinned, pulled on some gloves, and took the phone. "I don't know how you live without a smart phone."

"You don't miss what you never had." I searched the floor under where Kelly's body had dropped. There was nothing but a little blood high up near where her neck had been. I looked back at her body and saw a bloody hole near her left collarbone. "She's got one exit wound."

Susan looked up from the phone to glance around. "Where'd it go?"

I looked at the bedroom wall opposite the doorway. Nothing. Because of my position and the fact the bedroom door was open, I couldn't see the outside of the door. "Check the door. I bet it was closed when she was shot. The bullet exited near her collarbone and hit the door."

Susan turned and scanned the door, pointed. "There it is!" She pulled the door closed to look at the inside of it. "It didn't go through and through."

I turned to Melvin. "Can you cut that door open and recover the projectile?"

Melvin's eyes lit up and he nodded.

"Look in my crime scene kit that's in the hallway," I said. "Everything you need will be in there."

Melvin hurried into the hallway and set about ripping the inner panel off the door while Susan searched Kelly Dykes' cell phone. I completed the diagram I'd been working on and was about to offer Melvin some assistance when Susan let out a triumphant cry.

"I got it! I cracked her passcode!" Susan stared intently at the screen. "She did try to call nine-one-one, but she stopped at nine-one."

I moved closer to Susan and looked over her shoulder. "Can you look back to Friday and see her text messages?"

Susan smiled. "I'm on it."

She slid her thumb sideways across the screen and pressed on it until a list of names came up. "These are her contacts."

I was about to start reading through the list when a slide of Susan's thumb sent the list flying. "What're you doing?"

"Scrolling down to *H*." Susan then nodded and tilted the phone so I could see. "Hays Cain. He's actually listed as one of her *favorites*."

"Can we read their messages?"

Susan clicked on his name, whistled. "Yes, we can. There are a lot of them. These are from Friday."

"Can you go to the early hours that day?" I asked.
"Yeah. Here's the first conversation that day. It looks like it starts around four in the afternoon."
I began reading the messages.

_____

Hays: I'm out the house. Be seeing you later. Around 6 P.M.
Kelly: can't wait. why so late?
Hays: I need to take care of something first.
Kelly: what
Hays: I have a meeting to go to.
Kelly: u and ur secret meetings. where's the meeting
Hays: You know I can't tell you that.
Kelly: i don't understand what the big deal is. bet ur wife knows.
Hays: No.
Kelly: why won't u ever tell me?
Hays: I can't.
Kelly: i feel like u don't love me.
Hays: Of course I love you.
Kelly: then y don't u trust me?
Hays: I do trust you.
Kelly: if u trusted me u would tell me. u said ur self no secrets between us.
Hays: It's work related.
Kelly: now i know that's a lie!!! it's another woman isn't it? ur cheating on me!
Kelly: why won't u answer me?
Hays: I'm not cheating on you, sweetheart.
Kelly: prove it. tell me who ur meeting.
Hays: I can't.
Kelly: then we're through. i'm telling ur wife about us. it's over.
Hays: Baby, please don't say that. I love you and I want to be with you. Just give me a little time and soon I'll be all yours. You won't have to share me anymore.
Kelly: you mean you'll finally leave ur wife?
Hays: Yes. Just let me take care of an issue that's come up. It doesn't involve another woman. I just have to settle some things. I'm closing this business deal. After tonight I won't be attending any more of these meetings. You've made me realize what's important in life. All I want is you.
Kelly: that's so sweet!
Hays: It's true. I'm late for the meeting. I should be about an hour. I'll text you when I get out.

Kelly: k. luv u!
Hays: I love you, too!

***

"That's it for that conversation," Susan said. "Kelly tried to contact Hays three times at five o'clock, twice at six, and then once at eight. Here are the messages."

***

Kelly: where u at? r u standing me up?
Kelly: r u there?
Kelly: this isn't funny anymore. call me now or it's over.
Kelly: i don't want anything to do with u anymore. it's over. u never loved me. it was all a lie.
Kelly: oh, and i'm telling ur wife everything. i'm sending her the pictures u sent me.
Kelly: u should b careful about butt dialing my voicemail when ur lying. i heard ur buddies talking and i heard the boat. u weren't at no meeting. it's over! don't even bother calling back!

***

Susan and I looked at each other, and I pointed at the phone. "Please tell me you can find that voicemail."

"I'm trying." Susan's fingers danced across the glass screen for several seconds and then she held it up to her ear.

I leaned in and listened. The obvious sound of a boat running came through the little speaker for about five minutes. When it finally stopped, we could hear muffled voices. They sounded like men's voices, but it was hard to make out every word.

"Why'd...shoot him?" asked the first man.

"You heard...was going...cops and we can't...screw up the mission," said the second man.

"But he...to die."

"You want...jail?"

"No."

"...shut up and...cinder...other rope."

"What...noise?"

We heard rustling and it sounded like the phone was being handled. An excited voice said, "Holy shit! The phone called some—"

The call went dead.

"It was in his pocket," Susan said. "We've got the killers on tape!"

"That must be why they killed Kelly Dykes. We need to get this enhanced." I looked over at Melvin. He had just removed a part of the door panel and leaned it against the wall, and was shoving his hand into the lower portion of the door. "Melvin, you want to take a drive up to the city when we're done here?"

Melvin stopped, turned to look up at me. "Me? Take a road trip?" I nodded. "I've got a buddy up there who can work magic with recordings. I'll call and tell him you're coming. Just sign the evidence over to him and then go find something to eat. There's a café near the lab that's awesome. I'll give you food money."

A large grin split Melvin's face. "Thanks, Chief. You're awesome!" Melvin's mouth slid open as he wriggled his hand around in the narrow crack of the hollow door. He finally sucked in air, removed his hand from the door and lifted his arm triumphantly. Between his middle and ring fingers was a damaged lead projectile. "I've got it!"

"Great job!" I slapped his back, then dug money out of my wallet. After Susan had taken the projectile from him and secured it in an evidence envelope, I handed him forty bucks. "Here, you've earned this."

"Thanks again, Chief!"

"Call me Clint."

"I'm sorry, Chief—Clint it is."

Susan handed Melvin a clear plastic evidence envelope and a chain of custody form. "Make sure you fill it out and both of you sign it."

"Done!" Melvin took the envelope and evidence form and hurried out the door.

I smiled. "He's a good kid."

"He sure is. When he first started working here it took me about a month to get him to stop calling me ma'am and Ms. Susan."

I looked around the scene. "Let's wrap this up so the coroner can get Kelly's body out of here."

"Sure thing." Susan bent over and gathered up the other evidence packages, but she paused to look over at me. "I'm sorry about earlier. I was out of line."

"No, you weren't." I sighed. "In our line of work, it's important to know who you're going through the door with, so you had every right to say what you said. Just know this—I'd step in front of a bullet for you and every other person in this town."

Susan searched my eyes. "I know. That's what I'm afraid of."

I waved her off. "Let's get out of here. I'm hungry."

"Are you thinking what I'm thinking?"

"Yeah, I want to pay a visit to Hays' restaurant—see if we can't get inside his office."

CHAPTER 19

"Table for two?" asked the lady at the door of Hays Cain's restaurant. According to her nametag, she was Malory and she was head waitress.

"Are y'all still serving lunch?" I asked.

Malory shook her head. "Sorry, but you're a couple hours late. Dinner will be ready soon, or y'all can order off the sandwich menu."

I looked at Susan. "Want a burger or something?"

"Or something," Susan said. "I may take a salad. I have to watch what I eat."

Malory led us to a corner booth, and I took a seat where I could watch the door. Susan and I were the only customers. Malory left us after we were seated and returned with bread, butter, and oil. She snatched a notepad from a pocket in her green apron, then looked from Susan to me. "Aren't you the new chief of police?"

I smiled and nodded. "I'm Clint."

She pointed to the nametag. "This is me."

"When you're done flirting with my boss," Susan began, "you can get me a glass of water with lemon."

Malory gasped. "I'm not flirting!"

I felt my face flush.

"I swear," Susan said, "the women in this town act like they've never seen a single man before."

"That's because there aren't any in this town." Malory whisked away and returned with two waters. She wouldn't make eye contact with me as she set the glasses on the table. "If y'all are ready to make—"

"Actually," I said, "we'd like to take a look inside Hays Cain's office."

"I'm sorry?" Malory looked puzzled. "What on earth for?"

"We're following up on an investigation into his disappearance and we need to check his computer, calendar...stuff like that."

"His *disappearance?* He's missing?"

I nodded. "He hasn't been seen or heard from since Friday."

"Mrs. Cain came by and said he was out of town on business." Malory tucked a rebel lock of hair behind her ear. "He's done that before, so it wasn't odd."

"Well, we need to get into his office to see what's been going on in his life," Susan said.

"I don't know." Malory glanced over her shoulder, as though looking for a second opinion. "The manager's out."

"You mean Kelly?" Susan asked.

Malory nodded slowly. "She didn't show up this morning. I called, but it rang to her voicemail."

"Do you know where we can find her next of kin?" Susan asked.

"She's not originally from here. I think she moved here from Texas a few years ago. She doesn't even talk about—" Malory's mouth dropped open suddenly. "Wait—next of kin? Why do you need her next of kin? Is something wrong? Is she okay?"

Susan shook her head. "She's not okay...she's dead."

Malory recoiled in horror, grabbing at her mouth with both hands. "Dead? Kelly? Are you sure?"

I frowned. "I'm afraid so, ma'am."

Malory's eyes reddened. "What happened? Was she sick?"

"Why do you say that?" I asked.

"Say what?"

"Why'd you ask if she was sick?" I wanted to know.

Malory shrugged. "I just figured she was sick when she didn't show up this morning."

"We need to have a look inside that office to see if there's any connection between Kelly's death and Hays' disappearance," Susan explained.

Malory chewed on her lower lip. "Mr. Cain is very secretive. He'll fire me if he finds out I let y'all in there."

"He'll never know," I promised.

Malory sighed. She pulled a key from her apron and set it on the table. "Be quick about it."

Susan snatched the key off the table and slid out of the booth. I followed her to the office door, and we let ourselves in. It was dark and considerably cooler in the office. I felt along the wall, found the light switch, flipped it on.

"Damn," Susan said. "This place is a mess."

Paper seemed to be piled waist high on Hays' desk. I thumbed through it, while Susan fired up his computer. Much of the paperwork on the desk consisted of unopened mail that someone had apparently stacked there for him to open on his return. Other than bills and supply lists, there was nothing that offered a clue as to what Hays Cain was involved with.

"There's nothing on his computer that would explain the reason for his disappearance," Susan said.

"Any mention of meetings on his calendar?"

"None."

"Does he have a business calendar on his computer?"

Susan nodded. "But there's nothing about a meeting on Friday. In fact, there are no entries for Friday at all."

"What about emails?"

"I'm browsing through them now," Susan said idly. "So far, there's nothing worth noting."

I walked around the room and scanned the walls as Susan worked. I paused when I saw a picture of five men dressed in BDU pants. Four of them were shirtless, and the one to the right wore a white T-shirt. I moved closer. The picture was considerably damaged, looked old. "You think one of these guys is Hays Cain?"

Susan looked up from the monitor and squinted. "I can't really see from here, but if that *is* him, it's an ancient picture. He has to weigh at least two-fifty, and those kids look like they weigh between one-thirty-seven and one-sixty. It could be his son."

"What was his name again?"

"Allen," Susan answered, eyes fixed on the computer screen.

I turned back to the picture. They *were* skinny. Ribs and shoulder bones protruded like they'd been denied rations for weeks. A cigarette dangled from the corner of the guy's mouth to the far left. I didn't know if he was trying to look cool or if he was too haggard to hold it straight. Although they clearly suffered from malnutrition, I would've guessed their weights a little higher.

"What makes you such an expert on weight?" I wanted to know.

"I'm a fighter. It's my job to know weight."

"That makes sense." I looked at the wall across from Hays' desk and saw another picture. This one was large and framed, and the young man in the military dress uniform seemed to be staring down at Hays' desk. I approached it so I could make out the gold nameplate affixed to the bottom of the woodwork. It read, Allen Hays Cain, 19, KIA. "Damn, he was young."

"Too young," called a voice from the door. I turned to see Malory standing there, arms folded across her chest. "I don't know how he did it every day."

"What do you mean?" I asked.

"I don't know how he woke up and came to work every day, as though his life were normal." She frowned. "I still remember when Allen used to play in the restaurant after school—remember it like it was yesterday. He was such a funny kid. Although it's been two years, it's still so hard."

"People handle grief differently," I explained.

"Don't I know it. Mrs. Cain's life stopped dead in its tracks. She started drinking all the time. Stopped coming to the restaurant." Malory shook her head. "But not Mr. Cain. He handled his grief in a different way."

"How do you mean?" I asked.

Malory glanced over her shoulder, then looked back to me. "He started having new lady friends, if you know what I mean. There was a rumor he was dating Kelly, but we all thought it was just talk."

Susan stood from the computer and walked around the desk. "Nothing useful here."

"So, are y'all done?" Malory asked.

Susan nodded as she walked by her and into the dining area. I followed, but stopped to watch Malory lock up.

"Thanks for letting us have a look," I said. "I know you risked a lot."

"If it'll help find Mr. Cain and figure out who did this to Kelly, it's a small price to pay."

"Do you have any idea who might have a reason to hurt Hays Cain?"

Malory shook her head. "Everyone seems to like him."

"Has he ever messed with any married women? Maybe pissed off a husband or two?"

"I mean, he's messed with a lot of women. He throws his money around and that attracts certain types of women—some married, some not." Malory shrugged. "So, I'm really not sure."

I nodded. "Thanks for your help."

CHAPTER 20

After we'd eaten, Susan and I stopped at the hospital to check on Dexter Boudreaux.

"He's sleeping now," said the nurse in the intensive care unit. "His wife saw him earlier, and it really put a strain on him. The doctor doesn't want him getting too worked up, so he's limiting visitation."

"What's his condition?" Susan asked.

"It's improving. Slowly, but it is improving."

We took the elevator back to the first floor and walked out into the parking lot. Susan's phone rang and she answered it, spoke for a while, then handed it to me. "It's Melvin."

"What's going on, Melvin?"

"I delivered the phone, Chief. He listened to it and said it'll take some doing, but he should be able to extract the voices. He said to give him a couple of days."

"Did you tell him we didn't have a couple of days?" I asked.

Melvin was silent on the other end. Finally, he said, "Um…was I supposed to?"

"No, that's okay. If it'll take a couple of days, I guess we'll just have to wait." I handed Susan back her phone and we rode in silence to the police department.

"Clint, I need a favor," Susan said when I'd pulled my Tahoe into the sally port.

"Sure, anything."

"Can I have tomorrow and Friday off? I need to relax and game plan for my fight, and it's hard to do that at work."

"Absolutely! Take whatever time you need." I stepped out and followed her to the back door. "It's this Saturday, right?"

Susan nodded. "I'm fighting a girl from Texas. She's good. If I beat her, it'll elevate me in the sport."

I smiled. "You'll beat her, and I'll definitely be there to witness—"

"Where's Clint?" a booming voice asked from inside the police station, and I heard Lindsey stammering.

I hurried through the door and into the lobby. "I'm here, Mayor."

Mayor Landry wiped sweat from his head. "Jesus, Clint! What the hell is going on around here? I heard you were shot at. Is that true?"

"Susan, you can go ahead and leave. Have a good one. See you Saturday." I turned to the mayor and waved him into my office. When we were inside, I closed my door and took a seat at my desk. I filled him in on what had happened and the information we'd uncovered.

"Do you have an idea who shot at you?" Mayor Landry asked.

I shook my head. "No clue. I didn't get a good look at him or the truck he was in."

"Truck? He was in a truck?"

"Yeah, but I didn't get a good look at it. I don't even know what color it was."

"Take your Tahoe over to Randall's place. He'll patch it up until your new one is ready."

I scowled. "Mayor, I think Randall knows something. Hays texted his girlfriend Friday and told her he had a meeting to go to. Randall talked to him earlier that same day, so I think he knows something about the meeting."

Mayor Landry waved his hand dismissively. "The two of them were inseparable. It's not unusual that they talked that Friday. They've been friends—"

"Since high school and they served in the military together."

Mayor Landry smiled. "Look at that…we've been working together only a few days and we can already finish each other's sentences. I can't say that about my wife, and I've been married to her for thirty years."

"That's not the problem. The problem is this—Randall said the last time he talked to Hays was Wednesday or Thursday, but we have evidence he talked to him on Friday."

Mayor Landry's brows came together in a scowl. "Go careful with that one. He might have lied, or he might have made a mistake. He does a lot of work for the town, and I'd hate to make him mad by falsely accusing him of lying if it was only a mistake. I mean, I can't remember exactly what day you moved here for good. Was it Sunday or Saturday?"

"I moved Saturday, and we met at the police station on Sunday." He smiled. "You see? We old guys have a hard time remembering things, so go easy on him and don't accuse him of anything unless you have solid proof he did something wrong."

I nodded, not liking it, but realizing he was right. While there was something I didn't like about Randall Rupe and he might very well be keeping a secret, it certainly didn't mean he was a killer.

Mayor Landry stood to go, then stopped and pulled something from his shirt pocket. "I almost forgot. Here's your new phone. I'd appreciate it if you'd answer when I call."

"Sure thing." I took the phone and studied it. It was similar to Susan's phone. "What the hell is this?"

"Welcome to the new millennium, Clint, where phones are smarter than we are."

"I don't want this shit."

"You don't have to use all the extra features if you don't want to. Hell, you don't have to even use it to call anyone. Just answer it when I call." As he walked out, Mayor Landry called over his shoulder, "And I put it in a waterproof case if you ever decide to go swimming with all your clothes on again."

CHAPTER 21

Saturday, June 28

I stared at myself in the mirror. I was eight days from my thirtieth birthday, but even I had to admit I looked forty. Achilles whined at my feet. I looked down. He sat with his ears perked up, head cocked sideways. I smiled.

"No, little monster, you can't come with me."

I walked out of the bathroom and he followed, pushing up against my jeans as he always did when we walked. I stopped in the kitchen to fix his food and water, waved my hand toward the living room, where the guts of two sofa cushions were strewn about the floor. "If you don't stop tearing up my shit, I'm going to sell you to a cat lover."

Achilles barked like he understood me and, already knowing the drill, plopped his butt in the corner waiting for me to give the command. I smiled, proud of him. I'd never owned a German shepherd and I was impressed with how smart he was. Once I set the bowls down, I stood and crossed my arms. He stood, poised, ready to pounce. I waited longer than I had the last time and nodded, said, "Eat!"

Achilles gave an excited yelp and lunged forward. He darted clumsily toward the food bowl and tried to stop at the last second, but the smooth hardwood was like a slipping slide against his paws. He skidded into the bowl and some bits of dry food went flying. I laughed as he dove snout first into the bowl and ate like he hadn't done so in days. I squatted beside him and rubbed his neck while he crunched the food. I looked over at my work boots drying in the dish rack near the sink and leaned closer to him.

"And if you pee in my boots again," I warned, "you're going to wake up one night and find me standing over you giving you a golden shower to write home about."

Achilles finished crunching the food in his mouth and attacked the bowl once again.

I opened the back door, and Achilles' ears perked up and he darted out, barking as he ran. I chased after him, but his young legs were faster than I thought. He stopped at the tree line and I was able to catch up with him. I squatted and took his collar so he wouldn't run off. He let out a series of ferocious barks, his body jerking as he did. I squinted, trying to penetrate the depths of the woods. It was nearing dark, which made it difficult to make out much in the deep shadows.

"What is it, boy?"

Achilles continued barking. There were no squirrels jumping around. No birds chirping. Nothing at all. The wind wasn't even blowing. I stood and tugged on Achilles' collar. "Come on, little tiger. Let's go back inside."

Achilles let out a low growl that sounded more like a baby gurgling, and I couldn't help but admire the little man's efforts to sound intimidating. He finally lost interest in whatever it was he had seen and followed me back to the house after doing his business.

Once Achilles was in his crate, I grabbed my Glock that Melvin had recovered from the lake—and cleaned—and shoved it in the back of my waistband, then covered it with my shirt. I locked up my house and headed across town to the bingo hall. I was passing Hays Cain's restaurant when I spotted a familiar car in the driveway. My heart beat a little faster. Butterflies formed in my stomach. I glanced at the clock on my dash. I was two hours early for Susan's fight and I was hungry—it was all the excuse I needed. I smashed the brakes, turned into the parking lot, pulled up beside the red car. I hesitated as I stared at the front door of the restaurant.

What are you doing, Clint? You'll make a fool out of yourself for sure. Why are you even here, anyway? What do you expect will happen?

I shook the voices out of my head. "To hell with it!"

I shut off the Tahoe and stepped outside. I took a deep breath, walked inside, and stood just in the doorway for a second to let my eyes adjust to the dim light. Malory was working and walked up to me.

"Hey, Clint, how are you?" She smiled like she was greeting an old friend.

I nodded, casually looking around. "I'm good. What's on the dinner menu?"

"Fried catfish and white beans...they're to die for!"

"Okay, I'm in." I followed Malory to a booth in the corner of the room and took a seat. I scanned the large dining room and scowled. There were three families in the restaurant, but she wasn't among them. I suddenly didn't feel like eating anymore. I frowned...what was happening to me? I couldn't explain why I felt that way. It had been a long time since I'd felt anything at all, and I wasn't sure if I liked it.

I looked up at the giant clock on the wall. It was still early for the fight, but I could stop at the office and visit with the weekend crew. I was about to stand up to leave when a door opened behind me. It was Hays Cain's office. I turned and caught my breath, sinking back to my seat, mouth agape.

CHAPTER 22

She didn't see me at first, as she stepped out of Hays Cain's office and closed the door softly. She wore a light-colored sundress covered in little blue flowers. Her legs were bare, smooth-looking. Her ankle-high boots clacked against the square linoleum tiles when she turned from the door and started to walk away, but she stopped in her tracks when our eyes met. Her mouth fell open; she brushed nervously at her blonde hair.

"What are you doing?" I blurted.

"Um...I...I was just—"

"Hey!" Malory called, stomping across the dining room. "What were you doing in there?"

Chloe Rushing's eyes darted around the room as though she were looking for a place to hide. Without thought, I stood and touched Malory's arm gently. "She asked where the bathroom was located, and I told her it was the first door past the last booth. I meant to say the second door."

"She knows where the bathroom is," Malory said, eyeing Chloe. "Were you snooping around again?"

"Malory, you know how long it's been since I've come in here, and it's obvious you've remodeled the place recently."

"There's a giant sign over the bathroom door," Malory said, her eyes narrowing. After a long moment, she relaxed. "I didn't see you come in. Do you need a seat?"

"She can sit with me," I said—again without thought. I winced, not sure how Chloe would react.

"Yes, I'll sit with our new chief," Chloe said. She moved past me and slipped into the booth. "I'll take a tea with ice and lemon."

I took the seat across from her, and when Malory was gone, I leaned forward on my elbows. "What were you doing in there?"

Chloe's face reddened. "My job."

"What were you looking for?"

Chloe squinted. "Let's do this. I answer one of your questions, and you answer one of mine. We keep playing that game until someone gives up."

"I can't talk about an ongoing investigation. Protocol."

"Neither can I, but I'm willing to bend the rules for a little exchange of information." Chloe's bottom lip was full and she bit the corner of it. "Are you game?"

I hesitated. "I don't know."

"Look, I won't use any of the information you give me. I just want to verify some things I've heard, to let me know if I'm on the right track or not." She reached across the table and touched my forearm with her cold hand. "You can trust me…just ask anyone."

I smiled inwardly. She was cool—and hard to resist. "If I agree to play your little game, do you promise not to publish anything I say in your paper?"

"I promise. I just want to verify some information I heard."

I sighed. "Okay…shoot."

"Whose arm did y'all find in the lake?"

"You already know."

"So, it is Hays Cain?"

I nodded.

"I thought so." Chloe twirled a lock of her wavy hair. "Now it's your turn."

I shot a thumb toward Hays' office. "What were you doing in there?"

"I already answered that question. I said I was doing my job."

"You have to be more specific."

Chloe smiled, and her eyes seemed to twinkle. "I had to guess whose arm y'all found. If you can guess what I was doing, I'll answer truthfully."

I started to guess, but Malory walked up with our drinks. I waited as she placed the glasses on the table, then I took a long sip from mine. Malory turned to Chloe. "Do you want a catfish dinner, too?"

"Sure."

When Malory was out of earshot, I said, "You were trying to get into his computer or his daily planner to see what he's been up to."

"Close, but not quite." Chloe checked over her shoulder to make sure no one could hear, then fixed her blue eyes on me. "If you tell me one thing, I'll share with you some information I received, but only if you promise to keep it on the down low, as they say nowadays."

I shrugged. "Sure thing. Ask away."

"Did you find Hays Cain's body?"

I shook my head. "We've been on the water nonstop for the past two days—nothing. Not a thing."

Chloe's brow furrowed. She was looking right at me, but seeing through me, thinking. Finally, she asked, "Was there a murder in town, and was it Kelly Dykes?"

"Where'd you hear that?" I asked, the suddenness of my response giving me away.

Chloe smiled. "So, it is true."

"Who told you that?"

"I received an anonymous call from a blocked number saying Hays Cain was murdered, but that his murder was part of a larger scheme. The voice was disguised, muffled. It sounded like he was talking through a rag or something."

"It was a man?"

Chloe nodded. "I'm sure of it."

"Did you ask who it was?"

"Yeah, but he wouldn't say. He said he couldn't say who he was, that it was too dangerous—that his family would be in jeopardy."

I pondered this, then asked, "Did this person say if he knew who killed Cain? Did he give any indication at all who it might be?"

Chloe shook her head. "I told him I didn't believe what he was saying. I told him I wanted proof that what he was saying was true. He told me I would have to believe him. I asked him to tell me something that no one else would know to validate his claims."

"Did he tell you anything?"

"Yeah, he told me that Kelly Dykes was murdered because of what Hays told her."

"What did Hays tell her?"

"He didn't say."

We stopped talking when Malory brought our food and waited patiently for her to set it out in front of us. "Fried fish and white beans for each of you," Malory said. Steam drifted from the food, and the smell made my stomach growl. Once she had set out our silverware, Malory walked away.

I leaned toward Chloe. "When did this guy call you?"

Chloe reached into her purse and pulled out a notepad. She thumbed through it. "Around two o'clock this afternoon."

"Did he say anything else?" I asked. "Anything at all?"

"He did say something else. He said you interrupted Kelly's killer…that he was supposed to retrieve something and had to shoot at you to make his escape."

I sat quiet. The person who called her had to be the shooter, or someone close to the shooter. Other than me and my department, no one else knew about the shooting. I picked up my fork to signal the end of the question and answer session. "I trust you'll keep your word and not share this information with anyone."

"Ditto that. My editor would not take too kindly to me handing my exclusive to the chief of police." Chloe flipped her notebook shut and tucked it into her purse. She looked up at me and grinned. "Okay, enough about work. I want to hear about you."

"There's nothing to tell." I bit into the fried catfish. It was crunchy and delicious. I chewed it, savoring the flavor. When I swallowed, I grabbed up a fork full of white beans and ate it. "God, this is good."

Chloe nodded. Her cheeks were puffed out from the food she was chewing. "I used to eat here a lot," she said between mouthfuls, "but I had a disagreement with Hays over an article I wrote, and he told me I wasn't welcome in his restaurants again."

"Wait—he banned you from his restaurants?"

Chloe nodded.

"So, since he's dead," I joked, "you think you can eat in here anytime you want?"

Chloe smiled her perfect smile. "Something like that. I figure he can't poison my food if he's not around."

We continued to eat until Chloe glanced at her wristwatch, suddenly wiped her mouth on a napkin and started gathering her things. "I have to go! I'm going to be late for the fight." Chloe waved for Malory, calling out, "Can I get the check?"

"Wait…you're going watch Susan's fight?"

Chloe grinned. "Not just *her* fight—all of them. I'm covering it for the newspaper."

I felt my heart skip a tiny beat. "Um, do you want to ride with me? You can leave your car parked at the police department."

Chloe studied my face, her eyes slightly squinted. After a long, awkward moment, she nodded slowly. "Yeah, I'll ride with you. I can leave my car here, though. They won't mind."

CHAPTER 23

Once I paid Malory and left a sizable tip, Chloe followed me out to the parking lot and jumped into the passenger's side of my Tahoe. My palms were sweaty. My heart raced. I was very conscious of Chloe Rushing sitting right beside me, her left elbow resting on the center console almost rubbing against my arm. Neither of us said much as I drove, and we made it to the bingo hall with twenty minutes to spare. I bought a ticket at the door, and Chloe played the press card to get in for free.

I turned to her when we were inside the crowded room. "I guess you have a ringside seat or something. I'll go find a seat—"

Chloe smiled. "Don't be silly. I'm sitting with you."

I turned to scan the room. An octagon-shaped cyclone fence enclosure with padded corners was situated at the center of the room. Metal folding chairs surrounded the octagon-shaped fence. People milled around, drinks in their hands, talking loudly about who they thought would win each fight of the night. I pointed to a few empty chairs closest to the cage. "How about those seats? Can you see well enough from there?"

"Yeah," Chloe said, "that's perfect."

We squeezed past crowds of drinking fans and finally reached the empty chairs. I took the seat at the end and Chloe sat right beside me, her arm brushing against mine. I looked around, not expecting to know anyone. After all, I was a stranger in town and I'd spent more time in the water than on dry land up to that point. Out of uniform, no one even gave me a second glance. It was as though I was invisible, and I liked it. A familiar face caught my attention, and I craned my neck to see around one of the corner posts. "Is that the mayor?" I asked.

Chloe looked where I pointed. "Yep, that's him at the VIP table."

Mayor Landry was seated at a large table with five other men. Naturally, he was positioned at the head of the table. There was an empty chair to his left. Next to him to the right was a man I'd never seen before, but across from the mayor at the foot of the table was my father-in-law. "Who's that man sitting next to the mayor?" I wanted to know.

Chloe stood halfway out of her chair, placed a soft hand on my shoulder and leaned into me. I was as unfamiliar with women's perfume as I was with the study of alien life forms, but I immediately recognized it as the kind Michele used to wear.

"Oh, that's Walter Moore," Chloe said, sinking back to her seat. "He's an assistant district attorney here. The man to his right is Daniel Blackley."

"His name sounds familiar. What's he do?"

"You've probably seen the billboards in town advertising job openings. He's the CEO of Blackley and Sons Industries...a chemical plant on the river. They say his place has to stay on high alert because it's a potential terror target."

"William handled a burglary at one of his old warehouses in town."

"Really?" If Chloe had had ears like Achilles, they would've perked up. "What was stolen?"

"Nothing worth writing about." I looked at the man sitting across from Daniel Blackley—it was Randall Rupe. Next to Randall was another man I didn't recognize. "Who's the guy next to Randall?"

"Mark McNeal." Chloe pulled her notebook out and started making notes.

"Is he someone important?"

"I guess it depends on your definition—he owns some banks."

I was thoughtful, pointed out the empty chair. "I guess that's where Hays Cain would be sitting if he'd still be alive?"

"You're catching on, Chief."

I was still studying the VIP table when the announcer stepped to the middle of the cage and hollered into the microphone. He excitedly named some sponsors, identified who would be fighting in the main event, and thanked everyone in attendance. He then lowered his voice and nodded toward the table where Mayor Landry and the other men sat. "It's coming up on the two-year anniversary of the loss of six of Mechant Loup's finest soldiers. Let us now have a moment of silence to pay respect to those fine individuals and their families."

Everyone stood, bowed their heads. When the moment of silence was over, I asked Chloe what the announcement had been about.

She pointed to the table. "Two years ago, on the Fourth of July, six families lost kids who served in the national guard."

It seemed every man at the table was wiping tears from his eyes, including my father-in-law, Judge Miller. I scowled. Michele had never mentioned having a brother who died while serving. "They all had sons who died in the guard?"

"Except for Judge Miller and Mark McNeal." Chloe nodded. "Mark McNeal's daughter was killed. As for Judge Miller, he didn't have any kids who served in the military. From what I understand, he only had one daughter and she got killed in an armed robbery or something in the city."

I swallowed hard and tried to remain unfazed. "How'd they get killed? I mean, six of them all at one time? How'd that happen?"

"They were all together when—"

"Are you ready for the first fight of the evening?" the announcer screamed. "Let's hear it for…"

The announcer went on to introduce the fighters for the first match, and Chloe and I made small talk while we watched. It ended two minutes into the second round when one of the fighters put the other in a rear-naked choke. There were four more fights before the announcer called Susan's name. I caught movement at the end of the room and saw Susan walking toward the ring with a small army of people following her. Her hair was pulled back into cornrows, just as she wore it at work, but she looked nothing like she did in her uniform. She wore form-fitting shorts and shirt that accentuated her sleek, muscular frame. Her feet were bare, but she wore grappling gloves. The mouthpiece pushed her face into a scowl and that, along with the bruises on her toned legs, made for an intimidating presence.

I nodded my approval. "I'm glad she's on my side—she looks really tough."

"She's as tough as they get," Chloe said. "She's downright vicious. Did you know she's undefeated?"

I shook my head and watched as Susan jogged into the cage and bounced around on the balls of her feet. She looked relaxed out there, as though she were at home in the cage. I found myself envying what she had. How free and happy she looked. I tried to remember what it felt like to be happy—truly happy. Not the kind of happiness where I'd put on a fake smile and pretend to be fine, while my insides were on fire. Not the kind of happiness where I acted fine, but had to struggle to catch a deep breath because it felt like a boulder was crushing my chest. Not the kind of happiness where I was at ease in a room full of people, but was utterly lost and lonely on the inside. I wanted to breathe easy and free again. I wanted to have feelings again. To love...to worry...to care. *Yeah, I'd love to care again.* I frowned and shook my head. Those days were gone forever for me. The best I could hope for was an early end so I could see Michele and Abigail again.

CHAPTER 24

"Are you ignoring me?" Chloe's soft voice rescued me from my thoughts.

I jerked my head around to look at her. "What?"

She laughed. "I lost you for a minute. You were staring at Susan Wilson like you'd never seen a girl in tights."

"I didn't realize I was staring. I just... I just have a lot on my mind."

"I understand." Chloe put a hand on my knee. "You've been through a lot lately. I can't imagine how it must've felt to be nearly killed by an alligator. I could see the pain on your face that day—the first time I ever saw you."

I looked away from Chloe and back toward Susan. One of her trainers was applying some sort of grease to her face and then he checked her gloves and nodded. As I watched the action in the ring, I spotted a man in my peripheral vision. It appeared he was staring at me. I glanced in his direction—it was Beaver. He stood near the cage with his arms folded in front of his chest. He was glaring at me. I shook my head and smiled. When Beaver shifted his eyes from me to Chloe, they turned to mere slits. He mouthed something. I felt my heartbeat quicken.

"Why the hell is Beaver Detiveaux staring at you like he wants to kill you?"

Chloe followed my gaze, but quickly turned her head away. "He gives me the creeps."

"It looks like he hates you. Why?"

"I did a story on him a while back. It got him fired."

I gasped. "You were the reporter who got him fired?"

"Guilty as charged." Chloe chewed on her lower lip. "He should've gone to jail."

People in the bingo hall began to clap. I turned toward the cage just in time to see Susan and her opponent—some muscle-bound woman named Beatrix who looked like a German tank—advancing toward each other with evil intentions. When they clashed, there was a flurry of punches from both of them. In the middle of the action, and without warning, Susan jumped high into the air. She brought her right knee around in a whipping arc and it crashed into Beatrix' jaw. The impact was sickening. Beatrix stumbled backward. Like a hungry mountain lion, Susan pounced. She threw a jab and cross combination that felled Beatrix. I couldn't be sure, but it looked like Beatrix's eyes rolled back into her head on her way to the canvas. She didn't move after she hit the ground.

The crowd erupted. People jumped into the air. They whistled and screamed. I stood so I could see what was happening, and Chloe stood beside me, grabbed my arm and leaned close.

"What just happened?" Chloe asked, trying to scream above the roar of the manic crowd. Her lips brushed lightly against my ear and tickled. I shuddered as the sensation reverberated up and down my spine. It had been a long time since I'd felt a tingle like that.

I leaned into her. "Susan just knocked the piss out of that woman! I think she's dead."

"I missed it!" Chloe started writing frantically on her notepad, glanced up at a bank of televisions in the center of the room, waited for the replay. The crowd cheered again as the large screen showed the knockout in slow motion. When Chloe was done making her notes, she flipped her pad shut and shoved it into her purse. "Okay, that was the last fight. I'm ready."

I looked down at her, curious. "Ready for what?"

"To get out of here. Let's go do something." She grabbed my hand and started to drag me away when Mayor Landry appeared in front of us.

"Clint, can I have a word with you? Alone?"

I turned to Chloe. "Can you give us a minute?"

The smile faded from Chloe's face. She nodded and let go of my hand.

"What's up, Mayor?" I asked when we had moved out of earshot of Chloe.

"Any progress on the search for Hays?"

"None." I stepped closer to Mayor Landry. "You two were friends, right?"

"We've been friendly for years, but we grew really close after our sons were killed." He nodded his head toward the table where he had been sitting with my father-in-law and the others. "Tragedies bind people together, you know? Most of us barely knew each other before that miserable day."

I nodded my understanding. "I'm sorry. I didn't know."

"How could you?" Mayor Landry turned when a shadow fell over us.

"Hey, Clint, I see you're making yourself right at home here." Nick Miller approached us and extended his hand. "How've you been?"

"I'm good, Nick. Been busy, but good."

"How's the house treating you?"

"Good. I like it. I got a dog. Hope you don't mind."

"Not at all. A dog's a man's best friend, after all." He looked at Chloe standing alone near the exit to the bingo hall. "What's going on with her?"

Guilt tugged at my heart. "Um...nothing. She's just a friend."

"Well, it's good you're making friends. I hoped you would. It's time to move on."

I raised my hands. "Sir, it's not what you think. I'm not moving on or anything. We're strictly friends."

"Son, don't make the mistake I made. You're too young to carry this with you. Move on with your life. Trust me"—Nick grabbed my shoulder, squeezing it hard—"Michele would want it that way. She wouldn't want you to be alone." His voice shook; tears filled his eyes.

I pursed my lips and nodded slowly.

Nick Miller lowered his head and quickly walked away.

"It's not nice to keep a lady waiting," Chloe called from behind us.

CHAPTER 25

I didn't say much on the drive back to the restaurant. When we arrived in the parking lot, I followed Chloe to her car. "Why are you being so quiet now, Clint?"

I shrugged. "I'm just tired. I've worked six days straight and I have to be back out on the water in the morning. I have to find Hays Cain's body."

Chloe scowled. "You weren't tired twenty minutes ago."

"I know. It just hit me all of a sudden."

"All of a sudden after you talked to the mayor and the judge. Do you really think I'm that stupid?"

The question caught me off guard. "Not at all. You're extremely intelligent—that's why I like you."

"Oh, so you like me?" Chloe smiled and bit her lower lip, staring up at me.

"No...that's not what I mean."

"Oh, now you *don't* like me." Chloe crossed her arms in front of her chest. "Which is it, Mr. Chief of Police?"

I took a deep breath and exhaled slowly, as I collected my thoughts. "Look, I think you're really cool and I'd love to hang out with you all night, but I have to go to work—"

Chloe's eyes widened and her jaw dropped. "And now you want to spend the night with me!"

Before I could say anything, Chloe burst out laughing.

"What I meant was I'd like to spend more time with you, but I can't tonight. I have to get out on the water early in the morning, and I have to get home to Achilles."

Chloe's face scrunched up. "Who's Achilles?"

"My dog."

"I'm being passed over for a dog. Great."

I smiled. "Can I call you tomorrow?"

Chloe's eyebrows furrowed. "How do you know Judge Miller?"

"He's...um, he's my father-in-law."

Chloe's mouth fell open. "Oh, Clint, I'm so sorry! Now I understand."

"It's okay. I'd rather not talk about it." I opened Chloe's door for her, and she hesitated.

Finally, she slipped into the driver's seat of her car. "Why don't I cook dinner tomorrow and bring it over to your place? We can visit some more then."

My heart rate began to steadily increase. "Um...sure. That sounds great. As long as you make enough for Achilles."

"You've got a deal." Chloe pulled the door shut and drove away.

When I got home, Achilles was whining to get out of his crate. His tongue dangled from the corner of his mouth like a limp cigar and his tail wagged.

I opened the crate, and Achilles bounded toward me. I leaned over and scratched his head, then walked to the kitchen to grab a bottle of vodka. I twisted the cap off and opened the back door. "Come on, tiger. Get out there and do your business."

I sat on the back steps and pulled from the bottle as Achilles sniffed around in the grass. The evening air was warm, and there was a lazy breeze blowing. After a few seconds, I felt a pick on the back of my neck and slapped at it. I held up my hand until the light pouring from the back door illuminated it. I grinned at the tiny black smudge and spot of blood on my palm. "I got you, you little shit."

I wasn't grinning for long. "Damn mosquitoes are worse than vampires."

Thinking I was talking to him, Achilles started jogging toward me. He suddenly stopped and his ears came alert. I'd heard it, too—a large branch snapping. Only something heavy could've made that noise. I rested the bottle of vodka on the wooden steps and stood. I reached for my pistol, but cursed when I remembered I'd just returned from Susan's fight.

Another branch popped several yards beyond the tree line, and Achilles shot like a bullet toward the sound, barking as he ran.

"No! Achilles," I yelled, running after him. "Stop!"

The forest exploded with sound. Twigs snapped and leaves rustled as whatever it was ran off. It was black as sin and I couldn't see three feet in front of me. I could hear Achilles pushing through the underbrush, barking as he ran. He was about twenty yards ahead of me, but it sounded like I was catching up. A growl ripped from Achilles' throat. What was clearly a human gave an angry grunt and then Achilles let out a sharp cry.

"I'm going to kill you if you hurt my dog," I screamed.

Anger coursed through me and, although I was spent, it propelled me forward. I opened my mouth to yell again, but I smashed face first into what felt like a tree. The irony taste of blood was instant. My teeth jarred in my head and my knees gave out. I slid downward, the rough bark scraping my face as I fell. When my knees hit the ground, I jolted to a stop and collapsed onto my left side.

* * *

Something wet and slimy slid across my chin and lips. I stirred, then winced as pain shot through the front of my face. I opened my eyes. Everything was black. *Am I blind?*

A soft whimper in my ear told me Achilles was beside me. He nestled his cold nose against my face. I pushed myself to a seated position, but the blackness swirled around my head and I nearly vomited. I sank back to the ground. Achilles whined, trying to push me with his head. I rubbed his ears. "I'll be okay. Just give me a minute."

When my stomach had settled, I propped my back against the tree. I felt in the dark and pulled Achilles close, checking him with my hands to make sure he was okay. His coat was soft, but his young muscles were solid and ripped. When I pushed my fingers against the left side of his ribs, he yelped. "Somebody kicked you good, didn't they?"

I could feel Achilles lick the area.

"That won't work," I said. "You probably have bruised ribs. That'll take a little time to heal. You'll just have to suck it up."

Once I was sure Achilles was okay, I took the time to check on my own condition. My nose felt tender to the touch. I couldn't tell if it was broken, but blood poured freely from it. I pulled off my shirt and held it to my nose, leaning my head forward. Achilles' body squirmed rhythmically with the wagging of his tail. He sidled up to me and began to lick me aggressively. I didn't mind. "You're a brave little tiger, ain't you?"

After about fifteen minutes, and with the aid of the tree that had dropped me, I was able to stand slowly without vomiting. Blood still leaked from my nose and onto my chest, but I ignored it. I stumbled through the woods and toward my house. Having gained my night vision, I was able to distinguish the darker shadows from the lighter ones, which helped me pick my way through the trees. I stopped often to listen, but I didn't hear any sounds other than our walking and Achilles' panting.

When I reached the rear steps of my house, I snatched up the bottle of vodka and drank deeply of the smooth liquid. I dropped my arm, let the bottle dangle from my fingertips and stared up at the door to my house. There were only five steps between me and the porch, but I was still unsteady on my feet. Gripping the bottle of vodka in my left hand like it was a bomb, I held onto the railing with my right hand to keep from falling. I made my way one slow step at a time and finally made it to the top.

Once inside, I pushed the door shut and threw the deadbolt. I stumbled toward the couch and sat down hard. My bare chest and stomach were covered in blood, and blood had seeped onto my jeans. I took a long drink from the bottle of vodka. When I pulled it away from my mouth, I gasped for air. Vodka sprayed from my lips. I shook the bottle. There was only one swallow left and I didn't waste time. When the bottle was empty, I tossed it to the floor and stretched out onto the cushions. My head ached and the room spun.

Achilles leapt onto the couch and curled up on my blood-smeared stomach. I rested my hand over his neck and ruffled his hair. "I'm going to find that asshole who kicked you and I'm going to beat him to death."

Achilles squirmed higher up on my torso, his nails digging into my flesh. I didn't even flinch. My eyelids were heavy. I started to talk, but the words fell like bricks onto the floor.

CHAPTER 26

Sunday, June 29

"What in the hell happened to you?" Susan Wilson's hands were planted on her hips and her mouth was wide. Her gaze moved from my worn boots, up through my faded jeans and shirt, and rested on my battered face. "You look worse than I do right now—and I had a professional fight last night."

"You're an amazing fighter. I'm not." I walked by Susan and entered my office, with her on my heels.

"Clint, what happened?"

I sat behind my desk and lightly rubbed my nose with my fingers. "I ran into a tree."

"Bullshit! What happened?"

I sighed. The throbbing in my head was worse than any hangover I'd ever experienced. "Someone was behind my house last night."

"What do you mean?"

"I heard someone in the woods behind my house last night. Achilles took after them, and I tried to catch him, but I ran nose-first into a tree."

"Did you go to the hospital?"

I didn't want to explain why I couldn't get behind the wheel and drive, so I just waved a hand. "It's nothing a little time won't fix."

"Why didn't you call it in?"

I laughed, then winced when the pain stabbed at my face. "Who would I call? The cops? I am the cops. Besides, it's no big deal."

"No big deal?" Susan crossed her arms in front of her chest and paced back and forth in front of my desk. When she finally stopped, she whirled on me. "What if someone's trying to kill you? What if it's the same person who killed Kelly Dykes?"

I leaned back and stared at the ceiling. I hadn't thought of that. I figured it was someone with a good enough reason for being out in the woods at night. "Maybe it was a hunter or something. Maybe some kids playing hide and seek."

"What about Achilles? Did he come back?"

"When I came to, he was licking my face. Whoever it was kicked him hard enough to make his ribs tender, but he was more concerned about me than he was about himself. I tell you, that's one loyal little—"

"Wait—what? You were unconscious?"

"I don't know. I was stunned, I guess."

"If you lost consciousness, you need to go to the hospital. You could have a brain bleed."

I stood and grabbed my police radio. "Are you ready to hit the water again?"

Susan sighed. "You're one hard-headed man."

"Aren't we all?" I stood to walk out, but Susan caught hold of my arm.

"I saw you at my fight. Thanks. It meant a lot."

I nodded, then walked out of my office and into the break room where Melvin and Jack were at the table talking to a snowy-haired woman I hadn't met yet. I stuck out my hand. "I'm Clint Wolf."

The lady looked up and recoiled in horror. "What happened to you?"

Melvin looked up and gasped.

Jack twisted in his chair to see what all the fuss was about. He smirked. "It looks like you met Sergeant Susan Wilson."

"I didn't realize I looked that bad. I lost a fight with a tree trunk."

"Chief, no offense," the woman said, "but it looks like your face caught fire and someone put it out with a frying pan."

We all laughed.

"I'm Ethel," the lady said. "I'm one of your weekend dispatchers. I used to be a nurse, so you should let me look at that."

"I'll be fine, ma'am, but thanks. And it's nice to meet you." I turned to Melvin. "Any word on the recordings?"

Melvin shook his head. "Nothing since Friday. I'll call first thing in the morning and see if it's ready."

"I can take care of that," Jack offered.

"Nope. Melvin's got it." I could've sworn Melvin's face lit up. I grabbed the pot of coffee and poured a cup, drinking it straight and in one gulp. It burned my tongue, palate and throat, but it successfully redirected the pain from my nose. When I put the cup down, I glanced at the clock on the wall. "I'm going to head out to the lake with Susan and see if we can't cover more ground. We need to work the south bank a little better, I think. Melvin, can you head further down Bayou Tail?"

"Sure thing."

I shook my head. "I don't understand it. Hays Cain's body should've been floating by now."

"His body could've gotten tangled up in some debris or stuck in the mud," Jack offered.

"That's a real possibility." I started to walk out the break room.

"Hey, Chief," Melvin said, "I have a buddy who works for the sheriff's office. He's a canine officer and he's got a cadaver dog."

"Excellent idea, Melvin," I said. "You think he'd be willing to go out there with you?"

"He'd love it!"

"Great. Make it happen."

Melvin rushed out of the room, and I turned to Jack. "Did anything interesting happen last night?"

"Nothing much. It was pretty quiet." Jack scowled. "I did get another call about a suspicious man hanging around the gas station."

"Who called it in?" I asked.

"The clerk working the night shift. She said he came in and looked around, asked who the chief of police was, and then left."

"Asked who the chief of police was?" I echoed.

Jack shrugged. "That's what she said."

"Did she tell him?"

Jack smirked. "She told him she thought it was Beaver Detiveaux."

I scowled. *Who in the hell could be coming here asking about me?*

Jack stood up. "Well, I'm heading out for the day."

I nodded to Ethel. "You can get out of here, too. I'll wait here until Lindsey comes in."

CHAPTER 27

It was late in the day, and Susan and I were about to call it quits when Melvin's voice scratched over the police radio. "Chief, we got something!"

"Where are you?" I asked.

"We're still on Bayou Tail, about ten miles south of the lake."

Susan revved the engine and shot toward the southern end of Lake Berg. Misty droplets of water sprayed my face, making me thankful for the cool reprieve from the hot sun. The back of my neck burned. I glanced at my arms. "I'm going to have a farmer's tan," I called over the steady hum of the boat motor.

"I tried to tell you to use sunscreen," Susan said.

"I need sunscreen as much as you need a bodyguard."

Susan chuckled.

"I still can't believe how vicious you looked in that cage. You were downright mean. You went at her like she stole your boyfriend."

"I just did my job."

"Yeah, you did beat her like it was your job." I grabbed onto the edge of the boat as we hit some waves and rocked roughly up and down. When the front of the boat stopped bouncing, I leaned closer to Susan. "When are you fighting again?"

"I'm not sure. I need to meet with the promoter and my trainer. It's getting harder and harder to find opponents. The more I win, the harder it is to convince someone to take a fight with me."

"I can understand that." I pointed toward a sheriff's office boat tied to a tree along the banks of Bayou Tail a hundred yards away. "There they are."

As we neared them, I saw Melvin launch a large grappling hook into the air. It landed in the water with a large splash and quickly sank, dragging a long length of rope with it. Melvin allowed the rope to slide through his hands until there was slack in it. He looked up as Susan eased our boat beside theirs.

"Chief, this here"—he nodded at a young fellow dressed in dark blue BDUs—"is my buddy, Seth. And that ugly critter is Coco."

"Damn, Chief," Seth said. "What happened to you?"

"Nothing a little time can't fix." I glanced down at the critter. It looked like a saddleback German shepherd, only much smaller. "Is that a German shepherd?"

Seth nodded. "She was the runt of the litter, but she was so cute I couldn't pass her up."

"She doesn't look very scary," Susan said.

"She's not," Seth explained. "I use her strictly as a cadaver dog. I've got a large—"

"This is it!" Melvin's cheeks were puffy as he strained to pull whatever was attached to the grappling hook toward the surface.

I picked my way across our boat and stepped over to Melvin's boat. They both rocked gently as I changed over, and Melvin had to put out a hand to maintain his balance. I hurried beside him and grabbed hold of the prickly rope. Together, we dragged the heavy object toward us.

"It feels like we're pulling a dead whale," Melvin said between breaths. "I've never had a drown victim this hard to pull up."

"Hays only weighed about two-fifty," Susan said.

I nodded, leaned over to re-grip, and then pulled back on the rope. When I had pulled as far as I could, Melvin leaned over and took the next long tug. I wiped sweat from my forehead, said, "Maybe we're pulling up an old car."

"I claim it first if it's a treasure," Susan quickly said.

I started to respond, but stopped when I saw the crown of thick, curly hair break the surface of the muddy water. I leaned over and helped Melvin pull it closer and saw it was missing an arm. "It's him."

Susan maneuvered the back of her boat in our direction until she could reach the rope and helped us guide the body between the two boats. She pointed to some chains attached to Hays Cain's waist. "That's why it's so damn heavy!"

Hays' swollen torso had ripped the front of his button-up shirt open, but it was no match for the links of unforgiving chain. The skin at his waist had stretched around the chain and ripped in places. As

Melvin and Susan held Hays steady, I reached under his body and felt two ropes extending downward from the chain wrapped around his waist. I grabbed one of the ropes and tugged on it. Whatever was attached to the other end was heavy. "He's weighted down with something."

While holding onto the rope with one hand, I pulled my knife from my pocket with the other. I stretched my legs out for leverage as I reached under the water with my knife hand and sliced the rope. I scrambled backward and pulled the object from the water. It was a cinder block. I placed it at the bottom of the boat and retrieved the other cinder block. When it was also at the bottom of the boat, I straightened and rubbed the sweat from my eyes. "That's why we couldn't find him."

Susan grabbed the chain around Hays' waist. "Well, we've got him now. Help me get him onboard."

Hays' body was finally floating. Melvin gave a push and the front of his body glided toward me. I grabbed his good arm and looked over at Susan. She was breathing through her mouth to avoid taking in the rancid odor that emitted from Hays Cain's decayed flesh, but she grabbed a firm hold on his legs and nodded. We gave a hard pull and launched his body out of the water and over the side of the boat. We were a little overzealous in our attempt—most likely because of how hard it was to pull him from the bottom of the bayou—and his shoulder smashed into my knees, nearly knocking me over. I shoved him off my feet and stepped back to examine him.

Water gently lapped the sides of the boats and that was the only sound as we all stared down at what used to be Hays Cain. The skin around his lips had been eaten away by marine life and his eyes bulged.

"It looks like he's got a giant grin on his face," Susan said idly.

"God, Sue!" Melvin's face twisted in disgust. "That's a gross thing to say."

"No, look at it." Susan pointed. "That's what it looks like."

I scowled when I saw the hole in his forehead, leaned closer. "Single shot to the forehead. Chloe was right—he was murdered."

Susan's head snapped around. "What do you mean *Chloe was right?*"

"She got a call from someone who told her Hays had been murdered."

"And when were you going to tell me this?" Susan's eyes were narrow.

"I just told you. Look, she told me this yesterday—right before your fight. I wasn't about to interrupt your fight to tell you. I was scared you'd mistake me for that muscle-bound freak and attack me."

"Fat chance," Susan muttered.

"Hey!" Melvin protested. "I'm sure you can kick my ass, Sue, but I'm not going to let you call Chief Wolf fat. I'd have you know he humped out of these here swamps in alligator-infested—"

"Simmer down, cowboy." Susan started laughing. "I didn't call him fat, but it's nice to know you have his back."

"I'm sorry. I thought you said he was fat." Melvin scowled. "I'd have your back, too. We're a family. We should all stick together and get along."

I chuckled. "Well, brother and sister, let's get Mr. Cain out of here so we can get the autopsy done and put the poor man to rest."

CHAPTER 28

Monday, June 30

"So, what you're saying is," Mayor Landry began, "someone shot Hays Cain point blank in the forehead, wrapped a chain around his waist, tied cinder blocks to his body, and dumped him in the bayou?"

I nodded. "That about sums it up."

"Why in the hell would someone do that?" Mayor Landry leaned back in his chair and gripped the edge of his desk with large hands. "Do you have any leads? Anything at all?"

"We know he was shot with a nine millimeter pistol. We sent it off to be compared to the projectile we recovered from Kelly Dykes' murder scene." I hesitated, then said, "Chloe did receive an anonymous call before we found Hays' body. The caller said Hays had been murdered. He also told Chloe that Hays said something to Kelly Dykes about some secret he had and that was why she was killed—she knew too much. He was right about Hayes being murdered, so..."

Mayor Landry was thoughtful, then opened the top desk drawer, pulled out a set of keys, tossed them to me. "These are for your new Tahoe. Drive down to Randall's dealership and pick it up. It's solid black and fully loaded."

"I don't need a new vehicle. That Tahoe is plenty good enough."

Mayor Landry waved his hand. "That thing's cursed. It's Beaver's old ride. I don't want you sitting where that piece of shit sat. Besides, I'll need you to pick up the governor and his colonel from the airport when they come to town, and I don't want you picking them up in that old ride."

I stared down at Mayor Landry. "You want me to do *what?*"

Mayor Landry raised his hands. "Look, Nick told me you don't like the man, but this is bigger than you and him."

I don't like him? That's putting it mildly. "I'll get Melvin or Susan to pick him up."

"Clint, this is a big deal. First off, we can't have the governor or the colonel sitting in the backseat of a patrol cruiser. Second, and most importantly, if anyone less than you picks him up, it'll be viewed as an insult. Please—can I count on you?"

I pursed my lips, then nodded. "I'll handle it."

"By the way, what happened to your face?"

"It's just a scratch." I brushed the bridge of my nose with my thumb and shoved the Tahoe keys into my pocket. I walked out into the smothering morning air and took a deep breath to calm myself. I could only think of four people I hated more than the governor—and one of them was dead.

My phone rang. Still unsure exactly how to use the thing, I got it to stop beeping in my hand and held it to my ear. "This is Clint."

"Hey, you, what's up?" It was Chloe's soft voice.

I smiled and my muscles suddenly relaxed. "How are you, Chloe?"

"Good, good. Do you have plans tonight?"

"Not that I know of."

"What's that mean? Do you have people who work your calendar? Do my people have to call your people?"

"I mean, no, I don't have plans."

"Great. I'm picking you up at your house at six and I'm taking you to dinner."

"I thought you were cooking and coming over?" The words spilled from my mouth before I realized I was saying them. I slapped my forehead.

"Well, that sounded good at the time, but, to be honest, I can't cook worth shit."

I laughed. "We can do whatever you like."

"Great! See you at six."

My phone went dead, and I stood there with a goofy grin on my face. What was it about Chloe that made me feel that way? Happy, even. Was there something special about her, or was it simply the perfume? I shrugged and shoved the phone back into my pocket and jumped into my Tahoe. *Don't overanalyze it. Just roll with it.*

I drove to the office, parked along the highway and hurried through the front door. I found Lindsey leaning back in her chair with her feet on her desk. She had a book in her hands and was so engrossed in what she was reading that she didn't notice me walk in.

"'Morning, Lindsey."

"Shit!" She jerked in her chair and the book flew across the room and hit the wall with a thud.

I laughed. "It must be a good book."

"God, I think I had a heart attack." She rubbed her chest and looked up at me. Her eyes turned curious when she saw my nose, but she didn't mention it. "Why are you so happy? I've known you for a week and never seen you smile."

"No reason." I walked into my office, where Melvin was already waiting for me. "You got it?"

Melvin nodded. "He cleaned it up a little, but it's still difficult to hear. He said the poor quality of the original recording made it difficult to enhance."

I sat behind my desk and waited while Melvin set up the voice message from Kelly Dykes' phone. When he played it, I scowled. "It doesn't sound much different."

"He said it wouldn't."

"Well, we know for sure the second man talking is the shooter because the first man asked him why he shot Hays." I flipped my hands upward. "Other than that, we've got nothing."

Melvin placed the compact disc back into the evidence envelope. "What are we going to do next? I mean, where do we go from here?"

"Other than interview everyone who knew him? I'm not sure." I spun around in my chair and stared out at the street in front of the office. There wasn't much traffic. The sun was bright and reflected off my shattered headlight. I surged to my feet and walked closer to the window. "He wasn't trying to kill us!"

"Who?" Melvin wanted to know.

"The shooter from the other day...every bullet he fired at Kelly Dykes, who was running for her life, found its mark. She was a moving target, and he still hit her every time. That takes some skill."

Melvin grunted. "I couldn't do that."

I spun to face him. "Susan and I were sitting ducks when he fired the first shot. He could've taken us out easily—shot at least one of us—but he didn't. Instead, he blew out the headlight and taillight. Both were great shots from that distance." I shook my head. "That wasn't an accident. He deliberately missed us. He didn't want us dead."

Melvin frowned. "But why not?"

"I'm not sure. Maybe he just wanted to scare us enough to

facilitate his escape." I turned back to the window and stared thoughtfully at my Tahoe. "We need to find a good reason to kill Hays."

"Um, he's already dead."

I turned, smiling. "You know what I mean. Once we figure out why someone wanted him dead, it'll be easier to find out who killed him."

"I'm sure his wife wanted him dead," Melvin suggested.

"True, but it's definitely not her voice on the recording."

"Maybe she hired a couple of assassins to kill him for her. They only kill for money and certainly don't want to bring more heat on themselves, so they intentionally missed you and Susan."

"Ah, that is a thought."

"Chief, you…" Melvin hesitated.

"What is it, Melvin?"

"I don't know. You seem happy today."

I smiled. "It's because I am happy."

Melvin's face lit up into a giant grin. "You got a hot date or something?"

"Or something." I touched the outside of my pocket and felt a jagged object, suddenly remembering the Tahoe keys. I jerked them out. "I'll be back, Melvin. I'm going pick up my new ride."

I called Susan on the way to Randall Rupe's car dealership. When she answered, I asked, "Are you busy right now?"

"I'm just getting back from the crime lab. The firearms examiner said she'd have something by this afternoon."

"Great. Thanks. Now, do you want to go undercover?"

"It depends what I have to do. I won't do a prostitution sting or—"

"No!" I laughed. "Nothing like that. I want to kick a hornet's nest and want you to be there to see it, but I don't want anyone to see you."

"Sounds fun. Tell me what you want and I'll do it."

CHAPTER 29

"Well, look here. You finally decided to come get your new wheels. We've got you all fixed up and ready to go. I just need you to sign some papers and you'll be set." Randall Rupe slapped my back and led the way down the long hallway to his office, calling over his shoulder, "It looks like you got hit with an airbag."

"Something like that." When we were seated in his office, Randall shuffled some papers, stamped some forms, and then pushed a few to my side of the table to be signed. I signed the highlighted sections and slid them back.

"Malcolm told me he already gave you the keys—is that right?"

I pulled them from my pocket so he could see. "I've got them."

Randall stood and extended his hand. "Well, that about sums it—"

"Not so fast." I remained seated, leaned back in my chair. "I have a few questions for you before I go."

"Questions?" He slowly withdrew his hand and sank back into his seat. "About what?"

"Your good friend, Hays Cain, of course." I studied his face. His eyes were shifty; his neck jumped with each beat of his heart. "When was it that you last spoke to him or saw him?"

Randall looked up, licked his lips. "Um, I guess it was Friday."

"Spoke with him or saw him?"

"I...I didn't see him."

"So, you talked to him on the phone?"

Randall nodded, but didn't say anything.

"What did y'all talk about?"

"Small talk. You know how it goes with friends."

"Did he say what he was doing? Where he was going?"

Randall glanced at his gold wristwatch. "Excuse me, Chief, but I have a meeting in exactly two minutes with my sales team."

"I understand." I stood to go. "Thank you for talking with me."

"Anything to help a friend," Randall said, standing with me. He didn't extend his hand this time.

I started to walk out, but stopped at the door to stare Randall directly in the eyes. "You'll be happy to know that we have a solid lead on your friend's murder."

"You do?"

"We do." I nodded. "It seems Hays accidentally butt-dialed his girlfriend and the conversation between his killer and another man was recorded."

Randall's eyes widened ever so slightly.

"We sent the recording off for voice-recognition analysis." I said. "We should have the results back any day now. Hell, by this time next week, the murderer will be locked in a cell at the police station awaiting trial for murder."

The color drained from Randall's face.

"By the way, Randall, how'd you know Hays was dead?"

"You know how word travels in this town. I heard y'all pulled someone out the lake and figured it was Hays."

"I'm not talking about today."

Randall's thick brows turned to a V. "What, then, are you talking about?"

"I'm talking about when I interviewed you on Wednesday."

"I don't follow you, Chief."

"We found Hays' body yesterday, but you were speaking about him in past tense last Wednesday. What did you know that we didn't know?"

Randall glared at me. "I don't like the accusatory nature of your questioning."

"Well then, I guess I'll be in touch later." I held up the keys, smiled and walked out into the large garage where my new Tahoe was waiting. As I left the parking lot, I saw Randall watching me through the showroom window.

I grabbed my radio and keyed it up. "Heads up, Susan. I'm leaving."

"I'm in place," Susan replied.

"Good. Meet me back at the office later."

"Ten-four."

I stopped at the hospital before heading back to the office, and a nurse led me to Dexter Boudreaux's room. "How's it hanging, Mr. Boudreaux?"

Dexter lifted what remained of his left arm. The color had returned to his face. "Ain't nothing hanging on this side. It does look like I'm doing a little better than you, though. At least my moneymaker"—he rubbed his face with his good hand—"wasn't damaged."

"I'm real sorry about everything. I feel like my inexperience might have contributed to what happened."

"Nonsense! It ain't your fault, son. When you're getting after gators, sometimes you're the one that gets got." Dexter tapped the end of his nub. "If the Good Lord Himself was with me there's nothing he could've done to save this arm. It was meant to be."

I scowled. "I still don't like it."

"Well, like it or not, it can't be changed, so get over it." Dexter reached over with his good hand and grabbed a glass of water from the bed table. He drank deep from it and put it back. "Doc tells me I'll be out of here in no time. As soon as he lets me out of this prison, I'm going back after that gator."

"Do you think that's a good idea?"

"Chief, if a bad guy got away from you, would you just give up or would you keep going after him until you got him?"

I shrugged. "I guess you're right."

"Of course I'm right. Now, Denise tells me the town's been going to shit—said Hays Cain was murdered."

"That's right. His body was dumped somewhere along Bayou Tail last weekend."

Dexter's brow furrowed. "I was out on the water last weekend. Didn't notice anything out of the ordinary. It was quiet. I only saw one other boat. Maybe they saw something because I passed by early in the day and stayed at my camp that night."

"Did you know them?"

"One of them was a stranger, but the other man was Randall Rupe. They were in Randall's boat."

"Wait—Randall Rupe was out on the water last weekend?"

"Yeah. We were the only ones out there."

"Does Randall go out on the water a lot?"

Dexter shrugged. "I've seen him from time to time. He does a little fishing, but that's all."

"Did you talk to them?"

"No. I saw them from a distance. I was getting my camp ready for the alligator season and didn't have time to stop and talk."

"Can you describe the man?"

"Nope. Even if I did get a good look at him it would've been difficult to recognize him. He was wearing a ball cap and sunglasses."

"Were they moving?"

"No, they were stopped at the edge of the bayou. Randall had a line in the water and the other guy looked like he was messing with his bait."

I frowned. "Where on Bayou Tail?"

"South of the lake."

"How far south?"

Dexter shrugged. "About eight miles."

My blood ran cold. *Randall Rupe dumped Hays Cain's body!*

I rushed out of the hospital, dialing Susan's number as I jogged to my new Tahoe. She answered on the third ring. "What's up, Clint?"

"Where the hell are you? Are you still watching Randall? Did he go mobile?"

"Paradise Place...yes...yes."

"Where's Paradise Place?" I asked.

"The last street south of town. It doesn't look like much—just a shell road between two rows of cane fields."

"I'm on my way!" I pulled onto Main Street and smashed the accelerator, heading south.

"No! You can't come here."

"Why not?"

"It's too risky. They might see you."

"He's the one, Susan. Randall Rupe dumped Hays' body."

"What?" Susan asked. "Are you shitting me?"

"No. Dexter Boudreaux saw him this past weekend—right where we found Hays' body."

Susan was quiet for a long moment. "What do we do, Chief?"

"Where are you, exactly?"

"I'm parked in the middle of a cane field on the south side of Paradise Place about halfway down. I'm out of sight."

"Where's Randall?"

"He's in an old plantation home at the end of the street, and he's not alone."

"Who's with him?"

"I can't be sure. There're two cars parked in front of the house—Randall's and someone else's."

I sped through the heart of town, swerving around slower traffic. "Who owns the house?"

"As far as I know, it's abandoned."

"Can you get close enough to get a license plate on the other car?"

"No. I got out earlier and walked as far as I could without leaving the cover of the cane fields. I couldn't get close enough. Maybe if I had some binoculars…"

I slowed into the last curve on the southern end of town and coasted by Paradise Place. I strained to see the house at the back of the street, but couldn't. The street was clear. "I just drove by your location." I pulled to the shoulder of the road.

"I can't see the highway," Susan said. "Do you want me to stay here until he leaves and then see where he goes?"

I chewed on it for a minute.

"Clint, are you still there?"

"Yeah." I whipped my Tahoe around in the road and headed back north on Main Street. "Look, stay where you are and when Randall leaves, follow him."

"Are you driving again? What're you going to do?"

"I'm going type up an affidavit for Randall Rupe's arrest."

"You think we have enough?" Susan asked.

"Maybe not for murder, but definitely for accessory after the fact." I tossed my phone onto the console beside me and sped back the way I'd come.

When I reached the police department, I hurried inside and fired up my computer, then hammered away at the keyboard. It took about thirty minutes to detail the facts of the case and print out an affidavit and arrest warrant. With the documents in hand, I grabbed my keys and stepped out of my office.

As I rushed by Lindsey, I said, "I'm heading to the district attorney's office. Call my cell if you need me."

CHAPTER 30

The district attorney's office was twenty miles from Mechant Loup, but I got there in less than fifteen minutes, my mind racing faster than my tires spun. *Why on earth would Randall Rupe kill his best friend?* I parked my Tahoe in the visitor spot and snatched the affidavit and warrant from my seat. Once I'd entered the building, I asked for the assistant district attorney on duty.

Within seconds, a woman with long blonde hair and dark brown eyes opened a side door and—after doing a double take at my face—waved me inside. "Are you the new chief of police over in Mechant Loup?"

I nodded, held out my hand. "I'm Clint. Clint Wolf."

"Isabel Compton. I'm the first assistant district attorney here. I wanted to take the opportunity to meet you and welcome you to Chateau Parish. I've heard some good things about you and I'm looking forward to working with you. We've always worked well with the chiefs in the incorporated towns, and Mechant Loup is no different."

I nodded, held up the affidavit. "I need someone to take a look at this before I bring it to the judge."

Isabel's face turned quizzical. "That's unusual."

"What's that, ma'am?"

"In all my years of doing this, I don't think I've ever had an officer come to me *before* they got the warrant."

"I just want to make sure you'll go forward with the case before I present it to a judge."

"I usually review cases after the fact."

"That doesn't make any sense," I said.

"I know, right? I hate having to dismiss charges due to lack of evidence. The officers who worked the case usually get angry with me, and the defendants are usually emboldened because they feel they beat the system." She smiled. "This is certainly refreshing."

"It's always been my practice—whenever possible—to get with the district attorney's office before I move on a major case to make sure we're all on the same page. It's just common sense."

"I like it." Isabel took the affidavit. "Please, have a seat."

We each took a seat at opposite sides of the desk, and she began to read. A deep furrow formed on her brow as she read. She leaned over and punched an extension number into the phone. A man answered, and she said, "Walter, can you and Reginald come to the duty office for a minute?"

"Sure. Be there in a second."

Isabel looked up at me. "These are serious allegations against a prominent businessman in this parish."

"I know. That's why I thought you needed to see it."

The door swung open, and Walter Moore entered with a man I'd never seen. Walter looked different in a suit. When I'd seen him at Susan's fight he'd been wearing jeans and a pullover shirt. I stood, shook his hand. "I'm Clint Wolf, the new chief of police over in Mechant Loup."

"Walter Moore." Walter indicated to the man with him. "This is Reginald Hoffman. He's our chief investigator."

I shook his hand, too. "Pleasure."

"I saw you at the cage fights," Walter said. "Your officer can kick some serious ass. I tell you what, I'd be scared to be on the wrong side of her law." He nodded toward my nose. "It looks like you've already been there."

I nodded, appreciating the humor.

"Walter, check this out." Isabel handed him the affidavit, then tapped the desk with an index finger. "Tell me what you think."

Walter lowered his head to read it. When he was done, he rubbed a hand through his black curly hair and handed the paperwork to Reginald.

"This is crazy," Walter said. "I've known Randall Rupe and Hays Cain for years. Randall's not capable of murdering anyone, much less his best friend. I think you've got this all wrong."

"He might not have murdered Hays," I said, "but he sure was there when his body was dumped. At a minimum, that's accessory after the fact to murder."

"I just don't see it," Walter said. "If you told me Randall was involved in some white collar shit—like trying to bribe his high school football coach so he could get more playing time—then I'd say maybe, but murder? No way."

"He did that?" I asked.

Walter waved a hand in the air. "He tried to when we were in high school, but he got in trouble. The coach wasn't having any of it."

"What could a high school kid possibly bribe a coach with?"

"Money...cars. His dad gave him everything he wanted and he tried to use that to convince the coach to make him a starter." Walter chuckled. "Crazy little shit was a hoot."

"What witness saw him out there in the boat?" Isabel asked.

"Dexter Boudreaux."

"Isn't that the alligator man?" Walter asked.

I nodded.

Walter's brow furrowed. "I thought he died—got eaten by an alligator or something."

"No, he survived. He lost an arm. It'll be a long time before he can get around, but he pulled through."

Isabel took the affidavit from Reginald and read over it again. "Did Dexter see anything in the boat that could've been a body?"

I shook my head.

Isabel looked up at Reginald. "What do you think?"

"It's weak, but it looks like he's onto something."

Isabel drummed her finger on the desk, a tiny crease forming between her eyebrows as she pondered her decision. Finally, she pursed her lips and shook her head. "I'm sorry, but I don't feel comfortable moving forward with this just yet. I certainly can't tell you how to do your job, and you might find a judge who'll find probable cause, but it's a far cry from beyond a reasonable doubt."

"No, you're right." I took the affidavit and warrant from Isabel. "I don't want to waste time getting a warrant unless you'll file the charges."

"I agree with Reginald—it looks like you're definitely onto something. He might not be capable of murder, as Walter points out, but it's no coincidence he was seen where Hays Cain's body was dumped. Get me a little more evidence and we'll talk."

I thanked Isabel, Walter, and Reginald, stood to leave. Reginald stopped me. "Any leads on who the other guy is?"

"No, but I've got some ideas." My phone screamed from my pocket. I fished it out and saw Susan was calling. I nodded my goodbyes and said, "I have to take this. Thanks for seeing me."

"Hey, are you there, Clint?" I heard Susan's muffled voice ask from my palm.

I rushed out the door, shoving the phone to my ear. "I'm here. What's going on?"

"He drove back to the dealership. He didn't stop anywhere. Just left that plantation house and drove straight back."

"What about the other car? Did it leave, too?"

"Not while I was there. I tailed Randall and when he got back to the dealership, I doubled back to the plantation house, but the other vehicle was gone."

"Could you see what kind of car it was? When you were there the first time?"

"I was too far to get a good look at it, but I'm pretty sure it was a truck."

"That narrows it down for us—in a town where everyone from fishermen to nuns drives a truck." I slipped into my Tahoe and checked the dashboard clock. It was getting close to knockoff time. "You can call it a day. I think we'll bring him in tomorrow and squeeze him."

"Sounds good. See you at the office."

Thirty minutes later, I turned into the sally port and stepped out of my Tahoe, pausing to scan the area outside the double garage door. The street was quiet. The shadows were long, the sun making its slow dive behind me. A soft, warm breeze caressed my face. Had I not known better, I would've thought it was just another peaceful day in small-town Louisiana. But I did know better. I knew there was a killer on the loose, and I had to find him before he struck again.

"What're you doing out here?"

The voice startled me, and I turned to see Susan standing at the back door to the station. She strode up beside me and stared out into the waning daylight. Neither of us said anything for a long moment. Finally, I turned on my heels and walked inside. Jack and William were sitting at Marsha's desk talking with her.

Marsha lifted a finger when she saw me, grabbed some paperwork from her desk and handed it to me. "This was faxed over twenty minutes ago."

It was a firearms examination form. Susan sidled up beside me, leaning to read with me. "The projectiles match!"

"Yep," I said. "Whoever killed Hays Cain also killed Kelly Dykes."

"Who do you think it is?" William asked.

I shook my head. "Randall Rupe's involved, that's for sure."

"But what if he isn't?" Susan asked. "What if he's got nothing at all to do with it? After all, everyone said they were best of friends."

I had been a detective long enough to know the most obvious suspect was not always the correct suspect.

"Whoever it was, they were brazen enough to try and murder two cops," Jack said. "We aren't dealing with amateurs here."

I shook my head. "Whoever shot at us didn't want to hit us. They wanted us to duck down long enough for them to get away."

CHAPTER 31

I mentally punched myself in the gut when I pulled into my driveway at home and saw Chloe sitting on the front porch. I'd forgotten about our date. She wore a summer dress similar to the one she'd worn earlier, but this one was dark blue and shorter than the other one.

You belong on a magazine cover!

Chloe looked up from her phone when I stepped out of my Tahoe. I could hear Achilles barking from his crate. I grinned inwardly. He was trying so hard to sound like a big dog, but his shriek of a bark wouldn't scare anyone away anytime soon.

"Hey, look who finally decided to come home." Chloe's voice was cheery, seemingly unbothered that I was late. She shot a thumb toward the house. "Your dog is carrying on like I ate his lunch."

I pushed my door shut and walked toward her, stopping a few feet from the edge of the porch. "I had to work late. I'm sorry. It totally slipped my mind. You know, some work stuff came up and I had—"

"What the hell happened to you?" Chloe propelled herself toward me. She stopped inches away and gawked up at my nose. "Jesus Christ! Who did this to you?"

"It's nothing. I ran into something."

She poked it lightly with a finger. "Do you think it's broken?"

"Hard to tell." I apologized again for forgetting. "We've been busy in town, what with all that's going on."

"I guess you forgot what I do for a living." Chloe smiled. "I understand what it's like to have something drop in your lap at the last minute. When a story is hot, you've got to run with it. I totally get it. No worries."

I smiled my thanks for the understanding, then stood there not knowing what to do next.

"Well," Chloe said, "why don't we go inside and get you cleaned up. If you let me, I can put a little base on your nose so it's not so noticeable."

"Base? What on earth are you talking about?"

"Makeup."

I scoffed. "There's no way you're putting makeup on me."

"We won't call it makeup…we'll just call it war paint."

"You're not putting any of it on me." I tapped the bridge of my nose. It was still a little sore, but not nearly as bad as earlier. I looked down at Chloe and shrugged. "Well, I know it's later than you planned. What do you want to do?"

"Whatever you want. By the way, what's going on? Did you have a break in the case?"

"I can't really talk about it."

Chloe's brow furrowed. "What do you mean? You told me about Hays Cain and Kelly Dykes, and I told you about my source. We shared information. You didn't have a problem with it then."

"It's just that…" I rubbed my hands together, staring into her soft blue eyes. "Well, I don't want to become too comfortable talking shop."

"Why not?"

"If you received exclusive information from me about work and your competitors found out, they might cry foul. You know?"

"I guess you're right. I'd rather talk about you anyway. I want to know what makes you sweat, Chief Clint Wolf." Chloe put a cool hand against my cheek and smiled.

My pulse quickened. "Well, let me get cleaned up so we can go eat."

Chloe's face lit up. "Great! Let's do this."

I pushed open the door and walked to Achilles' crate. When I let him out, he rushed between my legs. I stumbled, and took a large step to avoid smashing him. He barked up at Chloe, sniffing her leg aggressively. His tail wagged, so I figured there was no danger of him trying to bite her with his needle-sharp puppy teeth. I hurried into the kitchen and snatched up the three empty bottles of vodka still out on the counter.

"Someone was thirsty," Chloe said. She had walked into the kitchen and stood behind me. "Celebrating something?"

Without saying a word, I dropped the bottles into the garbage can. Achilles' head jerked up when the bottles clanked against each other.

"Do you mind taking him out to do his business while I shower?" I asked. "I'll only be a few minutes."

"I'd love to!"

I hurried through a shower and then dressed into my newest jeans and pullover shirt—"new" meaning several years old. When I walked out, Chloe looked me up and down. "Black jeans," she said, smirking. "I didn't know they made those anymore."

I shrugged. "They were on sale somewhere about ten years ago. As long as they're not letting air in, they're still good enough for me."

"No matter...you make the nineties look better than they've ever looked."

I felt a stirring deep inside my gut. I approached Achilles' food and water bowls to reload them, but they were full.

"I filled his bowls after he pottied."

I smiled my thanks, then remembered the suspicious person in the woods and walked briskly to the back door to look outside. Everything seemed quiet in the dark shadows. Of course, a war party could've been hiding out there and I would've never known it. "Did Achilles bark at anything? Or seem interested in anything in the woods?"

"No. Why?"

"Just wondering." I squinted, trying to see beyond the glow radiating from the light that hung above my back door. Nothing. I turned away from the door and sent Achilles into his crate. "You ready?"

Chloe nodded and skipped out the door in front of me, the muscles in her slender legs rippling as she moved. There was a playfulness about her that excited me.

Before I locked the door and joined Chloe by her car, I looked back at Achilles. "Guard the house, little man."

CHAPTER 32

Chloe suggested a restaurant just north of Randall Rupe's dealership. I couldn't help but stare at the place as we drove by, wondering if I would be able to break him down the next day and get him to confess to his part in disposing of Hays Cain's body.

Chloe noticed. "Is he somehow involved in the murder of Hays Cain?"

"What makes you say that?"

Chloe shrugged. "They were best of friends, and I saw your Tahoe there more than once in recent days."

"Have you been following me?"

Chloe bit her lower lip and raised her eyebrows. "I think the correct term is *stalking*."

I laughed.

"It wasn't a joke."

I glanced sideways at the beautiful woman sitting beside me. I was feeling things I hadn't felt in almost two years—things I thought I'd never feel again. I was actually interested in someone—and not only as a friend. But was it fair for me to pursue something with her? I was damaged goods, and she deserved someone who was stable and knew what he wanted. And what would Michele and Abigail think, if they were up there looking down at me?

"Well?" Chloe asked.

"Well, what?"

"Is Randall involved?"

I sighed. "I thought we agreed—"

"You're right. No talking shop while we're out on a date. I'll call your office tomorrow during business hours and ask the tough questions then." Chloe smiled and poked my leg with her index finger.

She turned into the near empty parking lot of Seafood Sarah and parked her car in front of the building. When we stepped out, I looked up at the giant crab above the entrance. "I can't imagine what they serve."

Chloe giggled, grabbed my hand and led me through the double doors. A bar constructed of fine wood lined the entire left side of the room. A half wall separated the bar area from the dining area and a hostess dressed in black slacks and a tuxedo shirt led us to our table. I took the seat where I could see the door, and we ordered drinks.

"Thank you for agreeing to this," Chloe said. "I was afraid you wouldn't be interested in me."

"Are you crazy? Any man not interested in you is a fool...or likes guys."

"Thank you." Chloe's cheeks and neck turned bright red. "It's just that... Well, I would've thought Susan had gotten to you first."

I scowled. "I'm Susan's boss. She's off limits."

"Since when has that ever stopped a cop?"

I studied her face. "You have something against cops?"

"What do you mean?"

"You're talking about cops like they have no morals. It seems you've had some experience in that department."

Chloe opened her mouth to speak, but was interrupted when the double doors swung open and one of them slammed roughly into the counter near the entrance. I looked up and saw Beaver peering at us. I grunted. "Something's up with that dude."

Chloe turned to look. When she saw Beaver ambling toward us, she quickly turned back to me. The redness had faded from her flesh. "Oh, God. He's drunk."

I pushed my chair back from the table in case I had to stand up in a hurry. Beaver waved me off as he stopped by our table and stared down at us. "No need to stand up for me," he said. "This'll only take a minute."

"What will only take a minute?" I asked, noticing that Chloe's head was down. I wondered if he had threatened her after being fired. He certainly had the bully act down. I eased my hand under my shirt and rested it on the pistol tucked in my waistband.

Beaver shoved a hand in his shirt pocket and dug something out. He tossed it on the table in front of Chloe. I didn't take my eyes off him, but I could tell it was jewelry of some sort.

I heard Chloe gasp. "My grandma's ring! I've been looking for it everywhere."

"You left it at my house the last time you were over. You remember that last time, don't you? Sure you do. You slept with me and then left in such a hurry that you forgot your precious ring." A wicked grin spread across Beaver's face. "I remember wondering why you were in such a hurry, but I didn't have to wait long to find out, did I?"

My features remained unmoved on the outside, but my blood flowed like lava through my veins. I stole a quick glance at Chloe. Her head was still bent and tears dripped freely from her face, splashing on the varnished tabletop. She looked both angry and hurt. I removed my hand from my pistol, clenched my fist and looked back up at Beaver with steely eyes. "It's time for you to go."

"I'll decide when I'm done." Beaver held my stare for a long moment, and I realized the alcohol was making him bullet-proof. He finally broke the stare-down and chuckled. "It's a shame. I like you and I believe you and I would've made a good team. You're a lot like me. We would've gotten along under different circumstances."

I stood slowly to my feet, pushing my chair away with my right foot. "We're nothing alike. I told you once, now I'm telling you for the last time. It's time for you to go."

"You're a fool, Clint Wolf. She's using you for information like she did me. When she's finished with you, she'll chew you up and spit you out—just like she did to me." He stared down at her and shook his head. "She's nothing but a common whore. Instead of spreading her legs for money, this holster-sniffer bitch spreads her—"

My left fist was quicker than a rattlesnake's strike. It shot from my waist to Beaver's chin with the accuracy of an Olympic archer and the power of a mule's kick. The left hook sent him reeling. I stepped forward and threw a straight right that cut him down like a rotten tree in a tornado. He collapsed in a heap on the ground and didn't move. Blood oozed from an open wound at the bridge of his nose and poured from his broken lips.

Chloe gasped. The waitress, who'd walked up with our drinks, screamed and dropped her tray. Glasses shattered and liquid splashed everywhere. The waitress scurried back to the kitchen.

"Is...is he dead?" Chloe asked through her sobs.

"No. Go wait outside." I grabbed her hand, pulled her to her feet, watched her walk out the door.

A large man in a white apron was approaching from the back of the restaurant. He took a look at Beaver and stopped. He looked up at me, then back down at Beaver. A smile slowly spread across his face. "I've been waiting years to see this."

I looked around at the other patrons and frowned. "I'm sorry for ruining your night."

The man shook his head, waving his hand to encompass the entire room. "They would've paid to see that. Go on; take care of the pretty lady. I'll take care of this piece of shit."

I nodded my thanks and met Chloe in the parking lot. "Give me your keys."

Chloe didn't protest. She pulled the keys from her purse and handed them to me. I led her to the passenger's side and held the door for her. When she was seated, I closed it, walked around to the driver's side and paused before entering. What did Beaver mean when he said she was using me for information like she'd used him? That she'd dated him came as a shock to me—if it were true—and was a bit unsettling, but everyone dated someone at one point or another. I sighed when I remembered the way he'd looked at me at the fight. Things were finally coming into focus.

CHAPTER 33

When I got home, I turned off the car, and we sat in silence for several long minutes. The only sound between us was Chloe's soft sobbing. She sniffed, wiped her face with a tissue, and touched my arm. "No one has ever stood up for me the way you did."

"I wouldn't let any man talk to a lady like that."

"You don't believe him, do you?"

I looked into her troubled eyes. The light from my front porch reflected off the tears that streaked down her face. "Chloe, I don't know what to think."

"I would never use you!"

"At Susan's fight, when he looked at you that way, I asked about it. You told me it was because of your story, but you knew it wasn't. Why didn't you tell me y'all dated?"

"We didn't even know each other. We had dinner by accident and then we went to an event, and you expect me to tell you about all my past boyfriends?"

"You didn't have to say anything at all. You could've told me it was none of my business, but you led me to believe he was mad about the story."

Chloe took a deep breath and blew it out. "Have you ever done anything that you wish you hadn't? Something you really regret and wish you could undo?"

I didn't even have to think about it—the answer was instant. I turned my head away from Chloe, blinking away the moisture in my eyes.

"What am I saying? Of course you haven't. Only an idiot like me would make such horrible life decisions. My mom told me I'd end up with—"

"You're not an idiot." Images of Abigail's disfigured face and Michele's lifeless body flashed in my mind. I could smell the gunpowder like it was in Chloe's car. I shook my head to try to clear it. "We all make mistakes. We've all done things we wish we could undo."

"Yeah...right." Chloe scoffed. "What have you ever done that was bad? Fail to use your blinker?"

I bit back the burning in my jaw. "I've done something really horrible. Something I can never come back from."

Chloe turned to look at me. Her wet eyes were curious. "What is it, Clint? What have you done?"

I glanced at her with a suspicious eye. "You expect me to believe you didn't do a background check on me already? You're a reporter...it's what you do."

"I would never spy on someone I was interested in knowing, and I was interested in you from the moment I first laid eyes on you." She shook her head. "No, I want you to tell me about yourself. I don't want some reporter's slant on who they think you are based on something that happened to you."

"Well, maybe you should've done your research." I opened my mouth to speak, but my jaw trembled. I clamped it shut and swallowed the lump in my throat. When I felt controlled enough to talk without breaking down, I said, "I...I killed my wife and daughter."

Chloe gasped, recoiled in horror. "You did what? Do... Does anyone... Um, what do you mean?"

"It was my fault they died. I killed them."

I felt Chloe relax in the seat beside me. "You say it's your fault— does that mean you didn't actually kill them?"

"Of course not, but my actions got them killed. It was as if—" My eyes burned. I blinked several times. "It was as if I pulled the trigger myself."

"What...what happened?"

"I was a detective in the city. It was a couple of years ago at the height of the riots. We were eating out one night. It was a good part of the city, but some guys came in the restaurant wearing masks. Four of them. I'm a cop. I had to act. They were waving guns around and threatening people. I had to do something." I paused to let the trembling in my jaw subside.

Chloe's eyes were wide. "Did you confront them? You didn't confront them! It was four against one!"

"I waited until one of them got close. I told Michele to take Abigail and get under the table. They did, and I made my move when he was a few feet from me. I tried to disarm him, but he was stronger than I anticipated. We fought for the gun—"

"Y'all fought for *your* gun?"

"No, his gun."

"But why didn't you just shoot him with your gun? Why would you try to take his gun away?"

"I didn't have my gun—thanks to that idiot governor we have. He basically disarmed all off-duty police officers in the state."

"Are you talking about the bill he orchestrated where police officers couldn't carry their weapon in a private business?"

I nodded.

"But I thought that law was overturned?"

"It was—much later. A lot of people had to die before that stupid bastard realized what he'd done."

Chloe gulped. "What— So, what happened?"

"I finally got on top of the robber and was about to rip the gun out of his hand when one of the other men yelled at me to stop. He...he told me he would kill my baby if I didn't stop."

I turned my head away from Chloe and wiped a tear from my left eye with my shoulder. "I looked...I looked up and saw him holding my baby girl. She was afraid. She was crying and saying, 'Daddy, help me. Don't let him hurt me!' I told her everything would be okay. I told her I would protect her." I squeezed my eyes shut as tears threatened to spill freely down my cheeks. I couldn't let Chloe see me cry. I took several short breaths, willing away the burning. Finally, I said, "I lied. I didn't protect her."

Chloe was bawling beside me. She stripped off her seatbelt and leaned across the center console to wrap her arms around my neck. She pressed her wet face against mine. "Oh, my God! I'm so sorry!"

"I did what they said to do. I dropped the gun. I raised my hands and stepped back." I took a shuddered breath, blowing out forcefully against the side of Chloe's neck to try and maintain my composure. "They didn't care. They killed her. Just shot her right there in front of me and Michele. Point blank in the face. When...when Michele started to scream, they shot her, too." My whole body was strained by that point, as I fought to stifle my sobs. Chloe's arms tightened around me.

"I...I died right there with them. I didn't care about anything after that. In that one instant, I was no longer a husband...no longer a daddy. I would never get to hear Abigail's innocent little voice call me Daddy again."

I don't know how long Chloe held me, but it felt like forever. I was tempted to let the tears flow, but I dared not.

I took another deep breath and leaned back. "Jeez, I've never really talked about it before."

Chloe touched my face with soft fingers. "You need to talk about it. You can't keep that sort of thing inside. It'll kill you."

I looked into her swollen eyes. "Want to come in?"

She nodded.

Once we were inside, I let Achilles out the back door to take care of his business and then locked him in my bedroom. I joined Chloe on the sofa. "Do you want something to drink?"

She bit her lower lip. "What happened after? What did you do when they did that?"

"They heard sirens and started to run out the building, but I got...um, I caught one of them. He fired three shots at me, but missed every time. I don't... I...I just can't understand it. How'd he miss? I just don't know." I shook my head. "I fought with him over his gun. He was stronger than me, but I was so overcome with rage. I took his gun away and...and I shot him. A lot. I shot him until the gun was empty. I dropped the gun and lifted Abigail into my arms and stared down at her." I squeezed my eyes shut and shook my head. I opened my eyes, but could still see that horrific image. "I can't see her face anymore. I know she was beautiful. I remember she was beautiful, but after that day, I couldn't see her face. I only see blood and broken flesh. I have to look at her pictures to remember what she looked like."

Tears were flowing down Chloe's face again. Her blue eyes glistened. "I'm so sorry, Clint! I had no idea what you'd been through."

"I can hardly close my eyes without seeing Abigail's torn face. I... It haunts me all the time. I...I can't sleep."

Chloe looked toward the kitchen garbage can. "Is that why you have so much vodka?"

"I need it to sleep. I used to drink a few shots, and that would help. But eventually that wasn't enough. I upgraded to a glass and—" I frowned. I wasn't about to admit to downing a bottle a night, so I stopped talking.

Chloe pushed me back onto the sofa and stretched out beside me. I twisted onto my right side to make room for her to lie next to me. Our faces were inches apart. She stared into my eyes for a long moment. With a sigh, she buried her head in my chest and slung her right arm over me, began rubbing my back.

"Just close your eyes and focus on me," Chloe said softly. "Hear my breathing and let it rock you to sleep."

I did as she said. Although my eyes were shut, I was able to feel her face in front of mine and could smell the soft and inviting scent from her perfume. She spoke in whispered tones, telling me it was okay and that she was right there with me. Her hand slid up and down my back. "Feel me next to you."

As she continued to speak, her voice began to fade until it was nothing but a low murmur. When it dragged to a halt, my eyes fluttered. I caught my breath when Abigail's distorted face popped into view. I lunged to a seated position, glanced around. The room was dark and Chloe's breath was low and steady. Panic grabbed at my throat. I needed a drink.

Taking great care, I eased off the sofa and padded to the kitchen in my bare feet. I grabbed a bottle of vodka and allowed Achilles to roam around the backyard while I sucked it down. When it was empty, I tossed the bottle under the house so Chloe wouldn't know and locked Achilles back in my room. My eyes were heavy when I stumbled to the sofa, and I had a hard time feeling my way around, but I managed to squeeze beside Chloe without disturbing her.

I sighed as the alcohol's numbing powers began to spread through my body.

CHAPTER 34

Tuesday, July 1

Pain shot through my shoulder and up into my neck. I groaned, tried to turn over, couldn't. I pried my eyes open. *What the hell?*

"Good morning, Clint." Chloe's hair was messed up just enough to be sexy.

I looked around the room and it all started to come back to me. Light spilled through the windows. "Did we sleep here all night?"

She smiled. "We did."

Guilt tugged at my chest. I pushed myself up on my elbow, stared down at her. Her sundress was twisted, exposing her black bra and part of her left breast. I quickly averted my eyes to focus on her beautiful face. She noticed and smiled, but didn't adjust her dress.

Chloe brushed her fingers lightly across my face. "Wow...your nose is already looking better."

I nodded. "I heal up well. Good genes, I guess."

In lazy fashion, Chloe eased her legs off the sofa and brought herself to a seated position. "I have to get to the newsroom. I'm late."

I jerked my head around to look at the clock hanging in the living room. "Shit! I have to get to the office!"

Chloe stood and straightened her dress, glanced down and giggled. "It looks like I slept in this dress."

I stood, too, and watched her.

She turned toward me, and we faced each other for a long and awkward moment. "Well," I finally said, "I hope we can do it again."

She smiled and leaned in for a hug. She pressed her breasts against my chest and stayed there. I squeezed her back. We were caught in a game of chicken—each waiting to see who would let go first. I finally gave in and let my arms fall. Before she stepped back, she planted a wet kiss against my neck—a chill shot down my spine—and hurried off. The door slowed her escape, as she struggled with the lock.

I walked briskly to her and took her by the shoulder, spun her around. She gasped and looked up at me, eyes half closed, lips parted. I pushed my mouth to hers and kissed her like I meant it. We were locked in fervor, exploring each other's mouths with our tongues, for what seemed like a small eternity.

*　　*　　*

Jack, William, Melvin and Susan were all sitting in my office when I walked in. They had dragged in two extra chairs from the lobby. I tossed my keys on the desk. "How was the night shift?"

Jack said, "Quiet."

"Any more suspicious subject complaints?"

He shook his head.

I studied each of their faces. Susan had a pretty good poker face, but there was no way Melvin could hide anything from me. He was squirming like Achilles did when he had to pee really badly. "So," I said slowly, "any action over at Seafood Sarah last night?"

"Come to think of it, there was." William tried to sound casual.

"Somebody knocked the piss out of Beaver," Melvin blurted.

William elbowed him. "Why didn't you let me tell him?"

"I couldn't help it! The suspense was killing me."

"It was awesome to see him sprawled out on the ground with blood squirting from his face." William smiled and stared at the ceiling like he was reliving the moment. "I can't count the number of times I wanted to do that to him."

I nodded. "Who did it?"

Jack eyed me. "Well, Beaver claims he was drunk and slipped, and all the witnesses say they didn't see what happened, but that's bullshit."

"It had to be an outsider," Melvin said, "because nobody in this town has the balls to mess with Beaver. Well, except for Susan." He realized what he'd said and turned to Susan. "Sorry, Sue—no offense."

Susan hadn't taken her eyes off me. "None taken."

"What are you talking about?" Jack scoffed. "I'd kick his ass right now!"

"Sure you would," Melvin said. "He's lying in a hospital bed and can't defend himself."

"A hospital bed?" I winced, knowing I'd given myself away with my surprised reaction.

"By the time I got there, the ambulance had already taken him away," Jack said.

I lifted my eyebrows. "Wow. He must've fallen really hard. He should lay off the sauce."

"He didn't fall," Jack said. "Those witnesses are covering up for someone."

I tapped my fingers on the desk in front of me. I figured the townspeople hated him and were happy to see him get an ass-whipping, so that would explain the collective amnesia. But why would Beaver keep his mouth shut to protect me? Pride? I dismissed the thought and turned to Susan. "Ready to get to work? We need to put the squeeze on Randall."

"Sure. Let me get my—"

The door to my office burst open, and I heard Lindsey's voice call out from her desk, "Sir, you can't go in there!"

Red McKenzie stared wildly about the room. "Chief, I need someone quick. My boys are missing. They left last night to check their trout lines and never came home. I've looked everywhere. I can't find them."

"Do you know where their trout lines are?" I asked.

Red nodded. "I checked the area, but they're nowhere."

I walked around my desk, took Red by the arm and escorted him out into the lobby. "I want you to go home and wait for my officers. Call all your friends and ask them to meet them there, as well."

Red's chin quivered. "Them boys are all I got."

"I know, sir. We'll get them back for you. Contact everyone you know and meet my officers at your house."

Red nodded and darted out the door. I returned to my office, then pointed to Susan and Melvin. "Get the boats and get out to Red McKenzie's house right away. And watch your asses—that damn alligator is probably back."

"What about Randall Rupe?" Susan wanted to know.

"I'll take care of him. You're better on the water than I am—all of you are. Take separate boats so y'all can cover more ground." I turned to Jack and William. "Go get some rest and be back early. I have a feeling we're going to be busy."

Susan chewed on her lower lip. "Are you sure you want to go it alone with Randall Rupe?"

"No, I'd love to have you there, but we don't have a choice." I slapped her shoulder. "Now, go find those boys."

Susan and Melvin rushed out the door. Jack ambled out in their wake, but William stopped by the door. "Chief, thank you."

"For what?"

"For giving that bastard Beaver what he deserved."

I studied William's face. "What'd he do to you?"

William dropped his gaze. "We had a Christmas party one night a bunch of years ago and we all got drunk. He...um...my ex-wife was drunk, you know? And he took advantage of that."

I pursed my lips. "I'm sorry, William. Had I known that, I would've hit him three times."

"I appreciate you saying that." William waved goodbye to Lindsey on his way out the door.

I grabbed a fresh notepad and drove to Randall's dealership.

CHAPTER 35

I found Randall Rupe in his office and he looked surprised to see me. "Chief, what are you doing here?"

I helped myself to a chair, sat, and said, "I need to talk to you about Hays Cain's murder."

Randall's face twisted into a scowl. "I told you yesterday that I didn't know anything."

"Who'd you hear it from?"

"What are you talking about? Who did I hear what from?"

"You said you heard the rumors about a body being found and you figured it was Hays." I leaned an elbow onto his desk. "Who'd you hear it from?"

Randall's eyes became slits. "I don't remember, Chief, but I don't like your tone."

I waved him off. "You'll get used to it. Now, are you saying you don't remember who told you Hays was dead two days ago?"

"That's right."

"I see." I scratched my nose. "Your best friend dies and you don't remember how you found out about it?"

"Sure, I know how—someone called me."

"Right, but you don't remember who?"

"Of course not. I talk to hundreds of people every day."

"What did you do Friday?"

"Last Friday?"

I tilted my head and lifted an eyebrow. "Did you think I meant *next* Friday? Yes, I want to know what you did last Friday."

"Beginning when?"

"Early that morning."

Randall cleared his throat. "Well, I cut grass first thing in the morning. The weather was nice for it. Then I went to the restaurant and checked on the place. Everything was fine, so I left."

"Where'd you go?"

"Excuse me?"

I smirked. "I know you heard me—where'd you go after you left Hays' girlfriend's house?"

Randall's face turned red. "I didn't say anything about Hays or his girlfriend. I said I left the restaurant."

"Fair enough. Where'd you go?"

"When?"

"When you left the restaurant?"

"Oh, I went home. Straight home, as far as I can remember."

I clucked my tongue. "That's not entirely true, is it?"

"Are you calling me a liar?"

"I didn't," I said, "but I can if you need me to."

Randall Rupe glared across the desk at me. "I think it's time for you to leave."

I met his gaze with a cold one of my own, shaking my head. "I'm not going anywhere until I get the answers I'm looking for."

"Do you know who you're talking to?"

"Quite frankly, I don't give a shit who I'm talking to."

Randall pounded his fist on the desk and stood to his feet, as he pointed to the door. "Get out of here now!"

I rose and leaned close to Randall. "If you don't sit your ass down right this second, I'm going to take it as an act of aggression."

Randall gulped and sank back into his chair. He shot a glance toward the phone in the corner. His fingers twitched. "I don't think the mayor would be too happy about this," he said in a shaky voice.

"This is a law enforcement matter. The mayor's got nothing to do with it." I settled back into my chair. "Now, tell me again where you went when you left the restaurant? And don't say straight home because we both know that isn't true."

"I went home. You can ask my wife."

"Don't you remember going out on the water?"

Randall's thick eyebrows lifted ever so slightly. "Why would I want to go out on the water? It's the middle of summer and the fish aren't even biting right now."

"Good point. There's no reason to go out on the water, unless you want to dump the body of a man you just killed."

"I didn't kill anyone!"

"Maybe not, but you definitely helped dump Hays Cain's body—

and I can prove it. At a minimum, you're looking at principal to murder and life in prison without the benefit of parole, probation or suspension of sentence." I waved my hand. "Enjoy your freedom while you can. It won't last long."

Randall only shook his head.

"If you tell me who actually killed Hays, maybe I can get the district attorney to go easy on you."

"You've been in town just over a week. What makes you think you've got any clout with the DA?" Randall scoffed. "You can threaten to kick my ass and you can even arrest me, but it'll never stick—and it'll be me asking the DA to go easy on you."

I sighed, as I rose to my feet. "Well, I guess I have no choice, then."

Randall's eyes were wary. "What are you doing?"

"You leave me no choice." Taking a huge gamble, I pulled my cell phone out of my front pant pocket, set it on the desk and pressed the play button on the recorder. Randall's voice bled through the internal speaker.

"You've been recording me the whole while?" Randall's eyes widened. "That's illegal! I'll sue you!"

"You clearly know nothing about Louisiana law. But that's the least of your worries." I dug a compact disc out of my pants pocket and set it on the table. "Do you know what this is?"

"A disc."

While Randall's focus was on the disc, I eased my finger toward my phone and pressed the record button again. "Do you know what's on the disc?"

Randall shook his head slowly, staring at the compact disc as though it were a bomb vest set to go off at any moment.

"This is a recording of you and another man dumping Hays' body. It was recovered from Hays' girlfriend's phone."

Randall smirked. "Yeah, right."

"You don't remember Hays reaching out from the grave and butt-dialing his girlfriend? She caught the whole conversation on her voicemail." I walked around his desk and opened the compact disc port on his clock radio, slipped the disc in, and hit play. Randall's face turned ash gray when he heard the voices. I nodded. "That's definitely you and the killer on that recording."

"You...you can't tell that's me."

"Actually, I can." I removed the disc from the player and returned it to my pocket. "I sent the original copy to the city to be enhanced, and they did a great job. My officer told me he can tell it's you without a reference sample, but we're going through the extra trouble of proving it's you beyond any doubt, which is why I recorded you today. Once the lab gets this copy containing a known sample of your voice, they'll be able to positively identify you as one of the men on this tape."

"Wait, wait! Please, let me think about it."

I shook my head. "Nothing to think about. You either tell me who killed Hays or I'm going to arrest you for accessory after the fact to murder and then I'm going to put out a press release saying you're singing like a bird."

"But that's not true!"

"You think the media will care?" I decided to play dirty. After all, he was a murder suspect, and murder is dirty business. "You know what else? I'm going to leak to the press that you told your wife everything and I'm going to say she's cooperating with the investigation."

"But that's not true! She doesn't know anything."

I shrugged. "Maybe, maybe not, but it's my story and I'm sticking to it."

"But...but they'll kill her!"

"Who?"

Randall looked like a man who had been told he had minutes to live. His shoulders drooped; his eyes sagged.

I lifted my phone to show him it was recording again. "You said, 'They'll kill her.' Who'll kill her?"

Randall's face twisted in desperation. After a long moment, he sighed and nodded his resignation. "Okay, I'll talk. Just leave my wife out of this. She had nothing to do with it."

"As long as you tell me who killed Hays Cain and Kelly Dykes, I'll forget you were even married."

"If I talk, you've got to get my wife someplace safe."

"You'd better not feed me a line of shit."

"I won't."

"I'll have to verify your information—"

"Call Chloe Rushing. She can verify it."

My heart skipped a beat at the mention of her name. "What's she got to do with this?"

"I called her. Gave her some information without naming myself." Randall scowled. "I'm serious, Chief. They'll kill me and my wife if they know I talked."

"Who's 'they'?"

Randall pursed his lips. "Can I have a cigarette to calm my

nerves? Then I'll tell you whatever you want to know."

"Sure, smoke away."

Randall stood and started to walk around his desk. "I have to get my pack of cigarettes out of my car."

"Not without me." I followed him through the back door and to his car, watched carefully as he leaned in and retrieved a pack of cigarettes, kept my hand close to my pistol.

Randall tapped the pack of cigarettes against the palm of his left hand and a cigarette slipped out. He tossed the pack on the seat of his car and pushed the car door closed. I relaxed. Randall lit the cigarette and took a long drag from it.

He shoved the lighter into his front pant pocket. The door to the shop opened, and I turned to see a mechanic exit with a large cardboard box. He nodded at me, and I nodded back. I turned toward Randall, sucked a lungful of air, choked on it. He had removed a small pistol from his pocket and was shoving it up toward his chin.

"Holy shit!" the mechanic screamed, and the box fell from his hands.

"Drop the gun!" I ordered, lunging forward. It was too late. Randall pulled the trigger and the bullet entered near the right side of his jaw line. He collapsed to the ground, convulsing. I dropped to my knees beside him and cursed out loud, reaching for the bloody hole. Randall's body struggled against death's chokehold, but after taking a final wheezing breath, he lay still, eyes open and sightless.

"Call an ambulance!" I hollered. Blood oozed from the wound in Randall's jaw and began to saturate the front of his shirt. I felt for a pulse...there was none.

CHAPTER 36

It had taken an hour to calm Julie Rupe down enough for her to talk. She refused to sit and just paced back and forth in her living room, repeating the same phrase, "I just can't believe he would leave me alone like this. That cowardly bastard!"

"Honey, you're not alone," her white-haired, frail mother said, trying to calm her, but it was no use.

I waited patiently, questions swimming in my mind. I had tossed Randall's office, but found nothing of evidentiary value. I glanced at the grandfather clock in the corner of the room. *Three o'clock.* When I'd called Susan earlier to let her know about Randall's suicide, she'd told me they hadn't made any progress in locating the McKenzie boys. I wanted to call her back while waiting for Julie Rupe to calm down enough to take a statement from her, but thought better of it.

It was another fifteen minutes before she sat beside her mother and looked up at me, face streaked with tears and flushed with sorrow. "Why did he do this? Why did he leave me?"

"I'm very sorry for your pain, ma'am. If you're ready, I have a few questions for you that might help us understand what happened."

"Randall left me all alone—that's what happened! Just like he did when our son died. He's a coward!"

I allowed her to settle down somewhat and asked about Randall leaving when their son died.

"He was emotionally distant. Would drink constantly." She pointed to a recliner in the corner of the room. "He would just sit there and drink. Sure, he'd still go to work and did his job well, but when he'd get home he'd die in that chair. We quit doing things on the weekends. Didn't take family vacations anymore. He just left me all alone."

Guilt tugged at me as I witnessed how one man's actions could affect the lives of everyone around him. "Had he ever threatened to kill himself?"

"Many times—back then. It wasn't until recently that he quit drinking, and he hasn't threatened suicide in about six months."

"So, he'd gotten better?"

Julie rolled her eyes. "In one way, yes, but he was still distant. That didn't change. Instead of sitting there getting drunk and ignoring me, he was always off at some secret meeting or working late at the dealership."

Had I been a dog, my ears would've perked up. But I wasn't, so I just played it cool and, in a casual voice, asked, "What was he working on at the dealership?"

"Who knows? He could've been lying about work. He could've been out there screwing around—"

"Julie!" her mother scolded. "Don't talk like that in front of our guest!"

Julie fixed her mother with cold eyes, and I thought I saw the older woman sink back into her seat. Julie turned back to me. "As I was saying, he could've been sleeping around on me. We'd both been through a lot with Randall Junior's death, and I didn't have the energy to worry about what he was doing, so I just decided to believe he was working."

"These meetings you mentioned—what were they about?"

Julie scowled. "I'm really not sure. Whatever they were about, they gave him a renewed sense of purpose. He was definitely a changed man. He reminded me of the Randall I'd married—the one who was bound and determined to build a dealership where everyone said a dealership couldn't be built."

"Do you know of anyone else who attended these meetings or where they were held?"

Julie shook her head. "I have no idea where they were held, but I do know Mark came by and picked Randall up for a meeting one day."

"Mark?"

"Mark McNeal. I was in the flowerbed pulling weeds one afternoon—I started planting things after Randall Junior died. It helped me get through the early days. Anyway, I was out pulling weeds, and Mark came over to pick up Randall. When I asked where he was going, he told me he was going to his meeting." Julie shrugged. "So, I guess Mark went to the meetings, too. It could've been some alcohol treatment place, since he stopped drinking, but I'm really not sure."

I drummed my pen on my notepad. "The name Mark McNeal sounds familiar."

"It should," Julie said. "He only owns every bank in this—and the two surrounding—parishes."

"That's right," I said. "I saw him at the cage fight. He was actually sitting next to Randall."

"They were good friends," Julie acknowledged. "They grew even closer after our kids were killed."

"I knew your husband was good friends with Hays Cain," I said. "And Hays' son also died while serving in the national guard, correct?"

"Six of our kids died that day." Julie snapped her fingers. "Just like that, six families were ripped apart. It nearly took this town to its knees."

"I'm really sorry about your loss. I understand how you feel."

Julie scoffed, her eyes welling up with tears again. "You couldn't possibly know what it feels like to lose a son and then a husband. No one knows how I feel."

I suddenly realized I was okay to talk about it. I knew that Abigail and Michele would want me to help others in similar situations. "Ma'am, it's true I don't know how it feels to lose a son and a husband, but I do know how it feels to lose a daughter and a wife."

Julie's jaw slowly dropped. "Your wife and daughter died?"

I nodded. "They were killed—murdered—in an armed robbery that went bad."

"You poor soul! You're so young to have suffered so much."

"It's okay. I…I found a way to go on. To get through it. It's what they would want me to do, you know?"

Julie nodded. "You're right. Of course you're right. Randall Junior would want me to go on. He would want me to be happy."

"So would your husband. He would—"

"To hell with him!" Julie spat the words. "That selfish bastard left me alone! I hope he's burning in hell right now for what he did to me."

A woman scorned, I thought to myself, as I closed out the interview and left Julie Rupe to seethe. I stepped out into the afternoon air. The clouds overhead were starting to gather. It smelled like rain. I walked to my Tahoe and sat in the driver's seat to dial a familiar number. It was the only number I'd never programmed into any phone I'd owned, because it was forever burned into my brain.

"Hello?" came an uncertain and tired voice.

"Mom, it's me…Clint."

There was a long pause, and I thought I heard a soft sob. "Clint? Is it really you?"

"It's me, Mom."

"Oh, Clint, it's so good to hear from you. It's been so long. I've been worried every night about you. I didn't know if you were okay or not. One of my friends drove me by your house earlier this year, but the house looked empty. I tried calling the phone number for you, but it was disconnected. I didn't know how to get in touch with you. I was so scared that something bad happened to you."

I frowned. "I'm sorry, Mom. I…I know I should've kept in touch. I'm really sorry."

"But what've you been doing? Why didn't you call me before?"

"It's…it's just that, you know, every time I looked at you, I…you reminded me of what I didn't have any more. You reminded me of Abigail and Michele. And it killed me. I tried to get it out of my head. Tried to distance myself from everything that reminded me of them."

My mom was bawling on the other end of the phone. She had a million questions, and I tried to answer all of them on my drive back to the office. When I pulled into the sally port, I cut her off. "Can I call you later? I'm at the office."

"The office? What office?"

"I'm the chief of police in a little town called Mechant Loup."

After more excited chatter, I was finally able to get her off the phone. Feeling better about myself, I hurried into the office to write my report on Randall Rupe's suicide.

CHAPTER 37

I was just putting the finishing period on my report when Chloe called. I couldn't answer it fast enough. "Hey, what's up?"

"Nothing much. I've been working on a story about the vanishing coastline. Not as exciting as the suicide of a prominent businessman."

"I bet not," was all I said on that subject. "Want to hang out again? Maybe tomorrow night?"

"It's why I called. Your place or mine?"

"My place at eight o'clock?"

"Why so late?" Chloe asked.

"It'll give me time to cook up something special." I hit the print button on my computer and swiveled in my chair to catch the report as it spat from the printer.

There was a long pause from the other end. "Is it true you were with him when it happened?"

"Did you call to talk to me or pump me for information?" I joked.

"I called because I'm worried about you. No one should have to see something like that—especially you."

My door swung open, and Melvin and Susan trudged in.

"Clint? Are you still there?" Chloe asked.

"Yeah, but I have to get back to this report."

"Okay, I guess. So, I'll see you tomorrow night then?"

"For sure." I pressed the button to end the call. "Any sign of the boys?"

Susan shook her head and sank onto a chair. "Where're William and Jack?"

"They're already out on patrol." I looked from Melvin to Susan.

"Any ideas?"

"We looked everywhere. Red McKenzie's fit to be tied. He's certain that killer alligator got them."

"I'm not so sure about his theory," Melvin said.

"Why's that?" I asked.

"We searched every square foot of the bayou and the lake and didn't locate an oil slick."

Curious, I gave him my full attention. "What's that mean?"

"If that alligator got them, their boat would've sunk. When a boat sinks, the fuel and oil from the engine leak out into the water and eventually float to the surface." Melvin pointed to me. "That's how we found Dexter's boat."

"Can we rule out the alligator attack?" I asked.

Melvin shook his head. "Not entirely, but I think we need to expand the search area."

"Yeah," Susan said. "Melvin thinks we need to consider the possibilities the boys ran away of their own will or were taken."

"And you?" I asked.

"I think they're alligator bait."

I nodded, studied both of them. "Well, I think we can do both. Tomorrow, we'll hit the waters again, and I'll contact the media and circulate pictures of the boys"—I nodded toward Melvin—"just in case you're right."

Melvin smiled, then glanced down at his buzzing phone. His face quickly fell. "Oh, can I cut out? My wife's been calling all day. She's not feeling well and needs me to pick up some medicine on my way home. She's pregnant."

"When is she due?" I asked.

"Early August."

I nodded. "Go on...get out of here."

When Melvin was gone, I updated Susan on the Randall Rupe suicide case.

"We need to find out about these meetings."

"We know for sure that three men were attending these secret meetings—Hays Cain, Randall Rupe, and Mark McNeal—and two of them are dead. We need to interrogate Mark." I scowled. "If he doesn't talk, the case could very well have died with Randall."

"You know what they say," Susan offered. "Three people can keep a secret—"

"If two of them are dead." I nodded. "Mark could be the killer."

"Which means we need to find the gun in his possession or we need him to confess."

An idea found its way into the recesses of my mind. "Unless…"

Susan's eyebrows rose. "Unless what?"

I dropped my boots to the ground and slowly stood. "I'm going out to the plantation home at the end of Paradise Place. I need to get inside that building."

"For what?"

"It has to be the secret meeting place, and it might be where Hays was killed."

"Good luck finding a judge to sign a warrant. We've got no evidence whatsoever that the building—"

"I'm not applying for a warrant." I snatched the Tahoe keys from my desk. "I'm going in dark. I'll see you in the morning."

"You're not going without me," Susan said.

"What I'm about to do is illegal, and I don't want you involved."

"I'm already involved." Susan led the way to my Tahoe, then we raced across town. Traffic was light, but Mechant Loup was a small town at the end of the world, so I figured it to be normal for a Tuesday night.

I shut off my headlights as we turned onto Paradise Place, slid all of the windows down. Gravel crunched under the tires and an occasional rock popped against the undercarriage. I steered the Tahoe off the road to the right, where grass lined the street and made for a less conspicuous approach. The going was slightly bumpier, and we jostled side to side with the sway of the vehicle. Tall sugarcane blades lapped at the passenger's side of the SUV.

"It's up ahead," Susan whispered.

I gently smashed the emergency brake so I wouldn't light up the area, and we eased to a stop. With the Tahoe still in drive, I killed the engine and left the key in the ignition. We both leaned forward and peered ahead, trying to penetrate the utter darkness on the other side of the windshield.

"Can you see anything?" My voice was a hoarse whisper.

"No."

I flipped the switch on the interior lights to off so they wouldn't come on when we stepped out. "Together, on three," I said, grabbing my door handle. "One, two, three…"

There was a low metallic click as we simultaneously pulled on our door handles and inched them open. When we were outside the Tahoe, we swung the doors until they were almost shut and then met up near the hood. I could barely see Susan, but the distinct sound of a snap breaking and metal dragging against leather let me know she had palmed her pistol. I did the same, and we slunk toward the large shadow that loomed in the distance.

Blades of sugarcane sliced at my face and arms as we pushed our way along the outer edge of the rows. Mosquitoes buzzed in my ear and an occasional prick let me know they were drinking freely from my blood supply. I could feel Susan behind me. She bumped me several times when I stopped to listen and ran into me again when I stopped at the edge of the clearing. Although the clouds in the night sky blocked much of the light from the moon and stars, enough seeped through to paint the open area around the plantation in a ghostly hue.

"Everything looks quiet." Susan's breath was hot on my neck.

"Cover me." I said.

Susan patted my back, and I took that as a signal that she was ready. Crouching low, I scurried across the open yard. I was careful to skirt the outer edges of the shell driveway, keeping to the soft grass. When I reached the corner of the plantation home, I dropped to my knees and looked to Susan's location. I couldn't make out anything. I dug for my phone, but before I could find it, a shadow emerged from the darkness and skidded to a stop beside me.

"Everything looks clear," Susan whispered.

We knelt beside the plantation home for several long minutes, listening. Other than the crickets chirping and the sounds of other night critters, all was quiet. I holstered my pistol and Susan did the same. We walked the perimeter of the large home, testing the doors and windows, but everything was locked. There was no sign of life from inside.

"What do you think?" Susan asked.

"It looks empty. Let's try the back door." I led the way to a large screened-in porch and pulled out my knife. I planted a foot on the wooden steps, and they rocked beneath my weight. When I'd reached the top step, I cut the screen along the edge of the wooden frame—where it wouldn't be as noticeable—and squeezed my arm through the opening until I felt the lock. I flipped it up and pulled on the screen door. Susan sucked her breath and I froze as the vintage hinges squawked loudly and shattered the stillness of the night. Sweat poured from my forehead and dripped into my eyes. I blinked it away, but didn't move. I strained to hold the door in its half-open position, while listening for the slightest movement from inside. I heard none.

After a minute or two, we both relaxed. Susan said, "It's got to be empty. I'm pretty sure those hinges woke every dead person in the cemetery at the other end of town."

I rubbed the sweat from my forehead and slipped through the doorway and onto the wooden porch. My boots echoed on the hollow surface as I made my way to the back door. Susan joined me and pulled a flashlight from her back pocket to illuminate the doorknob. I pointed to the shiny deadbolt and knob combination that was oddly out of place on the weathered door. "That's fresh."

Susan nodded, her face appearing ghostly against the light from her phone. "Someone's definitely using this old place for something."

I shook on the handle, but the door was solid, and I wouldn't be able to fit a credit card in the crack. The top portion of the door was constructed of quarter panel glass. A thick curtain prevented us from being able to see inside. I pulled out my pistol. "Step back, Susan. This is going to be loud."

"Are you sure you have to—"

I smashed the barrel of my pistol into the bottom right panel and glass exploded. We waited for a few more minutes, but my actions evoked no response from inside. "We're good." I eased my hand into the broken window and unlocked the door from the inside.

Once I'd pulled my hand out, Susan turned the knob and walked in first. She shone her flashlight around. We were in a large family room. It was unfurnished and looked abandoned, as did the surrounding rooms. A spiral staircase was directly in front of us, and I walked toward it. "I'll check upstairs."

"I'm going with you," Susan said. "Haven't you watched scary movies? You never split up—ever."

The stairs creaked as we made our ascent, Susan's flashlight stabbing at the darkness and lighting our way. When we reached the top, we found ourselves in a small room that opened into a larger room to the right. To the left was a doorway that opened into another room. A staircase extended upward in front of us.

"Where does that go?" Susan asked.

"Who knows? Maybe it's—"

A solid thump and a muffled cry sounded from above, and we both jumped back and drew our weapons. My heart pounded in my chest. I glanced over at Susan. Her eyes were wide and her pistol trained on the door at the top of the stairs. I waved to her, got her attention. "I'm going up," I whispered. "Cover me."

Susan nodded, moving her pistol down so I could cross in front of her. As I passed her, she handed me her flashlight, and I aimed it up the staircase. I took the stairs one painstaking step at a time. My muscles were tense. My breathing was shallow. The thumping sound occurred at least twice more as I approached the door and tested the knob—it was locked. Taking a deep breath, I leaned back and shot a front kick that landed inches from the inside of the knob. The door crashed open. Slivers of splintered wood shot into the air. I rushed in, gun at the ready, and quickly scanned the room. When the flashlight swept the center of the otherwise empty attic, I gulped out loud. "What the *hell?*"

CHAPTER 38

"What's going on?" Susan asked from below.

I rushed to the squirming figures wrapped in tarpaulins, dropping to my knees beside them. I put my pistol on the ground and whipped out my knife. "Susan, radio for Jack and William to get out here right away!"

"I don't have my radio," Susan hollered, stomping up the stairs. "You told me we were going dark ops or some shit!"

"Hold still," I told the first figure, as I felt around to find what was holding the tarp in place. The flashlight had rolled to the other side of the attic and it was hard to see what I was doing. Whoever was inside was mumbling and struggling. "It's the police...calm down."

"Holy shit," Susan said when she stepped into the room. "Is that—"

"Grab the light!" I indicated with my head. "It's over in the corner."

Susan rattled off our location to someone on her phone while doing what I'd asked. She then hurried to my side and shone the light on the bodies before me. A rope was wrapped around the legs and the shoulders of both of them. I quickly cut the ropes off the first body and then moved to the second, while Susan peeled away the tarpaulin on the first. I was just starting to tear open my tarpaulin when Susan said, "Easy now, little fellow. It's okay. We've got you now."

I turned and saw the youngest of the McKenzie boys protruding from a slit in the tarp. Susan had pulled a blindfold down off his eyes so it dangled loosely around his neck. His eyes were wide. A piece of tape had been shoved over his mouth. His hands were tied behind his back and his feet were bound together—as though the rope on the outside of the tarpaulin hadn't been enough.

"This is going to hurt a little," Susan said, as she began to gently pull the tape off the younger boy.

I turned back to my tarp and stripped it away from the oldest McKenzie boy, then sighed. He was also moving and seemed to be in decent health, given the circumstances. He, too, had a blindfold and gag, and his feet and hands were bound. I removed the blindfold, and he blinked away the light from the flashlight, squinting. "It's okay, little man," I said. "You're about to be free."

Sirens sounded in the distance and drew nearer. By the time we had freed the boys and stood them to their feet, the sirens went dead right outside the house and boots pounded on the hardwood floors.

"Where the hell are y'all?" called Jack.

"Up here," Susan answered.

Jack and William clambered up the stairs and bumped into each other as they hurried through the door. "Holy crap-shit," William said. "The McKenzie boys!"

The youngest was crying, and Susan guided him down the stairs, while I followed with the oldest. "Seal off this place," I called over my shoulder. "We need to find out who the owner is and get a search warrant."

"Yes, Chief," both men said in unison.

When we were outside with the boys, we sat them in the back of Jack's cruiser. Susan was trying to soothe the youngest, and I knelt by the open door to talk to the oldest. "What's your name, son?"

"Zeke."

"Okay, Zeke, I'm going to ask you some questions. Is that okay?"

Zeke nodded, as he rubbed his wrists where the rope had dug a deep furrow.

"Good…good. Now, do you remember how you got here?"

Zeke nodded again.

I waited, but he didn't say anything, so I asked, "How'd you get here?"

"We were fishing… me and my brother. We found a little canal that went off the bayou and took it. It went for a long ways. And then we saw this big house that we never saw before, so we docked the boat in the marsh grass and walked to the house. We sneaked around the house to explore because it looked spooky, like a haunted house. That was when…when…"

Zeke's eyes began to tear up. He wiped them with a dirty palm and hung his head.

"What happened next?" I asked softly.

"Some man came after us. We ran, but he got Paulie. I couldn't leave my little brother behind, so I went back." Zeke sniffled and rubbed his nose on his sleeve. "The man told us he was going to kill us and feed us to the alligators for snooping around."

My mind raced. The way the boys were wrapped up, it appeared they were left to die. Killing a grownup was one thing, but killing a kid—two of them—was something different. It might've been just the incentive Randall needed to end his own life.

"Look, Zeke, I need you to think really hard," I said. "If you saw this man again, would you recognize him?"

Zeke shrugged, his face scrunched into a pout. "Mister, will my dad be mad at us?"

I smiled, rubbing his disheveled hair. "No, buddy. Your dad's going to be proud of you for going back with your brother, and he's going to be happy to see y'all again."

This seemed to cheer him up a little. I turned to Susan, who said, "Photo line-up, right?"

I nodded. "This was either Randall Rupe or Mark McNeal."

"Just what I was thinking."

I stood and walked back toward the house. William and Jack had secured the doors shut and wrapped the area in crime scene tape. They turned to me, and Jack said, "That does it. It's wrapped tight like a Christmas tree."

"Good. Take turns guarding it, and we'll be back in the morning with a warrant. And stay out of sight. I don't want whoever kidnapped them knowing we were here."

Jack looked around at all the commotion. "You don't think they know already?"

I followed his gaze, shrugged. "They could, but if there's even a slim chance we can catch them flatfooted, I want to take advantage of it. So, stay out of sight and call me if anyone comes down that road—even if it's a grandma driving a moped."

They both nodded, and William called, "I've got first watch!"

"No," Jack said. "I'll take first watch. Meet me back here in two hours."

William grunted, but nodded.

"William, can you drop the boys off at the hospital for me? Just to make sure they weren't harmed?"

This seemed to cheer him up. "Absolutely!"

I pulled Jack aside. "Look, don't you let your guard down, you hear?"

"I know what we're dealing with."

I squinted, my blood pressure rising slightly. "Don't go taking this for granted. Anyone willing to kidnap kids won't think twice about pumping a cop full of holes."

"I've got it."

I walked to William's cruiser and saw that Zeke had scooted closer to his brother and they were talking softly. When Susan stepped up beside me, I said, "I need you to go to the clerk of courts office first thing in the morning and find out who owns this place."

"What are you going to do?"

"I'm going to put together a couple of photo lineups and start drafting the search warrant. Once you get me the owner's information, I'll get the warrant signed, and we'll tear that place to the ground." I nodded in Jack's direction. "I'll get Melvin to relieve them in the morning. We need to keep a close eye on this place until we can toss it properly."

Susan leaned against William's cruiser and stared at the large plantation home. "There's definitely something worthwhile inside this house—they were willing to kill a couple of kids to keep it a secret."

"You're right," I said. "I can't imagine what it is, but it must be huge."

Just then, an old rusty pickup truck roared down the street and skidded to a stop several feet from my Tahoe. The driver's door squeaked open and Red McKenzie jumped out. Even in the faint glow from the headlights I could see his face matched his name. "Where the hell is the man who took my boys?"

I quickly caught up to him as he barreled toward the police line and grabbed his arm. "Red, calm down. Please. We've got your boys and they're fine. A little shaken up, but unharmed."

"But where's the bastard who took them? I want his ass all to myself!"

"We don't have him yet. We don't know who it is, but we're working on it."

Red pushed his face close to mine. "You'd better find him before I do!"

"I will." I pulled him by the arm and guided him toward his boys. "I need you to go with William. He's going to take your boys to the hospital."

"I thought you said they were unharmed?"

"I did, but I want them checked out anyway."

Red nodded. "Okay, but I want them riding with me."

"That's fine. And look, I need you to get them to the police station in the morning. I need a formal interview from them, and I want them to look at some photos. As for tonight, make sure they get plenty of rest."

"We'll do whatever you need us to do to catch this bastard."

I heard William tell Zeke and Paulie that their dad was there and stood back as they rushed to Red and nearly tackled him in a group bear hug. Red dropped to his knees and cried.

CHAPTER 39

Wednesday, July 2

It had taken most of the morning to put together two photographic line-ups—one that included Randall Rupe and another that included Mark McNeal. When I'd finally finished, I called Red McKenzie and asked him to bring his boys down to the police department.

"I'll be there a soon as I can," Red said. "Oh, and Chief..."

"What's that, Red?"

Red's voice cracked. "No matter what happens from here on out, you saved my boys' life, and that's something I'll never forget. I owe you my life."

"You don't owe me anything, Red. I was just doing my job. Now, hurry and get here so I can go after these assholes." I placed the receiver in its cradle on my desk and looked out the window. I groaned inwardly when I saw Mayor Landry park in front of the office. He hurried out of his car and jogged up the sidewalk. I figured he must've just heard about the kidnappings. I turned in my chair just as he entered my office.

"What in God's name were you thinking, Clint?"

"About?"

"Knocking the piss out of Beaver in front of half the town?" He pushed the door closed and dropped to a chair. "I don't need to be firing my second consecutive police chief over some stupid shit."

I shrugged. "He had it coming. He doesn't know how to talk to a lady."

"Well, lucky for you he's not pursuing charges."

"Lucky for him there was a crowd of witnesses. Otherwise, he wouldn't be talking at all."

Mayor Landry stifled a chuckle. "It sure was nice to see him busted up. There're a lot of folks in this town who would've paid to have seen it—myself included."

Just then, Lindsey stuck her head in my office. "Chief, Red McKenzie's here with his boys."

"Have them wait in the interview room." I turned back to Mayor Landry to explain what had taken place.

"Kidnappings? Here in Mechant Loup?" He rubbed his face with his hands. "What in the world is going on?"

"I'm not sure, but I'm about to find out."

"Just try to get this wrapped up before Friday. We don't need any distractions."

"Friday?" I scanned the deepest recesses of my brain, trying to remember what was happening that day. "What's so special about Friday?"

"Don't you remember?"

"Remember what?"

"I even reminded you. Didn't you get my message?"

I shook my head.

"I called you and left a message on your phone," Mayor Landry said. "I even texted you."

"What the hell is a text?" I asked.

"Stop messing with me, Clint."

I pointed to the mess on my desk. "We've got a lot going on here. Seriously, I don't remember what's happening on Friday."

"The unveiling of the new town hall building. The dedication ceremony." Major Landry slapped his forehead. "I can't believe you forgot!"

"Oh, that?" I scoffed. "I knew about that."

"Well, you do remember that I need you to pick up the governor at the airport, right? Nine sharp. You can't be late."

I shook my head. "I've got too much going on, Mayor. There's no way I can do it."

"Clint, this is a priority! It has to be done. You need to go get him for me."

"Look, I can get Susan to take my Tahoe and—"

"Absolutely not! I need you to do this one thing for me." Mayor Landry stood. "Clint, this is important to everyone in this town, but especially to me and the other parents who lost kids. You know how that feels. You know how we feel. Please, do this one thing for me…to help me honor them."

I frowned, then nodded. "Okay. I will."

"Thanks!"

I snatched the photographic line-ups from my desk. "Well then, let me get back to work so I can put this case to bed before the governor comes to town."

I followed the mayor out of my office. When he'd left the building, I met with Red, Paulie, and Zeke in the interview room. "Red, I'll need to speak with them one at a time. Can you step out with Paulie, so I can show the line-up to Zeke first?"

Red looked at Zeke. "You tell this man everything you know, you hear, son?"

Zeke nodded.

Red patted his head, then took Paulie by the hand and led him out into the hallway.

I smiled at Zeke. "How're you feeling, little man?"

"I'm okay." He looked on the verge of tears. A hospital band still clung to his wrist.

"Want a soda pop or some candy?"

Zeke shook his head and stared wide-eyed at the folders in my hand. "What's in there?"

"I have some pictures I want you to look at." I placed the folders on the desk and took my seat across from him. "There're six pictures in each folder. They're numbered one through six. I want you to look at them carefully. Take your time. There's no rush. If you see someone you recognize, I want you to point to the picture and say the number. I'm going to then ask you where you know that person from and I want you to tell me. Okay?"

Zeke nodded. "Is the bad man who took us in there?"

"I'm not sure. Look, I need you to understand something…if you don't recognize anyone in the pictures, that's okay, and all you have to do is tell me you don't see anyone you recognize. I don't want you picking someone just to pick them. Understand?"

"Yes, sir."

I opened the first folder—it contained the picture of Randall Rupe—and turned it so Zeke could see the pictures. He leaned away from the folder as though he thought it would bite him and looked away. Finally, he turned back to look at the photographs. His eyes narrowed and he studied it for a long moment.

"Do you recognize anyone in the pictures?" I asked. "If you don't see anyone you recognize right away, then you've probably never seen anyone of these men."

As though I hadn't said a word, Zeke continued examining the pictures for a full minute. He pushed the file away and shook his head. "No, sir. It wasn't none of them men."

"Are you sure?"

"I'm positive."

I closed the first folder and opened the one with Mark McNeal's picture and turned it so Zeke could see. By that point, he felt more comfortable and took the folder in his hands and pulled it close. I watched his eyes move from one picture to the other. He touched each picture and shook his head, then handed the folder back to me. "It was none of these men that took us."

I frowned. "Are you sure? Maybe you'll want to look again."

Zeke shook his head. "I'm sure."

Shit! I thought. Now what?

I stood and led Zeke out into the hallway. Red was standing just outside the door with Paulie—listening, no doubt. I ruffled Paulie's hair, and he frowned, pulling closer to his dad. "You ready, little man?"

Paulie turned away from me. Red nodded. "He's ready."

"Okay." I waved for Zeke to follow me. "Come sit in my office while I talk to Paulie and your dad. You can play on my computer. Just don't go meeting a girlfriend on some dating website."

Zeke's somber expression cracked into a smile, as he followed me down the hall. "I already got a girlfriend."

"No way! What's her name?"

"Bethany. She's in my class."

"Do you get to see her during the summer?" I opened the door to my office and stepped back so Zeke could enter.

"Not that much. I saw her at the baseball field the other night."

When Zeke was seated at my desk, I returned to the interview room, where Red and Paulie had already made themselves at home. I went through the same process with Paulie and met with the same results.

"Are you sure?" I asked when he couldn't identify anyone in the pictures.

His head bobbed up and down. "I'm sure."

I closed the folders slowly and stood to see them out. When we were by the front door, I shook Red's hand. "I'll do everything I can to find who did this."

"I know you will. And when you find them," Red said in a low, but deadly voice, "I want you to kill them."

CHAPTER 40

I worked at a furious pace on the search warrants and was almost done when my cell phone rang. Without looking, I pushed it to my ear. "This is Clint."

"Hey, handsome, how's your morning going?" It was Chloe.

"Not good. I've got a lot going on at the moment."

"Do you have a break in the case?"

"We found the McKenzie boys."

Chloe was quiet for a long moment. "Are they okay?"

"They're fine. Back home with their dad. Now I need to find out who took them."

"I'll let you go."

"Okay, thanks for calling."

"Oh, and Clint…"

"Yeah?"

"Please be careful. I just met you and I don't want to lose you before I get to know you."

I hesitated, as I took in the moment. I could hear Chloe's soft breathing and smiled. I was lucky—really lucky—to have someone like her fretting over me. "You know, I'll be careful. Just for you."

I thought I heard her smile—if that was even possible—and she said, "Thank you so much. And will I still get to see you tonight?"

"I'll do my best to finish before it gets too late. I want to see you really bad."

"Time means nothing to me. I don't care if it's three o'clock in the morning—wake me up."

"Will do." I called Susan next and asked how the records search was going.

"I'm waiting on the lady to dig up the records."

"Okay. Call me as soon as you know who owns it."

We said our goodbyes, and I hurried home to check on Achilles before having to head to the courthouse. I didn't know what time I'd get home that night and I didn't want him having to roll around in his business.

I could hear Achilles barking inside from the moment I stepped out of the Tahoe. "I'm coming. I'm coming."

Achilles was pushing against the walls of the crate and whimpering as I got the door open. I quickly drew my pistol when I realized my back door had been kicked in.

I crossed the living room and squatted beside the crate. I allowed Achilles to lick my left hand through the wires while I trained my pistol toward the back of my house and listened for any signs of movement. I heard nothing but the sounds of my heart beating heavy in my chest and Achilles' panting. I leaned toward Achilles and, in a low voice, said, "Quiet, boy."

I tiptoed into the kitchen. Once there, I glanced back at Achilles. He was sitting with his ears perked up, watching my every move. I figured he'd still be barking if an intruder was inside, but I couldn't be certain. I slipped into my bedroom and scanned the area with my pistol at the ready. Nothing appeared disturbed. My gun closet was closed. I opened the door and checked on my gun safe. Everything was exactly as I'd left it. I sighed, holstered my pistol and returned to the kitchen. A quick check of my personal stuff revealed nothing had been taken.

I examined the back door. It looked to have been kicked in. Could it have been the work of the suspicious person from the woods? I let Achilles out and, together, we walked into the backyard and looked around. Achilles marked his territory and sniffed around the perimeter of my property, but he didn't seem alarmed. I tried to pierce the shadows of the trees, but saw nothing that looked suspicious. There were no sounds out of the ordinary.

"Did you scare them off, little tiger?" I asked. Achilles' head whipped around at the sound of my voice and he loped toward me. I rubbed his ears. "You kept our place safe, didn't you? You deserve a good treat for that. I might grill you a thick steak later on—show off my cooking skills to Chloe."

When Achilles didn't respond, I went into the little work shed behind my house to retrieve my tool belt and a box of nails. The door was unlocked, and I frowned. I thought I'd remembered to lock it. I opened the door expecting my stuff to be missing, but everything seemed to be there. I grabbed the tool belt and strapped it around my waist, then shook my head. My career as a construction worker had been so brief that I hadn't had a chance to wear out the leather on the pouch.

"Get inside, boy," I said to Achilles, and he complied. "I have to hurry and get back to work."

I followed him in, repaired the door jam and reattached the knob. When I was done, I tugged on it to test its strength. It was solid—enough. I tossed my tool belt and the box of nails in a bottom cabinet, fed and watered Achilles, and locked the front door on my way out.

I then headed back to the office and waited for Susan to call. I didn't have to wait long.

"You're not going to believe this," she said when I answered the phone.

"What?"

"I got the deed to the plantation house and…"

"And what? Who does it belong to?"

"You…it belongs to you."

I nearly dropped the phone. "What are you talking about?"

"It's…it's in your wife's name."

I opened my mouth to respond, but nothing came out. Michele had never told me she owned anything, much less a big plantation home. *Why did you keep that from me?*

"Clint? Are you there?"

"Can you bring the paperwork in? I need to see it."

"Sure thing. I'll be there in a jiffy."

The phone went dead—like my mood. I stared blankly at the wall, unsure what to think or what to feel. I don't know how long I stared, but Susan walked in before I moved.

"Clint? Here it is." She slid the paperwork across the desk toward me.

I hesitated. I didn't know if I even wanted to look. With hands that shook slightly, I picked up the stapled papers and saw that it was an Act of Sale. From the looks of the form, the parties involved had printed it off the Internet and then found a notary to execute it because the notary's name had been handwritten on pre-designated lines throughout the form and was impossible to read.

I forced myself to look at the buyer's name. My heart sank even further when I saw that Michele had signed her married name, which meant she'd made the sale behind my back. *When did you do this? How?* The woman I loved, the mother of my child, was a fraud. "I can't believe she did this behind my back. I trusted her! When would she have even done this?" My mind was a mix of confusion, hurt, and anger. I checked the date—six months before her murder.

"Well," Susan said softly, "maybe she was trying to surprise you. Did she ever come here to visit her dad without you?"

I shrugged. "Sure. A lot."

Susan raised an eyebrow. "Maybe she purchased it on one of those trips. If she were trying to surprise you, she certainly wouldn't do it while you were with her."

I flipped through the form until I found the sale price, then shook the document in front of Susan. "The house cost five hundred thousand dollars! There's no way we could afford that."

Susan lowered her dark eyes. "Did you see who the seller was?"

I thumbed back through the form, caught my breath. "Hays Cain! What the hell was she up to?"

"There may be a good explanation, Clint. Don't start doubting—"

"The only two people who could explain it are dead."

"What about the witnesses or the notary?"

I shook my head as I studied the notary's signature. "It's chicken scratch. I can't make it out. Can you?"

Susan took the form and inspected it.

I rubbed my eyes, felt dizzy. *Why did you lie to me?*

Susan frowned. "I can't make this out."

I felt betrayed. I thought I'd known everything about Michele—at least everything that mattered. She certainly knew everything about me—even the things that didn't matter. I looked up at Susan. "Would you hide this kind of thing from your husband?"

"I'm sure there's a good explanation for this, Clint. If she didn't tell you, it was for a reason."

I sighed. "Whatever the reason, I'll never know now. She's gone. I'll never be able to ask her about it."

We were both quiet for a while and then Susan said, "Well, there is one positive thing that came out of this revelation."

"What could that possibly be?"

"We don't need a search warrant for the property. It now belongs to you."

I mulled it over for a long moment. I finally nodded. "Why don't you take Melvin out there and start searching the place?"

Susan stood, hesitated. "What are you going to do?"

I grabbed my Tahoe keys. "I'm going pay my father-in-law a visit. He's got to know something about this. Hell, it was probably bought with his money."

We walked outside, and I watched Susan amble off and get into her Charger. I then drove to the courthouse, but had to wait in my father-in-law's lobby for about twenty minutes before being buzzed through the door.

The tall, brown-haired woman who opened the door smiled. "Judge Miller will see you now."

She pointed the way down a narrow hall and into a cozy office, where I found Nick Miller sitting at a large desk cluttered with books and legal-sized documents. He looked up from an official-looking file. "What are you doing in these parts, Clint?"

"I need to talk to you." I hefted the Act of Sale in my hand, then tossed it on the desk in front of him.

Nick ran a wrinkled hand through his stringy salt and pepper hair. "What's this?"

"What do you know about the plantation home at the end of Paradise Place?"

Nick folded his hands like a tent in front of his mouth. "Paradise Place...is that the street on the southern end of Mechant Loup?"

I nodded. "That's the one. The road is lined with cane fields—both sides of the street—nearly all the way down, and at the end of the street there's a large plantation home."

"I don't know that I've been back there since high school. That road used to be popular with us teens, if you know what I mean. I didn't realize that house was still standing. It was in bad shape when I was a kid—can't imagine what it looks like now." Nick picked up the Act of Sale. "Why do you ask?"

"Because it belongs to Michele."

Nick Miller swallowed hard, and I thought I saw his eyes glisten. He cradled the papers in hands that trembled slightly and thumbed through them carefully, as though he thought some part of Michele was still attached and he didn't want to disturb her. "I...I had no idea. Where'd y'all get the money for this?"

"I have no clue," I said.

Nick looked up at me. "What do you mean?"

"I didn't know anything about it. I thought you gave her the money."

"How's that possible? It was purchased before Michele...before she passed, but after you two were married. You must know something about it."

I hung my head. "She kept it from me."

"Michele wouldn't do that." Nick slid the Act of Sale back toward me, nodded positively. "She was an honest girl. She'd never keep something like this from you. You had to know about it."

"The date on it is six months before Michele was killed. It had to be when she came out to visit you."

"Unfortunately, I was always working. She'd call Sandra before Sandra passed and they'd go shopping or do whatever it was that they did." Nick sighed. "Maybe Sandra would've known something about it."

Great, I thought. Everyone who knew about the sale was dead. I thanked Nick and left. It was starting to drizzle, so I drove a little slower on the way back to the office. I had a lot on my mind, and none of it had to do with the case at hand. The rain began to fall harder and it matched my mood perfectly.

CHAPTER 41

The only person at the police department was Lindsey. She was sitting at her desk reading a book and it wasn't the same one from Monday.

"Damn, you read a lot."

She jerked and yelped at the sound of my voice. "Shit! You're like a ninja! I never hear you walk up. Why can't you drag your feet or wear squeaky shoes like a normal person?"

"I don't know." I looked around, as I brushed the rain from my face. "Is Susan out at the house on Paradise?"

Lindsey nodded, bent a corner of the page and closed her book.

"How many books do you read each week?" I asked.

"As many as I can. Probably four a week, depending on how thick it is."

"Damn, that's a lot." I ducked into my office and grabbed my camera. I checked the battery and memory card. The battery was full and the memory card nearly empty. I then headed for the door.

"Are you going to the kidnapping scene?" Lindsey asked, without looking up.

"Yeah. Hold down the fort while I'm gone."

She shoved her hand in my direction, a note dangling between her fingers. "Tell Melvin to stop ignoring his wife's calls. She wants him to pick up some pickles, peanut butter, cherry tomatoes, and mayonnaise on his way home."

I screwed my face into a knot, took the note and shoved it into my pocket. "That's a strange combination."

"Pregnant women for you. My sister had a baby and she had all kinds of weird cravings. She would think about two or three different types of foods and they just didn't seem right to her unless they were all mixed together. Crazy."

I thought back to when Michele was pregnant with Abigail. I'd been shoved violently awake many times in the middle of the night and sent on urgent missions to find dark chocolate bars, and not just any dark chocolate—it had to be exactly seventy-two percent cocoa. I shook my head, frowning as the images of Abigail being gunned down rushed into my mental theater. I shook my head to clear it and hurried out the door.

As I stepped out onto the front porch, I cursed myself for not parking in the sally port. The rain was falling heavier, and I wondered if it would disrupt the ceremony on Friday. This brought me hope. "Maybe I won't have to see that prick after all."

Hitting the unlock button on the keyless remote, I sprinted to the Tahoe—as though running would somehow minimize the amount of rain that fell on me—and jerked the door open smoothly. Once inside, I closed the door and pushed rivulets of water off my face and forehead.

"What a perfect day for this shit." I pulled onto the highway and travelled the few miles to Paradise Place.

I drove my Tahoe around to the back of the house. Shoving my camera under the front of my shirt, I sprinted for the back door. Cold droplets splashed against the back of my neck and slid down my back. I shivered, pushed through the screen door and slowed to a stop. I shook the rain off me like a wet dog, and stomped my feet on the hollow wooden porch to dry them.

I looked up to see Susan and Melvin at the door with guns drawn. I raised my hands; they relaxed.

"Shit!" Melvin said. "We thought the killers were back."

I nodded and joined them inside. The lights were on, and I cast a curious glance around. "There's power here?"

Susan nodded. "Whoever comes here apparently shuts the power off at the outside breaker when they leave."

"Did y'all find anything?"

"Follow me," Susan said.

She and Melvin hurried up the spiral staircase to the second floor, and I followed. There was a huge room to the right of us with a large wooden table positioned at the center of it. Seven chairs were situated around the table.

I pointed to the furniture. "I didn't notice the table and chairs last night."

"I didn't either." Susan made a beeline for what looked like a newspaper at the head of the table. She snatched it up with gloved hands and handed it to me. "You need to see this."

"What is it?" I pulled on a pair of latex gloves Melvin handed me and took the newspaper from Susan. I gasped when I realized what the article was about. It was at the top of the front page—big as shit—and the article was accompanied by a large picture of me. I didn't need to read it. I knew what it said, could cite it from memory.

A woman, her child, and an unidentified man were all killed last night after gunshots erupted inside River Seas Seafood Restaurant on the corner of Twenty-Third and Rank. Witnesses inside the restaurant say four masked men who were heavily armed stormed the establishment and demanded money from the cashier. According to one witness, an off-duty cop interceded and things turned deadly.

"I don't know what he was thinking," said the witness, who agreed to speak under the cover of anonymity. "The cop started fighting with one of the robbers and it looked like he was getting the best of the robber. Then one of the other robbers grabbed this little girl—I think it was the cop's daughter—and threatened to shoot her if the cop didn't stop fighting. The cop stopped, but the man killed the girl and the lady right there in front of him. The robbers ran out, but the cop caught one of them and somehow got his gun away and killed him. It was terrible."

"All we wanted to do was go out to dinner and celebrate my daughter's birthday," another witness told reporters, "but then those men came in with masks on and tried to rob the place and all hell broke loose. If somebody in the place would've had a gun, those thugs could've been stopped."

This most recent robbery is the fourth in a string of restaurant robberies that have occurred in the city over the past three weeks, and authorities believe it is directly related to the riots sparking up all over the state. It is the first robbery to end in bloodshed. Governor Lester Katz said the actions of the off-duty officer most likely escalated the situation and caused the deaths of the woman and child. He would not comment when asked if his anti-gun policies and denigration of the police were to blame for the riots that have been popping up all over the city.

"There is no direct evidence that this incident had anything to do with the comprehensive gun laws that have been enacted as a result of my commonsense approach to governing, and my tireless efforts to keep the people in my state safe," Katz said today in a statement. "Rather, the evidence suggests the off-duty officer's actions were ill-advised and directly contributed to the deaths of the victims at the

scene Had everyone in the restaurant complied with the robbers' demands, no one would've been hurt."

The police chief said his police officer did what he was trained to do, and, using strong language, he rebuked the governor's assertion.

"It's easy for [Governor Katz] to sit up there in the safety and security of his mansion and fan the flames of police hatred—a mansion that is being protected by the very police officers he is throwing under the bus. But we will no longer stand for this type of lawlessness. It's time for us to take back our city. I'm ordering all of my men to carry their firearms everywhere they go—on duty or off-duty. If anyone interferes with them, they are to meet force with force. I am also encouraging every law-abiding citizen in this city to exercise their right to bear arms and protect their family and property. Beginning today, we are waging war on the lawless thugs who have taken over this city and we are going to bring peace back to our streets. Enough is enough!"

The governor could not be reached for follow-up comment on the police chief's accusations and plan of action.

The names of the victims were being withheld pending notification of loved ones. The robber killed at the scene was identified as Thomas Parker, a convicted felon who was paroled three years ago after being convicted of attempting to kill a police officer on the east side of the city during a daytime shootout. Police have named Parker's three brothers, David, Simon, and Taylor as suspects in the restaurant robberies. Anyone with information on their whereabouts is urged to call police on their toll free hotline.

CHAPTER 42

Susan put her hand on my arm. "I'm sorry you had to see this garbage again."

"I've read this article a thousand times," I said. "Seeing it isn't a big deal. But what I want to know is…" I paused and slowly scanned the room. It was empty except for the table, chairs, and the lone newspaper article. "What the hell is it doing here? In this house—a house that's in Michele's name?"

"Look over here." Susan walked near the head of the table and pointed to a small pool of blood on the floor. "We took samples to send to the lab for confirmation, but my bet is this is where Hays Cain was murdered."

"Randall told Chloe that Hay Cain's murder was a part of something bigger." I looked from the article to the blood, frowned. "What were you bastards up to?"

"Pauline Cain might know something about this place," Susan offered.

"You're right. I'll talk to her tomorrow." I looked around the room. "Are y'all done in here?"

"We need to fingerprint the table and swab it for DNA," Susan said.

While they set about processing the table, I decided to check out the attic where we found Red McKenzie's boys. Once up there, I shone my light around the room. Cobwebs dangled eerily from the ceiling rafters. Dust coated the rough floor, except for the area where the boys had been bound and covered. I examined it closely for possible evidence—a shoeprint, fiber, anything—but it was clean. I then began searching the remainder of the house for evidence, while

Susan and Melvin dusted every inch of the large table in the meeting room. It seemed nothing in the house had been used in years except for the upstairs area.

It was late in the day when I rejoined Susan and Melvin in the meeting room. Susan turned to me, wiping her face with a shirt sleeve. A mixture of sweat and dust left a streak across her forehead. "All of this is connected to you somehow. This house being in Michele's name, the article about you on the table...all of it stinks to high shit."

"I wonder if the break-in at my house is also connected to this."

Susan's head snapped around. "What break-in?"

"Someone broke into my house sometime this morning. I found my back door busted open when I stopped to check on Achilles."

"Why am I just hearing about this?" Susan's chin hung nearly to her chest. "Did you call it in?"

"Call it in to who? Myself?" I scoffed. "I'm not going to waste time making a report."

"But what about documenting it in case any future incidents happen?"

"I already know about it...and now so do you."

"You need to make a report," Susan said. "Just in case something else happens. At least let me ride by and take some pictures and do a write-up on it."

"Not necessary. Nothing was missing. All they did was bust up the door. It looked like Achilles might've scared them off. Besides, I already fixed the damage and cleaned up the mess."

"You're one hardheaded man." Susan was almost finished packing up the crime scene equipment.

Melvin hoisted two large bags that contained dozens of individual evidence packages. I walked downstairs with him and held the doors for him, then opened the trunk to his Charger. The rain had stopped, but the yard was soggy and we sloshed around in the muck. The one thing I missed about the city was the solid ground.

After he'd secured the evidence in his trunk, Melvin and I returned upstairs and helped Susan bring the crime scene equipment to her cruiser.

I nodded my thanks. "See y'all tomorrow morning."

"I still think you need to make a complaint about the burglary," Susan said.

"Okay." I started to walk away, then suddenly remembered. I pulled the note from my pocket and stopped Melvin. "Lindsey said your wife called with this demand letter."

Melvin took it, his face relaxing into a smile. "She does this all the time."

"And as long as you keep fetching her list like a good little puppy, she'll keep doing it," Susan called over her shoulder.

"I'd fetch her list any day," Melvin declared.

"I bet she made you wear matching shirts on your honeymoon," Susan chided.

Melvin nodded. "And hats."

Susan laughed out loud. "Boy, does she have you whipped!"

"I love her." Melvin was unapologetic. "I'd do anything to make her happy, and she'd do anything to make me happy."

I smiled inwardly, then thought of Chloe and remembered our date night. I called her to say I was on my way home and told her where I hid the spare key.

Next, I stopped at the office to brief Jack and William on the happenings of the day. Melvin and Susan were putting away the evidence when I arrived. "Don't forget that list," I said to Melvin, then called Jack and William into my office. When I'd let them in on what had happened, I turned to Jack. "I want you to stay home tomorrow night and work the day shift Friday."

"The *day* shift?" He said it like I'd asked him to castrate himself.

"Yeah. The ribbon-cutting ceremony is that day and I'll need you to take care of something for me."

"Take care of what?" Jack looked skeptical. "Traffic? Get some fat-cat his coffee?"

"No, I'll need you to drive to the crime lab and pick up some evidence and a report. Melvin and Susan will be busy at the ceremony and won't have time to run to the lab."

"What evidence do I have to pick up?"

"The tarpaulins and tape from the kidnappings of the McKenzie boys. We sent them off for DNA and fingerprint analysis, and they said they'd be done by Friday. Hopefully they were able to recover something."

Jack looked at William, then back at me. "Why don't you make him go? That's a boring assignment."

William frowned and gave Jack an angry stare.

"Because I told you to do it." I walked out, leaving Jack and William standing in my office mean-mugging each other.

Once inside my Tahoe, I raced home and found Chloe's car already parked in the driveway. She turned from the kitchen sink when I opened the door. "It's about time you came home."

I smiled as I tossed my keys and phone on the end table in the living room. "What're you doing?"

"Washing dishes."

Achilles was lying on his back at her feet, pawing at her ankles. I snapped my fingers and he twisted to all fours and covered the short distance in two hops. He planted his paws on my legs and licked at my hand.

"He's so adorable." Chloe wiped her hands on a dishtowel she'd dug from one of the drawers and strolled to where I stood tussling with my dog.

"I wouldn't call him adorable."

She cocked her head sideways. "Oh, really? What would you call him?"

I shrugged. "I don't know. I guess I'd describe him as vicious or a tiger or—"

"There's not a vicious bone in his body!" Chloe laughed. "Face it...you have a puppy that's as loveable and sweet as you are. Sure, you might want people to think you're tough and mean, but under all of that"—she waved her hand back and forth in front of me—"you're just a cute little puppy who wants a little attention."

I pushed Achilles off me. When I turned toward Chloe, our lips immediately locked. I pulled her tight, her firm breasts pushing against my chest. She caressed my face as we kissed, and I allowed my hands to explore her back. I became excited, and she moaned when she felt it. She pushed forward, forcing me back toward the sofa. I went with it, but lost my balance when the back of my foot made contact with the sofa. We fell hard to the cushions—our bodies melding together as one—but our lips never parted.

I heard Achilles whimper, felt him tug at my arm. I quickly sat up and pulled Chloe into a straddle position. "The bedroom," I whispered.

She nodded, then kissed from one side of my neck to the other. Gripping the bottoms of her thighs and pulling her tight, I stood and walked with her to my bedroom. I was surprised how easy it was to lift her. She leaned back as I carried her and ripped the front of her shirt open. I heard tiny objects bounce off the floor and knew it was her buttons. When I stepped through the doorway, I kicked it closed behind me and spun to pin her against the wall. She let out a startled cry and her legs locked together behind my back. I reached around and unsnapped her bra with my left hand. She shrugged out of it, then grabbed me firmly behind the neck and pulled me close. My tongue explored hers. I ran my hands up along her soft waist and rubbed the sides of her heaving breasts. She dipped her right shoulder low, wriggling her hand into the front of my pants. My stomach jerked violently inward at the touch. She shoved her hand deeper into my waistline, then gasped when she felt how much I wanted her.

CHAPTER 43

Thursday, July 3

Bright light bled through the blinds and stirred me into semi-consciousness. I attempted to stretch, but couldn't move my right arm. I tried to wiggle my fingers; they were numb. Grunting, I tried to slide toward my left, but something had my arm anchored to the bed. I pried my eyes open and squinted through the morning sunlight. When my eyes came into focus, I gasped, gawking at what lay beside me, cradled in my right arm.

Chloe was completely naked, her backside turned to me. The sheets had gathered at the foot of the bed and her entire body was exposed. I explored her unblemished porcelain figure with my eyes. Her skin was so milky pure the sun reflected off it like virgin snow. Her curves were long and flowing. I'd known she had a nice body—it was obvious through her clothes—but I hadn't prepared myself for that degree of perfection.

I didn't move. Tried to will my heart to beat even quieter. I didn't want to do anything to disturb that moment—wanted it to last forever. As all good things must, the moment was rudely shattered by a sharp bark from Achilles. I'd let him out in the middle of the night while I secretly downed another bottle of vodka, but that had been hours ago. He yelped again.

Chloe moaned and turned her upper torso toward me, eyes half open and dreamy. "Good morning, sweetheart."

I smiled down at her, trying to erase the guilt I felt. How long could I keep hiding it from her? Would she follow me outside one day and catch me drinking? If so, how would she react?

Her blonde hair dangled across her shoulders and teasingly covered portions of her breasts as though each strand had been painted perfectly in place. "You're so beautiful."

Chloe blushed and lifted her arms above her head to stretch. The movement pushed her full breasts out into firm mounds, and I felt my excitement growing. Without thought, I leaned over and kissed her left breast softly, while cupping her right one firmly in my hand. She arched her back and smiled. My body yearned for her. I became more aggressive, and she moaned her approval.

She then reached for me and pulled me on top of her, whispering, "I want you again!"

With hands that trembled, I shoved her legs apart—a bit rougher than I'd intended. She responded by screeching and digging her nails into my lower back. She dragged her nails across my skin, leaving a burning sensation in their wake. I bent my head and bit one of her nipples gently. She dug her nails deeper into my flesh and forced me closer.

*   *   *

When we were done, Chloe rolled off and plopped onto her back beside me. We both lay there gasping for several minutes, our bodies slick and sweaty.

"God, you're amazing," Chloe said between breaths. "Your recovery time is unbelievable!"

"It's you...you excite me that much." I grabbed the nearest pillow and wiped rivulets of sweat from my face, before tossing it aside. I took a deep breath and slowly exhaled to try to lower my heart rate. "Wow! I don't think I've ever been that worked up before."

"Can we just die here for the rest of the day?"

"I might have to—my knees are shot. I doubt I can even walk." After about fifteen minutes of lying there enjoying Chloe's presence, I sat up and threw my legs over the side of the bed, remaining in that position for a moment to gather myself. I looked over at her glistening body. I had to avert my eyes for fear I'd want her again. "Are you hungry?"

She grabbed her belly. "Can you hear my stomach growling?"

"No." I stood to my feet and searched the floor for my boxers. Achilles was whining from his crate. "I can't hear your stomach growling over the sound of my ferocious dog whining."

I pulled my boxers on and stretched. Chloe sat up and looked around like a drunk woman.She plopped her feet to the floor and just sat there on the side of the bed, shoulders hunched over. "God, I'm so exhausted, but so relaxed."

I grunted my agreement and pulled on a pair of jeans. Chloe stood and started stumbling among the debris field of shirts, shoes, socks, and pants.

"Where's my bra?" she asked, her hands planted on perfect hips.

I spotted it under the edge of the bed and snatched it, handing it to her. "I'd love to help you back into it," I offered, "but I only know how to take them off."

"Hmm..." Chloe eyed me suspiciously. "I was pretty impressed with that one-handed escape move. It was as though you'd done it a few times—or a million."

"I had a lot of practice back when I wore a bra."

Chloe giggled and continued pulling on her clothes. When she got to her shirt, she gasped and held it up. "Shit! The buttons are gone! What am I supposed to do? I can't go out like this." She pointed to her shirtless torso.

I opened the top drawer of my dresser, pulled out the first T-shirt I grabbed, tossed it to her. "Will this work?"

She caught it, pulled it to her face and sniffed deeply. "It smells like you! I'm keeping it and never washing it."

I smiled and walked to Achilles' crate. I opened the door and he dashed out, rushing back and forth from me to Chloe, his tail wagging so violently I thought he would throw out his hip.

Chloe dropped to her knees, and Achilles took a clumsy leap into her lap and attacked her face with his tongue. She giggled and tried to hold him at bay.

I left them to fight it out and set about cooking breakfast. "How do you like your eggs?"

"You making me breakfast?" Chloe asked.

"Yes, I am...a complicated blend of eggs and bacon. I might even toast some bread with grape jelly if you're lucky."

Chloe's bare feet slapped the floor as she walked into the kitchen. "What can I do to help?"

I nodded toward the back door. "Can you let him out to do his business?"

"Come on, Achilles!" Chloe clapped her hands and hopped toward the door. Achilles mimicked her movements, and they bounded outside together.

I finished breakfast and set the plates out on the table. I had to push some paperwork aside to make room for an extra person because I wasn't used to having guests. Once Chloe and I were seated, she examined the eggs in front of her and nodded her approval. "How'd you cook these without breaking the yolk? I break it every time I flip the damn thing."

"That's my secret...I don't flip them."

"Then how do you cook them?"

"I heat the oil and splash it onto the top of the egg—"

"Holy shit!" Chloe had glanced at the stack of paperwork on my table and lifted a thin sliver of paper, her mouth wide and a forkful of eggs and bacon dangling from her hand. "Why on earth do you have a check for fifty thousand dollars just sitting here on your table?"

I frowned. "I need to give that back to my father-in-law."

"It's in your name. Why haven't you cashed it?"

"I don't want his money—don't need it."

Chloe studied my face, nodding slowly. "I understand not wanting to take a handout. My mom and dad tried to pay for my college, but I refused to take their money. They worked hard all of their lives and struggled to make ends meet most of the time, so I couldn't do that to them."

"That was admirable of you. Most kids wouldn't think twice about draining their parents dry to get what they want. Some even feel like it's owed them."

Chloe placed the check back on the table and continued her breakfast. We ate mostly in silence after that, and when we were done she helped me wash the dishes. "Are you going into the office today?"

I nodded, as I spread the dishtowel on the counter to dry. "I have to figure out who kidnapped the McKenzie boys. It's connected to the murders, I know, but I'm not sure how yet."

Chloe hesitated, then finally looked up at me. "Is it okay if I come over again tonight?"

I hesitated for a brief second when I thought about my sleeping problem, but then nodded. "I would love that."

CHAPTER 44

I was about to step inside the office when Melvin appeared in the doorway with a large evidence box in his hand.

"Bringing that to the lab?"

He nodded. "Susan went back to the plantation house to recover Red McKenzie's boat. Red called today to ask about it."

"Alright. Be careful." I waved at Lindsey on the way to my office, pushed the door shut. I pulled out the Act of Sale again and studied the signature of the notary. Try as I did, I couldn't make out a single letter. It was worse than my own handwriting. I scowled and tossed it aside. I turned to stare out the window. *What does this case have to do with me?*

I knew I needed to interview Mark McNeal because he was the only other living person with a connection to the meetings. I sighed. If he refused to talk, I'd be back to square one, but I had no other choice. "It's time to shake the murder tree."

I drove to Pauline Cain's house to see if she knew anything about the plantation home. I glanced to the sky as I parked my Tahoe. *At least it's not raining today.*

Stephen Butler led me to the back of the house, where Pauline was lying on a lounge chair in a bikini that looked like it was missing some parts. Dark sunglasses covered her eyes and a straw hat shaded her face. A tall glass of some type of fruity drink—no doubt heavy on the alcohol—rested on a glass-topped table next to her.

"Mrs. Cain," Stephen said. "Chief Wolf is here to—"

"Thank you, Stephen. I can see who it is." Without moving, Pauline waved me to sit in a chair next to her. "Please, Chief, sit and join me. Would you like a drink?"

"No, thanks. I'm here on business."

Pauline reached a hand to her sunglasses and pulled them down to see me more clearly. "And what business might that be?"

I pulled the Act of Sale to the plantation home Michele had purchased without my knowledge and handed it to her. "Do you know anything about this?"

She sat up and swung her long legs in my direction, cradling the deed in her lap. Her finger slid across the pages as she read. I knew when she reached Hays' name because her mouth dropped. "What the hell? When did he purchase that place? Why didn't I know anything about this? And who's this woman? Is it another of those sluts he was—" Pauline stopped, eyes squinted. After thinking about it for a full minute, she looked up at me knowingly. "This is your wife, isn't it?"

I nodded.

"I'm so sorry, Clint! May I call you Clint?"

I waved her off. "No need to apologize. Did you know anything about this?"

"No. I was hoping you could tell me more about it, but it looks like you were as much in the dark as I was."

Pauline read over the document again and huffed. "How could I not know about this? What else did he do that I didn't know about?"

"I know how you feel. I've been asking myself the same thing since I found out. I don't know how I missed it. I don't know when she had the opportunity to make this deal, much less how she paid for it. We never had that kind of money."

We both sat in silence for a while—Pauline staring at the Act of Sale and me staring at the ground, trying to keep my eyes from drifting to the vast amount of skin not covered by the tiny slivers of cloth that constituted her bikini.

Pauline finally handed the deed back over to me and shook her head. "I'm sorry, but I have no idea what this is about. I wish I could help, I really do. It sucks losing someone who kept so many secrets from you...so many lies." She paused to take a long drink from her sweaty glass. Frowning, she put it down. "I hope you get some resolution."

I thanked her and turned to walk away, but she stopped me.

"Clint, if you find out why he died and what he was involved in, please tell me all of it—the good, the bad, and the unbearable."

I only nodded, returned to my Tahoe and drove to the nearest store for a bottle of ketchup. I stopped at the plantation house and walked upstairs to the meeting room. After squirting ketchup on the floor, I scrawled a name into it and let it dry for a bit. When it looked right, I took a picture with my phone. I then headed out of town.

Mark McNeal was my last hope. If he couldn't—or wouldn't—tell me about the meetings, this case and my wife's secret would likely die with Hays Cain and Randall Rupe.

I walked into Platinum Star Bank in the central part of Chateau Parish and asked the teller at the counter if Mark McNeal was in. She studied the badge and gun strapped to my jeans, then glanced to her left at a woman with a nametag that read Branch Manager. I slid down the counter until I was in front of the manager. "Ma'am, I need to speak with Mr. McNeal right away. It's urgent."

The woman lifted the phone and dialed an extension. "Mark, there's a man here with a gun and badge, but no uniform, who says he needs to speak with you. Should I call the sheriff's office?"

My blood pressure started to rise, but I only smiled. "Do whatever makes you feel comfortable."

Although Mark McNeal couldn't see her, the woman nodded and hung up. She pointed across the spacious lobby to a door centered on the wall to my left. "Mr. McNeal said he'll see you."

Mark McNeal was not what I'd expected a bank owner to look like. While he was dressed in a spiffy suit, his face was weathered and his hands hard. He definitely spent a lot more time outdoors than he did behind his desk. I couldn't help but notice the giant canvas on the wall behind him. The gold nameplate tacked to the lower arm of the frame read, Gina Rochelle McNeal, 20, KIA.

I extended my hand. "Clint Wolf, chief of police in Mechant Loup."

"Nice to meet you, Clint." He took my hand and squeezed—a little too hard, as though he were trying to gain some psychological edge. I didn't care and didn't squeeze back. When he let my hand go, he waved me to the chair across from him. "Please, sit down."

I took a seat and made a casual scan of his desktop, but froze when my eyes came upon a five-by-seven picture frame containing a photo of five men dressed in BDU pants—only one wore a shirt, and he was positioned on the right. I pointed to it. "I've seen that picture before."

"I'm sure you have," Mark said in a casual tone. "You work for Malcolm."

"Malcolm's in here?" I studied the picture more closely. "None of them resemble him at all. Which one is he?"

"None of those kids resemble any of us anymore. That was a lifetime ago." Mark tilted the frame so he could see, stabbed the young man in the middle with a finger. "That was Malcolm back in the day."

"Shit, he's gained two people since then. He was a skinny kid, wasn't he?"

"We all were." Mark leaned back and the flaps of his jacket fell open, exposing a belly that tested the thread holding the buttons in place. "I've gained at least a hundred pounds since my days in the service."

"I graduated from the police academy at one-sixty, so I get it."

"You can't be more than—what?—one-ninety?"

"I'm one eighty-five." I turned my attention back to the picture on the desk. "Who are the others?"

"From left to right it's Randall Rupe, Daniel Blackley, Malcolm, me and Hays."

I leaned close to the picture, squinted. "What's Daniel Blackley holding?"

"TNT. He was always playing with explosives." Mark nodded. "Best explosives technician I ever met."

I nodded to indicate the picture on the wall behind Mark McNeal. "Is that your daughter?"

Mark turned his chair to stare up at the picture frame. "My oldest. When she died, the rest of us died with her. It's difficult to pull yourself together and go on after that happens. My other daughters and my wife were so lost. They still haven't recovered."

"I know the feeling."

Mark eyed me, but said nothing.

Something suddenly occurred to me. "I don't know if you know why I'm here today…"

I waited to see how Mark would respond. He only shrugged, while he stared coolly at me. I held the silence, waiting to see if Mark would feel the need to say something—anything. He didn't, and I realized I was dealing with a crafty one. I'd have to bullshit him a bit.

"You're aware that Hays Cain and Randall Rupe are dead, correct?"

"They were good friends of mine. Of course I'm aware they're dead. I was at their funerals."

"Are you aware that Hays Cain's murder was part of a larger plot?"

"What are you talking about?"

"Randall spoke to me before he died." I paused. I thought I saw Mark's complexion fade just a little, but his face was like stone.

"Randall told me Hays' murder had something to do with the meetings y'all were having about a secret operation."

"What meetings?" Mark seemed bored. "What secret operation?"

"The meetings that took place at the end of Paradise Place—at my house." I paused to let that information sink in. It was time to gamble. "He told me y'all were responsible for the murders of Hays Cain and Kelly Dykes and the kidnapping of two kids to protect the operation—to keep the secret. He also told me Hays was killed at my house."

"That's a good story, but I've never murdered or kidnapped anyone."

"You didn't get your hands dirty, of course, but your DNA is all over my house, making you an accomplice to everything that happened as a result of those meetings."

Mark McNeal—great poker player though he might have been—stumbled ever so slightly as his left eye twitched. "I don't know what you're talking about."

So, you were a part of the meetings, and those meetings had something to do with Cain, Dykes, and the McKenzie boys—but what was that larger scheme Randall told Chloe about?

I leaned forward. "Look, Mark, I know you didn't want any of this to happen. I know you didn't want your friend to die and I know you wouldn't hurt innocent kids, but those things happened and you're a part of it now—like it or not."

"You can't prove a thing." Mark's eyes shifted around the room, as though he were looking for an escape route, a place to hide. "That's conjecture, and you have no evidence to support any of it. My DNA could've been planted at the house. Hell, Randall, Hays and I were always together. If my DNA is really in that house, it could've been transferred from them." Mark's eyes were sparkling now. He was in charge again. "I suspect you are aware of cases where DNA has been deposited at crime scenes due to the transfer of trace evidence?"

"I am aware."

"Well, then you know these horrible events had nothing to do with me." Mark stood to end the meeting. "I wish you well in your investigation, but you are—as they say—barking up the wrong tree, Chief."

"Then how do you explain this?" I dug my phone out of my back pocket and accessed the last picture I'd taken, turned it up so Mark McNeal could see.

Mark tried to speak, but the words wouldn't come. Finally, he managed, "I...I didn't do that!"

CHAPTER 45

I returned my phone to my pocket before Mark McNeal had time to realize his name was actually scrawled in ketchup and not blood. Although I had intentionally taken a grainy picture to help disguise the fact it was ketchup, I didn't want to give him time to recover and get his confidence back. "Why then would a murder victim—your friend!—use his dying moments to write your name in his own blood?"

Mark sank to his chair, the life drained out of him. "It— I swear, it wasn't me. I don't even know what you're talking about."

"Look, it's not too late for you. Tell me what I want to know, and I'll talk to the district attorney for you—get you a reduced sentence."

Mark suddenly pursed his lips and shook his head. "Sorry, Chief, but I want my lawyer. I'm not talking today and I'm not talking ever."

Shit!

Although I was breaking dishes on the inside, I remained unmoved on the outside. "Have it your way, Mr. McNeal. When the house comes crashing down, you'll be buried under all the rubble." I pointed a finger at him. "And I'm going to enjoy watching your spineless ass be put to death for the murder of your friend—a man who served with you and who would've given his life for you."

Mark gritted his teeth, face red. "You won't be alive long enough to see it."

I stood and met his cold gaze with one of my own. "Are you threatening me?"

"Just exercising my right to free speech is all. No offense meant."

I nodded, flashed a disarming smile and leaned over, extending my hand to shake his. "No worries, sir, and no hard feelings. I'm just doing my job."

Mark hesitated, but finally sighed and reached up with his hand. We shook and, as he relaxed his hand to let go, I raked my fingernails roughly against the inside of his wrist and palm. He jerked his hand back. "Hey! You scratched me!"

"I'm sorry…just exercising my right to collect DNA from you."

"Wait— What did you say?" Mark leaped to his feet. "You can't do that!"

He continued to protest, but I walked out, allowing his threats of a lawsuit to fall on empty air.

I took great care to do everything with my left hand—open the bank door, fish out my keys, open the Tahoe door, remove a paper bag from my crime scene kit, carefully place the bag over my right hand, and use a rubber band to hold it in place. I then drove to the coroner's office and found Doctor Louise Wong leaning over the body of an elderly lady who had died of natural causes. Doctor Wong looked up, her face covered with a mask and shield.

I smiled, approached her. "I need you to scrape my fingernails."

"Excuse me?" she asked, her bloody gloved hands suspended above the body in front of her. "You want me to scrape your fingernails?"

"I scratched a murder suspect and have his DNA under my fingernails."

Doctor Wong quickly removed her gloves and washed her hands and arms. She removed a sex crimes kit from a top cabinet and ushered me onto a stool. She plopped into a saddle chair and wheeled up directly in front of me, then paused to look into my eyes. "I'm going to enjoy this."

I endured the process. Once she had packaged the cuttings and scrapings and sealed it as evidence, I signed the chain of custody form.

After thanking her and being forced to listen to her bitch about how little her husband did around the house, I drove to the office and filled out a crime lab submittal form for the clippings and scrapings Doctor Wong had recovered from my nails. As I wrote the information on the forms, the sensitive skin under my nails smarted from where she had rubbed the tip of the implement. I paused to stare down at my fingers, wondering if they would produce the results I suspected.

When I had finished filling out the form, I left it on Jack's desk, along with a note for him to drop the sex crimes kit off at the lab. On my way out, I stopped to check on Lindsey. "Anything going on today?"

"Nothing since this morning." Lindsey wrung her hands. "Chief, do I need to be worried? You know, I live alone with my little girl and my mom, and we don't even have a gun. Do we have to worry someone will come into our house and kill us, too? Like what happened to Kelly Dykes?"

"No, it's nothing you need to worry about. These killings were targeted—meaning, Hays Cain and Kelly Dykes were killed for a very specific reason. It wasn't random."

"What was the reason?"

I sighed. "I wish I knew."

"Then how can you say it was a targeted killing?"

I smiled and put my hand on her shoulder. "I promise...you don't have to worry."

I turned away from Lindsey's desk and walked outside to my Tahoe. I pursed my lips as I drove away. "It's got to be you, Mark McNeal...you're acting too guilty. Besides, an innocent man doesn't lawyer up."

I stopped at the town hall and met with Mayor Landry. He wasn't happy about my meeting with McNeal.

"Damn it, Clint, he's an important man in these parts. You can't just go accusing him of murder."

"He's acting like a guilty man."

"It doesn't matter how he's acting...you can't go scratching people to get their DNA. That's got to be illegal."

I shook my head. "It doesn't violate any rules of evidence or any of his rights. It's no different than if I had offered him a soda and then recovered the can for his fingerprints."

Mayor Landry sat with arms folded in front of his belly, a scowl cutting deep lines into his mug. "You really think he's involved?"

"He knows something. If he didn't kill them himself, he knows who did."

"Okay, but don't go near him again unless you have real evidence. We don't need a costly lawsuit during an election year."

I nodded my understanding. I glanced around the office. "Where's your picture?"

"What picture?"

I described the picture in Mark McNeal's office. "He said y'all served in the military together."

"We did."

"Hays Cain had that same picture in his office. Where's yours?"

"I don't keep that kind of stuff around. Those are days I'd rather forget. We can't talk about what we did, so I'd just as soon not have a conversation piece hanging around that might elicit questions I can't answer."

I nodded, staring at him as I sat deep in thought.

"What is it?" he wanted to know.

"I'm starting to wonder if that picture has something to do with this case."

"What do you mean?"

"Something's going on in this town, and so far, I know for a fact it involves three men—and all three of those men served together in the military. Now, two of them are dead and one's not talking, so that just leaves you and Daniel Blackley unaccounted for." I let that sink in. "Did something happen out there that would warrant these killings?"

"What are you getting at?"

"Let's say y'all did something while y'all were in the service that could land one—or all—of y'all in jail and y'all swore each other to secrecy. Let's imagine that later in life, Hays doesn't want to keep the secret any longer. Call it a guilty conscience, a change of heart, whatever. He decides he's coming clean, but some of y'all don't like it...and enough to kill Hays."

"You've got a hell of an imagination, I give you that." Mayor Landry laughed. "No, Clint, none of us did anything wrong out there."

"Randall Rupe was about to give up something big before he killed himself. I believe he was going to reveal the man who killed Hays Cain."

"What if he was about to confess to the killing, but he couldn't stand the thought of going to jail?"

I dismissed the idea with a wave. "No, he was scared of someone, that's for sure."

Mayor Landry frowned, but remained quiet.

"What were y'all meeting about?"

"What are you talking about?"

"The five of y'all...what were y'all meeting about? It had to be something important because two people were murdered over it and another killed himself."

"I don't know where you heard that nonsense, but we never had any meetings. The only time we get together is once or twice a year to honor our fallen children."

"Then tell me this..." I shot a thumb to the front of the building, where Mayor Landry's town car was parked. "Why was your car seen out at that plantation house at the end of Paradise Place with the rest of them?"

I thought I saw the front of Mayor Landry's neck jump in response to my bluff—right where his carotid artery was located—but I couldn't be sure.

"I don't know where you're getting these wild theories, but I don't appreciate your implications."

"It's no theory," I said with feigned confidence. "I can show you the surveillance logs."

Mayor Landry's eyes flashed. "Need I remind you that the chief of police in Mechant Loup serves at the pleasure of the mayor? In this case, that means you serve at my pleasure. If I tell you to tie my shoes and you refuse, I can fire you."

I stood and smiled. "Try giving me that order and see what happens."

"God damn it, Clint." Mayor Landry took a deep breath and blew it out forcefully. "Look, I brought you here because I need you— *want* you—to run this police department the right way. The way it should be run. You share my values and my vision for this town and we'll do great things together."

"I don't think we share the same values at all."

"You're right in that we don't share every single value, but the important ones are there." Mayor Landry stood to stare down at me. "For instance, I don't agree with the lies you told today, with the way you came at me, but I'm willing to overlook them and let bygones be bygones so we can move forward with tomorrow's ribbon cutting."

"What lies are you talking about?"

"The lies about my license plate being on some surveillance log. That vehicle has never been out that way."

I felt my own carotid artery pulsate and studied his expression closely. He was cool under pressure—that was for sure. As I wondered if I should acknowledge my bluff or double down, Mayor Landry lifted his hands in the surrender position.

"Look, I appreciate your tenacity. It's what we need around here. But the truth is I'm not dirty. I'm one of the good guys, just like you are. We're on the same team. I want you to solve the murder of my friend as bad you want it solved." Mayor Landry's eyebrows came together above the bridge of his nose. "I don't know anything about these meetings you keep talking about and I don't know who killed one of my closest friends, but when you find out, I want to be the first to know. As God is my witness, I'll be there when that asshole is put to death."

I nodded, sighed. If he knew anything about the killings, he certainly wasn't putting off any vibes. "I need to bring Mark in for questioning. I'll do it with a warrant if I have to."

"A warrant? For what?"

"He threatened me. Said I wouldn't be alive long enough to see him pay for his crimes."

Mayor Landry's eyes narrowed. "That does sound like a threat."

"I also need to bring Daniel Blackley in. He might know something."

"I agree with you." Mayor Landry dropped to his chair. "Can you at least wait until Monday to bring them in? I need you to focus your efforts on the ribbon-cutting ceremony, if you don't mind. This is important to everyone in town. I want tomorrow to be perfect. I want it to be the greatest day in the history of Mechant Loup. Not just for me, but for my boy." Mayor Landry quickly lowered his head and grabbed his face.

After several minutes of silence, I asked, "Are you okay?"

When he lifted his head, his eyes were red. "I miss Alex so much. If I do nothing else with my life, I just want to honor his memory and the memory of Mechant Loup's other children who died serving their country. This dedication that we're doing tomorrow…I've been working on it for several years. The day is finally here. It's finally going to happen. They'll finally get the recognition they deserve. And I don't want anything messing it up, so if you'll please put the case on the back burner for one day, I'll do whatever I can to help you break Mark down and make him confess."

I thought about it and finally nodded. If I could do something to honor the memories of Abigail and Michele, I sure wouldn't want anyone screwing with it. "I can do that. I'll suspend the case until Monday. We have some evidence to work up anyway."

"Thanks." Mayor Landry stared off into the distance. "I just wish Hays and Randall could be here to see it happen. Whatever they were into, they didn't deserve to die."

CHAPTER 46

It was sunny outside, but the light was waning fast. Even though I decided to call it a day, I stopped at the police department. William and Melvin were in the break room. "Where's Susan?"

Melvin looked up. "She's on a complaint."

"William, I put a note on Jack's desk along with a crime lab submittal form. When he gets in tomorrow morning, can you make sure he delivers the sex crimes kit to the lab?"

"Sure thing."

"How's your wife, Melvin?"

"She's good. She spent all day picking out paint for the baby's room, so guess what I'll be doing this weekend?"

"If you need help, let me know. Unless Chloe's got plans for me, I'll be free this weekend."

"Chloe, the news reporter?" William asked.

I nodded.

Melvin said, "I might take you up on that offer, Chief."

"Well, I'm heading out. Stay safe, William. Melvin, I'll see you in the morning." I turned to walk out of the break room, but Susan rushed in, and we nearly collided. She put both hands on my chest to stop herself, then looked up into my eyes. Her lips were parted and deep lines of concern were etched into her face. "Clint, we need to talk." She leaned to look behind me. "Y'all come with us!"

Susan turned on her heel and hurried to my office and held the door until Melvin, William, and I were inside.

"What's going on?" I asked.

She slammed the door shut. "Someone wants you dead."

I just stared, her words bouncing around inside my head.

"Wait...what'd you say?"

"You heard me. This is real—it's not a drill."

William and Melvin gasped, asking in unison, "Someone wants him dead?"

"Who?" I asked. "Beaver?"

Susan shook her head. "Pauline Cain called earlier, said she needed to talk to me or you right away—in person. You weren't in, so I drove out to her house."

"I was just at her house earlier today. I just saw her."

"She told me you were there. Anyway, it seems not long after you left, she receives a call from Jennifer McNeal—"

"Mark's wife?" I asked.

"Yeah. Their kids, Allen and Gina, had dated since high school, so Pauline and Jennifer are close. It seems Mark rushed home after you met with him and a man she'd never met showed up at the house. They were talking about you."

My brows furrowed. "What did the man look like? Did she say?"

"She didn't get to see him; she just heard them arguing. And then the man told Mark to settle down and not worry about a thing. He said..." Susan bit her lip, shook her head. "The man said you'd be dead by the weekend."

A chill reverberated up and down my spine. Sure, I'd been threatened many times in my line of work and it had never bothered me, but to be given a time frame—to be told you only had a couple of days to live? That made it real. Made it seem like a bullet was already in flight, heading my direction with my name all over it, and there was nothing I could do to stop it. I whistled. "Mark told me to my face that I wouldn't live to see him punished for his crimes."

"Mark McNeal threatened you?" Melvin asked. "I'll go out and kill his ass right now!"

"I'm with you." William smashed his fist on my desk.

"Simmer down, boys," Susan said. "We don't know who else is involved, so getting Mark will only tip our hand."

I took a seat behind my desk to ponder what I'd just learned.

"Randall told your girlfriend all of this was part of a larger scheme," Susan said. "You might be that larger scheme."

Melvin's head bobbed up and down. "She's right. There's nothing bigger than killing a cop—especially a chief of police."

Susan placed her palms on my desk, her face inches from mine. "Please listen to me. You need to keep your head down. Give yourself a few days off. Lay low until we figure out who wants you dead. At least until the weekend is over."

I scowled. "I will *not* let these bastards interfere with my life. If they want me dead, they can come for me. If they do, they'll be killed, and we'll know exactly who they are."

"That's what I'm talking about," William said. "I'm with you, Chief."

"Cut the bravado shit, William!" Susan straightened and crossed her arms in front of her chest. "This is not some shoot 'em up game. This is real life, where death plays for keeps. What would you do if someone threatened to kill me? Would you expect me to go to work as usual? Or would you make me stay home and avoid danger?"

"Sorry, Susan. I'm not going into hiding. If someone wants me dead, they know where to find me." I got up and started to walk past Susan, but she grabbed my left bicep. Her grip was firm. I looked down at her hand, then back up into her dark eyes. "I won't go into hiding."

"I'm not asking you to go into hiding. I'm just asking you to stay home. Give yourself a day or two off. You're constantly working overtime, so you definitely have time on the books you can take."

I smiled. "I'm salaried. I don't get overtime."

"Clint, this is not a joke. Someone wants you dead."

I turned from Susan to look at Melvin, who stood with jaw set, his face a few shades lighter than I was used to seeing. "Chief, you have to listen to her. If something happens to you, what's going to happen to us?"

"Okay," I said. "I'll pick up the governor in the morning and bring him to the new town hall. Then I'll head home."

"Not going to happen," Susan said. "Melvin will pick up the governor."

I shook my head. "Mayor Landry was explicit—I was to pick up the governor in my new Tahoe at nine sharp and bring him straight to the ribbon-cutting ceremony."

Susan shot her thumb at Melvin. With her other hand firmly on her hip, she said, "Give Melvin your Tahoe keys."

I hesitated.

Melvin stuck out his hand. "She's serious, Chief. You'd better do it."

"But what about the mayor? He'll be pissed."

"He'll never know," Susan said. "I'll meet Melvin in the parking lot and escort the governor to the ribbon-cutting area. And since when did you give a shit what the mayor thought?"

I glanced at the clock on the bottom corner of my computer screen. It was getting late, and I needed to hurry home to make dinner for Chloe and me, so I didn't have time to argue. "Fine, y'all win." *I'll come in tomorrow and settle this shit.* I fished my keys from my pocket and handed them to Melvin. He handed me the keys to his patrol cruiser.

I looked at Susan, raised my eyebrows. "Can I go home now, *Mom?*"

"Yeah, but go straight home—don't pass Go and don't collect two hundred dollars."

As I walked out, I heard Susan tell William to follow me.

"I don't need a babysitter," I called over my shoulder.

"It's called an escort," Susan retorted.

I called Chloe as I drove home. She answered on the first ring.

"Hey, Clint, how are you?"

"I'm good. Are we still on for tonight?"

"Absolutely. I'll be there in an hour."

"Great!" I said. "Dinner should be done by then."

I hung up, then stopped at the grocery store for two thick ribeyes and other miscellaneous groceries. I frowned when I saw William pull into the lot and park facing Melvin's car. I walked over to him and leaned into his window. "William, you don't have to follow me. I really believe this is just a hoax. Nothing to worry about."

"Chief, I know you're my boss and you can fire me if you want, but Susan can kick my ass." He nodded as if to reinforce his statement. "No offense, but I'm more scared of her than I am of you."

I laughed, nodding my understanding. "Well, thanks for the escort."

When I was done at the grocery store, I rushed home and lit the pit. While it was heating, I took Achilles out to pee. When we came in, I turned on the flat screen television in my living room and prepped the meat on the kitchen counter. The local news anchor was talking about the ribbon-cutting ceremony, and I groaned. *The mayor is going to be pissed at me when he finds out I'm not bringing the governor!* The thought of his puffy cheeks stretching to the point of ripping brought a smile to my face.

Achilles danced at my feet, his body wriggling with excitement. I looked down, nodded. "Yeah, buddy, I've got one for you, too."

CHAPTER 47

Twenty minutes later, I was on the back porch with Achilles and had just placed the slabs of meat on the hot grill. The steaks sizzled and the aroma of searing meat rose to greet me like an old friend when my phone rang. My stomach growled.

"Damn that smells good!" I pulled the phone to my ear. It was Melvin.

"I need to talk to you about something. It's serious."

"Did Susan put you up to this? She's really going too far."

"No. I came on my own." Melvin's voice sounded different, like he was upset. "I need to show you something."

"Wait...are you here? Are you at my house now?" I leaned over and stared through the back door glass to where I could see a shadow through the front curtain.

"It's urgent, Chief."

"Um...okay. I'm coming." I put the tongs on the table beside the pit, walked inside and through my house, opened the front door. Melvin stood there wringing his hands, a camera slung over his shoulder. I glanced across the street, where William was parked watching my house. I shook my head and turned to Melvin. "What's going on?"

"Chief, I don't know how to say this. It's kind of... I feel awkward being here."

"What is it?"

Melvin took a deep breath, exhaled. "You know that Chloe Rushing used to date Beaver when he was chief of police, right?"

I nodded slowly. "Yeah...and?"

Melvin stared at his boots. "I was on my way home and...well...I saw…"

"Melvin, just spit it out."

"I saw Chloe with Beaver. They were together in her car. They were parked at the end of the boat launch. It's where people usually meet for…you know…to…um…to have sex sometimes."

"That's not possible. You must've seen wrong. She should be heading this way right now." I pulled out my phone and started to dial her number.

"Chief, wait." Melvin removed the camera from his shoulder and messed with the buttons. "Look, I'm not wrong."

I slowly took the camera from him and looked at the display screen. It was a clear shot of Chloe's car. She was in the driver's seat, her body facing Beaver, who was apparently talking. His mouth was partially open, and his hands were in the air.

"I'm sorry, Chief." Melvin's voice was soft, nearly a whisper.

"It's okay. Thanks for telling me. I appreciate the loyalty." I handed him the camera and went back inside, then closed the door behind me. I stared at Chloe's number on my phone, frozen. *Do I call her? If so, what do I say?*

I pressed the call button and was still trying to figure out what I would say when she answered. It startled me, and I stammered.

"Clint? Is that you?" asked her sweet voice.

"Um…yeah, I was…um…wondering how long you'd be? The steaks are almost done."

"Oh, shit, I'm so sorry." There was a long pause. I thought I heard her whisper and a door slam, but the phone was muffled so I couldn't be sure. "Baby, I'm sorry. I'll have to take a rain check. Something's come up."

My heart sank to the soles of my boots. "Something's come up?"

"Yeah, I'm working on a story and it'll be a while. Maybe tomorrow night?"

"Sure." I ended the call and let my phone fall to the floor. I felt numb. My chest ached. *How could I have been such a fool?*

Achilles, sensing something was wrong, whimpered as he strode beside me. I walked to the back porch, stared down at the smoking pit, walked back into the kitchen. I stood there, the weight of my body pushing down on my haggard legs. Slowly, I sank to my knees, realization swarming over me. Achilles sidled up beside me and nestled his cool, wet nose in the crook of my arm. I'd been played— first by Michele and now by Chloe.

"God, I'm such a fool!"

Achilles whined as he tried to squirm closer to me. I rubbed his neck with an idle hand. I don't know how long I knelt there, but smoke billowing in the back door drew me from my stupor. My feet dragged as I made my way to the pit. Using the tongs, I opened the hood and nearly choked when the thick gray smoke engulfed me. My eyes smarted. The smell of burnt meat singed my nostril hairs.

Achilles barked beside me, as though he could somehow scare away the threat. I told him to sit, and he complied. I then pulled the steaks from the grill with the tongs and tossed them into the yard. Achilles followed the meat with his eyes and his ears perked up, but he stayed seated.

I left the hood open on the pit so it could air out and stood there staring at the smoldering meat, hands shoved deep in my pocket, shoulders slumped. My mind was blank. When the ribeyes appeared cool enough, I waved for Achilles to go get them, and he did. He attacked them with the same ferociousness I wanted to direct at Beaver. I clenched my fists in my pockets and felt the fabric stretch. *Do I call her and tell her I know about her and Beaver?* I shook my head. *That'll make me look crazy, like I've been following her. Besides, she doesn't owe me anything. No one said anything about exclusivity.*

I sighed, walked back inside. As I stared at it, my heart pounded against my chest. *Don't do it. It's too early.*

I stood there for a long time, staring at the handle to my liquor cabinet. It was dark outside and Achilles was scratching to come back inside before I turned my eyes away from it. I let Achilles in. He lapped up some water from his bowl, curled up in a corner of the living room to sleep—fat with content.

I should've been hungry, but I wasn't. I sat on the sofa and closed my eyes, trying to focus on nothingness. The television droned in the background. It didn't sound like the news anymore, but I didn't open my eyes to see. I felt myself slipping…

I jerked awake when Abigail's face returned to haunt my dreams. I glanced at the clock. *Shit!* I'd only been sleeping for five minutes.

A loud chirping noise sounded from the living room floor. I looked in the direction and saw my phone. I suddenly remembered. I grew nauseous. I stood and walked to the kitchen to dig out a bottle of vodka.

Like a man who'd just reached an oasis after crawling through the desert for days, I twisted off the cap and brought the bottle to my mouth with hands that shook. I drank deep, gobbling up the smooth liquid. I finally put the bottle down and gasped for air. It warmed my throat, and the warmth moved downward through my chest and into my stomach. I sighed, then took another drink. I grabbed a second bottle, because it felt like that kind of a night.

I returned to the sofa and stared blankly at the television as I drank, allowing the liquor to do its job. I felt it in my lips first. They began to tingle. The sharp pain in my chest slowly began to fade to a dull throb. My eyes slid shut and I started to drift off—*Damn it!* My phone again. I jerked up and rushed across the living room, snatched it from the floor and looked at the screen. *Chloe.* With a grunt, I flung the phone across the room. It smashed violently against the far wall and separated into dozens of pieces. Achilles yelped in surprise and darted into his crate and curled up in the corner.

I turned and realized the room was spinning. I stumbled back to the sofa, where I reached for the bottle of vodka. It was empty. I uttered another grunt and stretched out on the sofa to sleep.

CHAPTER 48

Friday, July 4

I thought I heard someone calling my name. I tried to lift my head, but winced at the shot of pain that stabbed through my brain. The backs of my eyelids were bright, so I knew it was morning. I forced them open and looked through the blur. I was in my living room. Alone. Something smelled awful. I glanced down and saw vomit on my shirt. It was still damp against my chest. "Shit!"

I started to sit up, then heard my name again through the haze. *What the—*

I nearly choked on my tongue when I saw my picture plastered on the television screen. It was a mugshot from my years working in the city, and there was a caption at the bottom that read, Clint William Wolf, Dead at 29. I was instantly alert, cocking my head sideways in confusion.

"…had recently joined the Mechant Loup Police Department as its chief of police. Sources tell us he lost his daughter and wife in a botched armed robbery two years ago and that his hatred for the governor stemmed from the governor's policy prohibiting law enforcement officers from carrying their weapons into privately owned businesses while off-duty. In other news, a shooting downtown has left three people dead and another injured. Police say—"

I scrambled across the floor, feeling for the remote. I finally found it and switched through the channels, searching for a news station that was still playing the story. I tried all the local stations, but they had moved on to other news. As I scrolled through the higher channels, I came across a national news channel and froze when I saw a picture of the governor beside a picture of me. Panic settled into my chest and smothered me as I listened to the anchorwoman talk.

"An explosion at a local airport has rocked a small community deep in south Louisiana and sent waves of panic across the entire state as officials confirm that Governor Lester Katz lost his life today in what authorities are calling a clear terror attack. Law enforcement agencies throughout the state, and even the country, are on high alert today as they anticipate other such attacks. Chloe Rushing is a local reporter for the town of Mechant Loup and is on the ground near the site of the explosion. She has more on this developing story. Chloe…"

Chloe appeared on camera wearing jeans and a T-shirt, her hair in a ponytail and a microphone in her hand. She stood in front of the plantation home Michele had purchased without my knowledge. I felt sick.

"Thanks, Jenn. Yes, state police officials have confirmed that the governor and his colonel were killed in an explosion early this morning at an airport in central Chateau Parish. They have also confirmed that Chief of Police Clint Wolf is a suspect in the assassination of the sixtieth…sixtieth governor of the…the…um…the State of Louisiana—"

Chloe's chin began to tremble, as she struggled to get another word out, but couldn't. She dropped her head and pushed the microphone against her face and wept. The camera quickly returned to the anchorwoman, who looked stunned. She quickly recovered when she realized she was live again.

"A very emotional day in that small community, as you can see there. What our affiliate has learned from a confidential source is that explosives were found inside an old plantation home belonging to Police Chief Clint Wolf's deceased wife, and they believe it is where he built the bomb used to kill the governor. Sources say Wolf had been at odds with the governor's policies ever since he worked as a homicide detective in the city, and he directly blamed the governor for the horrendous murders of his wife and daughter two years ago.

"According to news reports, the ex-detective was having dinner with his family when four gunmen—believed to be part of the riots plaguing the city during that time period—stormed the restaurant in an armed robbery attempt. Because of a bill that the governor had signed into law banning off-duty officers from carrying their weapons in private businesses, Wolf was unarmed when he interceded to thwart the robbery. He failed in his attempt and his wife and daughter died, causing the state legislature and the governor's office to reconsider their earlier stance on the issue.

"Authorities believe the disgruntled ex-detective attached a bomb to the undercarriage of his official police vehicle and detonated it when the governor and his assistant entered the SUV. Wolf was among the dead, and police are calling this a suicide bombing—"

"Melvin!" I lurched forward to my hands and knees and vomited on the floor. Clear liquid sprayed from my lips, splashing onto the floor. Images flashed through my mind...images of a young, pregnant wife waiting for her husband to get home with her latest craving...of her lying in a hospital bed with no one to curse during childbirth...a young child walking to the bus stop for the first time with only one hand being held...a teenager playing football or cheerleading with an empty seat next to Mommy...

Wave after wave spewed from my stomach. I gasped for air. My head pounded. Throat burned from the bile that spilled from my mouth. Through tear-blurred eyes, I saw Achilles pad over and begin licking the floor in front of me. I pushed at him between heaves, but he persisted.

"God, no! Not Melvin!" I clenched my fists and pounded the floor. My knuckles hurt at first, but soon they were as numb as my insides. I looked to the ceiling, screamed, "Why, God? Why did you do that to him? Why not me?"

As I struggled to come to grips with Melvin's death and calm my gut, the anchorwoman's voice buzzed in the background. I wiped my mouth on my sleeve and pulled myself to my feet. The threat on my life had been real, but I wasn't the target—I was the patsy. I scanned the floor for my phone, then noticed the pieces strewn about and grunted.

A picture of the governor and his family flashed up on the screen. As I stared through the haze, my cold heart wept for them. His kids were young. One had to be ten and the other couldn't be more than six. His wife was beautiful, but in a plain and wholesome way. They looked like a happy family. He looked like a caring father and a loving husband.

It suddenly hit me like a wrecking ball to the solar plexus—it was not his fault Michele and Abigail had been killed. His policies were a reflection of his life, his experiences. As reckless as I thought his policies were, I had to admit he had done what he thought was best for the state and for the citizens of Louisiana. His policies had nothing to do with the murders of my family—*he* had nothing to do with the murders. Bad people had taken advantage of his policies, but he had no way of knowing that would happen. And now bad people had left two wives—one pregnant—without husbands and three kids—one unborn—without fathers.

I gritted my teeth. "Someone's responsible for this, and they'll have to pay…with their lives!"

I ripped my dirty shirt off and started toward my bedroom when boots stomped on my front porch. I darted into my bedroom and snatched my pistol from the nightstand. I stopped in the doorway with my pistol aimed toward the front of the house. Someone pounded on the door. It shook on its hinges.

"Clint! Wake the hell up!"

I lowered my pistol, exhaling the lungful of air I'd been holding. It was Susan. I rushed to the door and opened it. "Did you see this shit?"

Susan jerked her head back to look me up and down. "What happened to you?"

I pulled her inside and slammed the door shut. "Melvin's dead! He took my place and now he's dead!"

"I know. I've been calling you all morning."

I pointed to the mess on the floor. "My phone's broken."

Susan frowned. "We need to get you out of here."

"I'm not going anywhere."

Susan charged into my living room and shot her index finger toward the television. "Someone just blew up the governor and pinned it on you. When they find out they got the wrong person—and that won't take very long—they'll be coming here to finish the job."

"They won't have to come here because I'm going to them."

"Them *who?* We have no idea who did this."

"Mark McNeal definitely knows something, and I'm going to find out what." I walked into my bedroom to grab a shirt from my drawer.

Susan stayed on my heels. "Clint, listen to me! They think you're dead—we need to use that to our advantage."

I slipped on the fresh shirt, opened my gun safe, pulled out my load-bearing vest and shrugged into it. I checked the ammo pouches—six thirty-round magazines in .223 caliber. I grabbed an extra pistol and secured it into the holster attached to the front of the vest, then slung the AR-15 over my shoulder.

"Clint, what are thinking?" Susan forced herself in front of me. She grabbed my shoulders and pulled my face close to hers. "Where do you think you're going?"

"Mark McNeal knows something, and I'm going to find out what—even if it means I have to kill him."

"You're talking crazy, Clint. You've got to chill out."

"Sue, they killed Melvin...Melvin! He'd never hurt anyone. I don't even know why he was a cop. He was too nice for this type of work."

"Look, I'll go talk to Mark McNeal—find out what he knows. Get a hat and sunglasses so no one recognizes you, and I'll take you someplace safe. We need to keep the fact you're still breathing a secret as long as we can. Once they realize you're alive, they will definitely come after you to finish the job."

"Good—then I'll know who's behind it."

"I'm not losing you, Clint Wolf!" Susan cupped my face with both of her hands, staring intently into my eyes. "For once in your stubborn life, can you trust someone other than yourself? As long as they think you're dead, we have an advantage. Let me do some snooping around and see what I can find out. I know what I'm doing."

Her hands were warm. "These people are dangerous, Sue. I'm not going to let you go out there alone."

"I won't be alone. I'll get William and Jack to come with me. Besides, we're not a danger to them. They didn't want us dead; they wanted you dead. We're invisible to them."

I stared into her eyes and began to melt in the warmth of her touch. That touch, that feeling...it was strangely familiar. I searched the recesses of my memory, desperately trying to recall where I'd experienced it. Finally, I sighed, pulling her hands away from my face. "Okay, we'll do it your way, but if you don't find out anything within twenty-four hours, we do it my way."

She nodded, then followed me into the living room. We both stopped when we heard Mayor Landry's voice on the television.

"It's so hard to believe that Clint Wolf did this. I never would've guessed it. He seemed normal, you know? I never would've hired him had I known how much hate he had for the governor."

Mayor Landry wiped his brow, shook his head, and continued. "He insisted on being the one to pick up the governor, but I didn't think anything of it. Now, I know why."

"That lying sack of shit! He's in on it." I spun to Susan. "I need to talk to him. You need to help me get inside the town hall so I can confront that cowardly bastard. That bastard is going to tell me what he knows even if I have to beat him to death!"

"No way! That place is crawling with SWAT from the state police and the sheriff's office. You wouldn't make it across the street without being arrested or shot."

She was right, of course, but I didn't like it. I looked at her standing there, fists balled up, shoved into her waist. I pushed my lips together. "Even Chloe thinks I killed the governor. Why don't you?"

"Because you're still alive, you dope."

"Good point." I grabbed a ball cap and a pair of dark sunglasses from my closet and walked out with Susan. Achilles tried to follow us, but I told him to stay put. "You can't come on this adventure, little buddy. It's too damn dangerous." I didn't even bother putting him in his crate. I was supposed to be dead anyway, so what did I care about a few sofa cushions?

CHAPTER 49

"Where are we?" I asked when we drove down a long street set back in the trees. Susan turned onto a driveway made of dirt.

"My place."

"Your place?"

Susan parked in front of a modest house, painted light green and trimmed in white. It was about a foot off the ground and a square porch was cut into the right side of the house. A yellow bench was positioned against the wall and a red punching bag hung from the center of the porch.

Susan shoved the Charger into park and killed the engine. "Yep, it's my little piece of paradise. You'll be safe here."

"I'm safe everywhere." I grabbed my rifle and walked down the cemented driveway behind Susan. She reached under a pot behind the bench, removed a key, and let us in.

"Make yourself at home." Susan tossed the key on the coffee table and waved her hand around. "What's mine is yours. There's food in the kitchen, the bathroom's down the hall, and the keys to my truck are on the ring by the back door, but don't go anywhere unless it's an emergency."

I nodded, then leaned my rifle in the corner nearest the door and shrugged out of my vest. I sank onto the sofa and my thoughts went immediately back to Melvin and his pregnant wife. I frowned, wondering if she even knew. I posed the question to Susan.

"I know it sucks, but we can't tell her anything right now. We need to keep your—"

"I get it. I get it. No one can know I'm alive. It just sucks." I clenched my fists. "I swear to you, Susan, when I find out who did this to Melvin, I'm going to kill them."

"What about the governor? He's dead, too. Would you kill them for him, too?"

"Yeah, he is dead, isn't he?" I sighed. "I didn't like him or his policies, but he didn't deserve to die."

Susan stripped the police radio from her belt and pointed to the channel knob. "Seven is the sheriff's office and nine is the state police. Flip this button and it'll scan all the channels."

I took it and thanked her. "What about you?"

"I've got an extra one in the car." Susan slid open a drawer under the coffee table and pulled out a cell phone, then powered it on. "This is an old throw-away phone, but it works. My number's programmed in the contacts."

I examined it and found the contact section with her number. "Yours is the only number in here. What if I need to call someone else?"

"I'm the only one who knows you're alive, so you shouldn't be calling anyone else. Now, I'll head to the town hall and see what the mayor's up to. I'll be back around lunchtime. Follow the radio traffic and stay inside." Before waiting for my response, Susan darted out the door and sped out of the driveway.

I spent a restless couple of hours pacing the floors, checking the volume on the radio to make sure it was working, and surfing the channels on the large flat screen television in Susan's living room. The police radio was silent, and the news channels were playing the same feeds as earlier, with so-called experts explaining my motivation for killing the governor.

I suddenly remembered my mom. I snatched Susan's phone from my pocket, but I just stared at it. I wanted to call to let her know I was still alive. Susan's words echoed in the back of my mind, and I knew she was right, but what if the news of my supposed death was too much for my mom's heart to handle? I started dialing her number, but stopped when I heard a noise outside.

I craned my neck, listened. Car doors slammed outside—*two* of them. I stalked to the doorway and grabbed my rifle. Boots stomped on the wooden porch. I dropped to a kneeling position in the corner, my rifle trained on the doorway. A key was inserted into the hole and the door swung open. I lowered the muzzle when Susan appeared behind the door.

"I thought I heard two doors slam," I said. "I must be getting—"

My jaw dropped to the floor when a man walked through the doorway behind Susan. "What the hell?" My rifle clanked to the floor. I stood slowly to my feet and stared in disbelief. "What the hell is going on? I thought you were dead!"

Melvin nodded, his eyes hollow, chin set. "I...I was all set to go get the governor, but Jack—" Melvin shook his head, then lowered it. His eyes grew moist.

Susan put a hand on his shoulder. "Stop beating yourself up over it. It's not your fault."

I rushed over and wrapped him in a bear hug. When I let go, I pushed him back and stared at him, my own eyes misting. "It's so good to see you, Melvin! I was so worried for your wife, and I thought your baby would have to grow up without a dad. God, it's so good to see you!" I took a deep breath and exhaled, relief flooding me with emotion. "So, what happened?"

"Jack...you know how Jack's always trying to order everyone around," Susan said. "Jack ordered Melvin to go to the crime lab and took your Tahoe to pick up the governor. He said since he was the lieutenant, he should be the one to pick up the governor."

"So, Jack's dead?" I asked.

Melvin nodded. "I tried to tell him that you wanted me to go, but he wouldn't listen. I even tried calling you, but your phone went straight to voicemail."

I slapped his shoulder. "Look, like Susan said, this isn't your fault. Some asshole planted that bomb and that's who's responsible—no one else."

"I know what y'all are saying, but it's just taking me a while to get over it. I mean, that was supposed to be me."

"No, that was supposed to be me." I pursed my lips. "Not Jack and not you. Y'all were completely innocent in all of this." I turned to Susan. "Did you find out anything?"

"It's not good." She closed the door and walked to the kitchen. While she made a pot of coffee, she told me what she had learned at the town hall. "They ran a search warrant on your house and found a gun under your mattress."

I scowled. "I don't keep a gun under my mattress."

"It wasn't your gun—it was the gun that killed Hays Cain and Kelly Dykes."

"What the hell?" I leaned against her counter. "How'd that get there? They must've planted it."

"They didn't have time. I was there with them."

"What—you think I did this now?"

"No, not at all," Susan said quickly. "While I know the gun was planted at some point, it wasn't planted today. Reginald Hoffman is leading the investigation and he's not dirty."

"Reginald Hoffman?" I nodded. "I met him."

"He's the chief investigator for the district attorney's office. He worked for the sheriff's office for years. After he broke this one murder case that no one else could break, the district attorney hired him to oversee all of the major cases in the parish."

"He's the best investigator in Chateau," Melvin said. "And he's fair. He'll figure this out and clear your name."

"I'm not as optimistic. The evidence is damning, and people in high places have their hands in this." Susan took out three coffee cups and started to fill them.

I waved mine off.

She handed one to Melvin and sipped on the other, then nodded toward me. "So, we need to figure out who had the chance to get into your house and plant that gun."

"No one comes to my house," I said.

"Well, there was one person," she said slowly.

I shook my head. "Nope. Chloe would never do that."

Susan raised an eyebrow. "Do you really know her? Melvin told me about last night. We all know Beaver's dirty. Hell, she's the one who exposed him. He must have something on her. He might be in on the whole deal and he could've used her to plant the gun."

I couldn't argue with her, so I just clamped my mouth shut.

"Is there a reason why Chloe would want you dead?" Susan asked.

I shook my head. "This is not about me. It's about the governor. We need to figure out who'd want the governor dead."

"You mean besides you?"

I grunted with amusement. Susan's bluntness was a quality I appreciated.

"Tell him about the explosives," Melvin offered.

I looked from Susan to Melvin. "What explosives?"

"They found some empty containers with the logo for Blackley and Sons Industries in your shed," Susan said. "There were traces of ammonium nitrate in the containers. Daniel Blackley is now claiming they were stolen in the burglary out at his warehouse. I remember reading the report. He said nothing was in that building."

I suddenly straightened. "The burglary…the one at my house! They didn't break in to steal anything. They broke in to plant that shit!"

"That makes sense." Susan shoved a loaf of bread in Melvin's direction, and he began making sandwiches for their lunch. "But who did it?"

My mind raced. Something I'd seen and heard had haunted me from the moment I'd seen and heard it, but I hadn't been able to make sense out of it until just then. "Daniel Blackley—he was an explosives technician in the military."

Susan and Melvin both raised their eyebrows.

"So?" Susan asked. "He doesn't have a reason to kill the governor. The governor was about to honor his dead son by dedicating the new town hall to him."

I nodded slowly, the pieces coming together inside my head. We ate sandwiches as I told them my theory.

Susan whistled when I was done. "I think you're onto something. Now, how do we prove it?"

"I'll take care of that part." I bit into the last of my sandwich and stood to throw away my trash. Out of the corner of my eye, I saw Susan and Melvin exchange glances. "What's going on, y'all?"

Susan's eyes fell. "There's something I need to tell you. Something I should've told you right when we walked through the door."

"What?"

"Where's your bathroom, Susan?" Melvin asked. "I don't want to be here when you tell him."

Susan pointed toward the hallway. "Third door on the right."

Melvin hurried off.

"What is it?" I asked. "What's going on?"

"One of the operators on the state police SWAT team—a guy named Cade LeBlanc—he shot Achilles."

CHAPTER 50

My blood was still boiling six hours later, but I knew I had to concentrate on the task at hand. Susan and Melvin had long since gone back to the town hall to keep tabs on the mayor and to try to get word to Reginald Hoffman about the conspiracy, and they thought I was hanging out at Susan's house waiting on them to return. I wasn't.

After another hour, or so, Mark McNeal finally exited the bank and got into his car. He drove away, and I followed. We zigzagged through town for about ten minutes, until we came to what must've been his house. I parked two blocks away and snatched my rifle from the seat beside me. I locked Susan's truck. I crept through the neighborhood until I reached the sidewalk to his house, watching as Mark McNeal unlocked his front door. His phone was pinned to his ear with one hand and he worked the key with the other.

I took a deep breath, as I prepared myself for what was about to follow. As soon as his door swung open, I closed the distance between us in an instant, making no sound other than my boots scraping cement. He was preoccupied with his conversation and didn't know what hit him.

I shoved him hard and sent him reeling into the foyer, his phone flying from his hand. He crashed into the far wall and collapsed to the ground in a heap. Before he could turn around, I kicked the door shut behind me and leveled my rifle at the back of his head.

He spun around with deceptive ease, but froze when he saw the muzzle of the rifle. He lifted his gaze and gasped out loud when he saw my face. "What in the world? You're…you're supposed to be dead!"

I smiled. I didn't know what it looked like, but it felt like a wicked smile. "So are you if you don't start talking."

I approached Mark and jerked him to his feet, then spun him around. After slinging my rifle, I cuffed his hands behind his back and shoved him toward what looked like a living room. I forced him into a recliner and palmed my rifle again, sweeping the house, looking for signs of life. "Who's here with you?"

"No one. I'm alone."

"If you're lying to me..." I locked the front door and made my way to the other side of the room to glance down a long hallway. All was quiet.

"My wife and girls left earlier for Gatlinburg," Mark called from his seat. "We go every year for the Fourth."

After I tossed my rifle to the sofa, I stood for a long moment looking down at Mark McNeal. He didn't look the least bit intimidated. I pulled the coffee table in front of the recliner and sat on a corner, facing him. "Why'd you stay behind?"

"If you're going to arrest me, take me down to the detention center and book me already."

"We're not going anywhere until you tell me who orchestrated the events that transpired today. I want the name of the mastermind, I want to know the names of everyone involved, and I want to know what the hell I did to become the fall guy."

"I'm not telling you shit."

"You're going straight to the needle for killing the governor."

"I didn't kill the governor."

"Right." I crossed my arms. "Your wife—what's her name again? Jennifer? What a pretty name."

Mark stared at me, hate glowing from his eyes.

"And the twins...aren't their names Maci and Traci?" I stood and strode around the living room. "I heard they were seventeen, which means they'll be tried as adults."

Mark scowled. "What are you talking about?"

"Not only will they be tried as adults, but they'll be put to death like common murderers." I nodded like I was positive. "Yep, they'll die alongside you for sure. And it's a shame because they had such a bright future ahead of them. And your wife, I'm betting she'll die in jail before her—"

"Leave them out of this!" Mark's face was red. "They had nothing to do with anything."

"I can prove otherwise." I stepped back in front of him and plopped down on the coffee table again. "What would you do if I told you my officers interviewed several people within the last few hours, including Pauline Cain and Julie Rupe, who say your wife and daughters knew exactly what you were up to, but did nothing to stop y'all?"

"You're bluffing."

"Really? Just like your wife overheard you talking to someone yesterday about killing me before the weekend."

Mark's eyes shifted briefly.

"Yep, your wife's talking. She's running around town telling all kinds of secrets."

"She doesn't know anything!"

"What do you think Malcolm will say when I tell him I ran into your wife yesterday and she warned me not to go pick up the governor in my Tahoe?"

I saw the hesitation in Mark's eyes. I stood and pulled the throw-away phone from my pocket and made a show of dialing a number. I put the phone to my ear. "Hey, Susan? It's Clint. Let the mayor know Jennifer McNeal was the one who warned me about the bomb under my Tahoe. Tell him she's on her way to Gatlinburg and that she left…" I put the phone to my shoulder and glanced at Mark. "What time did they leave for Gatlinburg?"

"Wait! Stop!" Mark McNeal dropped to his knees in front of the coffee table, tears welling up in his eyes. He cast a nervous glance toward the corner of the room.

I followed his gaze to where his phone lay partially covered by a curtain.

"Please," he whispered. "I'll talk. I'll tell you whatever you want to know. Just leave my family out of this. They'll be killed, and they don't deserve to die. They didn't know anything. They're innocent."

"Susan, stand by," I said into the dead line. "Hold off for now."

I shoved the phone into my pocket, walked to Mark's phone, picked it up. The timer was running and the name displayed at the top of the screen was Malcolm. I ended the call, then turned to Mark. "Were you talking to Malcolm Landry when I came up?"

Mark nodded. "You've got to get me out of here. He'll kill us both."

"Don't worry about Malcolm. I'll take care of him. I just need you to tell me what his involvement is in all of this. As it stands now, this is all on you, Randall, Hays, and Daniel."

Sweat pooled on Mark's forehead. "Look, I'll talk, but you've got to get me out of here and you've got to get my family someplace safe."

"Okay."

"Say it—say you'll take them someplace safe. If Malcolm thinks for a second they know something, he'll have them killed."

"I'll take your family someplace safe, but if you try to bullshit me—even once—the deal is off and I'm turning them over to Malcolm." I straddled the coffee table. "Now talk."

Mark sighed. "Where do you want me to start?"

"Whose idea was it to kill the governor?"

"I don't know."

"That's it—no deal." I started to pull the phone from my pocket.

"I'm not bullshitting you!" Mark looked desperate. "It was after the funeral. After our kids were murdered. We were all sitting there talking and one of us—I'm not sure who said it—one of us said the governor had to pay for what he did. There was no hesitation. We all agreed. We were so grief-stricken that I don't think we really knew what we were saying. Besides, we'd all had a bit to drink. A few days later, I get a visit from Malcolm and Walter and they're asking me if I was serious when I said I wanted the governor dead."

"Wait a minute. Walter who?"

"Moore."

"The assistant district attorney?"

Mark took a deep breath and exhaled long and slow. Shoulders drooping, he finally said, "It was Walter who killed Hays."

I sucked wind. "Walter Moore? No way. He's a lawyer."

"He's crazy...and extremely dangerous. He was a sniper in the military." Mark shook his head. "He's unstable, unpredictable. He scares the shit out of me. He killed Hays simply because Hays threatened to go to the cops. At one of our meetings, Hays was saying he couldn't go through with it. He tried to walk out of the meeting...said he was turning himself in." Mark stared off like he was seeing everything happen all over again. "Walter walked right up to him and shot him in the head. Just like that. No warning. Pulled a pistol out of his waistband and put Hays down."

"Hays couldn't go through with killing the governor?" I asked.

"No, he was fine with killing the governor. That wasn't the problem."

"Then what was it?"

Mark indicated toward me with his head. "You...you were the problem. He didn't like that we were setting you up for it. He said you were an innocent man...that you'd been through the same thing we'd been through and the governor had to pay for what he did to you, too."

I took a long look inside of myself, then sighed. "The governor was an innocent man, too. He wasn't responsible for the murders of your kids, just like he wasn't responsible—"

"Bull shit!" Mark lunged to his feet, jerking on the cuffs that bound his wrists together. "That sonofabitch worked night and day to get laws passed that limited what cops could do and then he went out and publicly drummed up hatred for the police. It was his actions and his rhetoric that caused the riots two years ago—so, hell yeah, it's his fault my daughter is dead!"

"Wait a minute. I thought your daughter was in the national guard. I thought she died overseas in the war."

Mark shook his head as he sank back to the recliner. "She did two tours in Afghanistan—they all did—and came out unscathed. After all of that, she ends up dying right here in her home state. Can you believe that shit?"

Confused, I asked what happened.

"After the riots started, the governor sent in the national guard to support law enforcement."

"Yeah, we had some come to the city, but they only acted in a support role. They secured the precincts, while we worked to quell the unrest and stop the looting and burning. They weren't in any real danger."

"No real danger?" Mark scoffed. "Tell that to those of us who lost our kids."

"I didn't mean it that way." I leaned close, stared into Mark's painful eyes, felt like I was looking at my own reflection. "Tell me what happened."

"Gina was somewhere up north with Little Randall, Allen, Bragg, and Devin."

"Who're Bragg and Devin?"

"Bragg was Daniel's boy, and Devin was Walter's kid. They were eating at a local diner when a group of protesters marched through the street, but these weren't any regular protesters. These thugs were looking for trouble and started looting a gift shop across from the diner. Gina heard screaming and went outside to see what was going on. The old lady was trying to defend her shop, but one of the thugs hit her across the head with a bat." Mark's voice cracked; he squeezed his eyes shut. "The boys tried to stop Gina, but she ran to help the old lady. That's when someone in the crowd opened fired with a fully automatic. Killed all of them, including three of the other customers in the diner."

Tears were flowing freely down Mark's face. I stared at the floor.

"They never found who did it," Mark said between gasps for air. "But if you ask me, it was like the governor himself pulled the trigger."

I didn't say a word for a while, didn't argue. When Mark had regained most of his composure, I asked, "What did I have to do with all of this?"

"You hated the governor like we did. I mean, from what Malcolm said, the governor indirectly killed your wife and daughter, so you had as much hatred for him as we did. Malcolm had already made plans for the ribbon cutting to take place on the anniversary of our kids' murders and he'd arranged for the governor to come down to the ceremony. He hired you as the chief of police to make sure you'd go get the governor."

"Why didn't you or one of the others strap a bomb to your car and go pick up the governor yourself?"

"I have a wife and kids. We all do." Mark nodded toward me. "You had no one. We even read some report that said you were suicidal. We figured we were doing you a favor."

"You sick bastard!" I punched Mark squarely in the nose, snapping his head back. I winced at the pain in my knuckles from punching my floors earlier. I stood to cool myself. "Keep talking before I put a bullet in you right here and now!"

Mark McNeal coughed as blood poured into his mouth and he gasped from the pain. "I think you broke my nose!"

I grabbed my rifle and pushed the muzzle against Mark's left eyeball. "Tell me how y'all got the bomb under my Tahoe."

"Okay! Okay! I'll tell you everything!" Mark leaned his head forward when I removed my rifle from his face. "Daniel built the bomb. He did it in that old plantation house at the south end of town. Randall provided the new Tahoe. They secured it under the Tahoe, and Malcolm got you to get the Tahoe from the dealership."

"Wait a minute. I've been driving around for days with a bomb under my ass?"

Mark nodded.

"What about the gun that killed Hays and Kelly? How'd that get in—"

"Walter. He broke into your house and planted the gun and the containers from Daniel's warehouse."

"Who killed Kelly Dykes?"

"You did."

"Excuse me?"

"Hays butt-dialed someone when Randall and Walter were in the process of dumping his body. They must've dropped him or something to cause the phone to go off. They tried calling the number back, but the girl wouldn't answer. We all suspected it was his girlfriend, but none of us knew who she was until you blabbed it all over the police radio."

I glanced around the room. "You have a police scanner?"

Mark shook his head. "But Malcolm does. He kept tabs on every step of your investigation. As soon as that address was called over the radio, he had Walter go out there and silence her before you could get to her."

I was thoughtful. "But what about the McKenzie boys? Did Walter kidnap them, too?"

"Walter found them snooping around and thought they might've seen something, so he tied them up and left them for dead." Mark frowned. "That's when I knew Walter was losing it—he was going too far. I tried to stay away from him. I didn't know what would set him off next."

I squinted. "So, it was Walter who tried to kill me?"

Mark shook his head vigorously. "He wasn't trying to kill you. If he wanted you dead, you'd be dead. No, he couldn't kill you because we needed you to be our patsy."

I mulled over what I'd just learned. A thought occurred to me, something that had been bugging me all day. "Why'd y'all pick me as the fall guy? I mean, there must be hundreds of people who hate the governor just as much or more than I do."

Mark lowered his eyes. "At one of the—"

A twinkle of glass and a slight movement of the curtain to my left brought my head around. The sound was immediately followed by a sickening splat. Out of the corner of my eye, I saw Mark's head contort as blood, bone, and brain matter sprayed across the back of the recliner.

CHAPTER 51

I instinctively dropped to the ground and scurried across the floor as bullets from a fully automatic weapon ripped through the windows of the front room. Projectiles splattered against the walls and furniture. My pistol was already in my fist. I hugged the floor, trying to keep as much furniture between me and the front wall as possible. I lifted my head to get a bead on my rifle, but a heavier report sounded outside and a single bullet whizzed by, nicking my cheek. *That's a sniper rifle!*

I tried to bury myself into the floor and grabbed my face. Blood poured from a furrow that had been burned into my flesh. I craned my head to listen. There were at least two shooters—one spraying the house with fully-auto fire and another delivering pinpoint accurate sniper fire. Walter and Malcolm? What about Daniel? Was he involved like Mark suggested?

I crawled down the long hallway, my hand leaving smudges of blood on the plush carpet. I turned into the first opening I found and landed in what appeared to be a game room. A pool table was at the center of the room and the heads of large game lined the high walls.

A lamp was on in the corner of the game room and I darted for it, staying low. I reached up with a sticky hand and flipped the switch to off, then paused. I spat on my bloody hand and wiped it partially clean on my jeans. My shirt collar was wet. After I pulled off my vest, I lifted my shirt to dry my face. It was no use. Blood continued to flow freely.

I realized just then that the shooting at the front of the house had ceased. It could mean the shooters had changed positions or were moving in. *I need to get out of here. This is a deathtrap!*

I crawled the rest of the way to the door, threw the deadbolt, eased it open. Warm air rushed in. The night was quiet. I squeezed through the door and made my way to the corner of the house to my right…stopping every few feet to listen for danger. Once I made it to the corner, I quick-peeked around it and could see the street at the front of the house. A narrow patch of grass and a cyclone fence was all that separated Mark's house from the neighbor's house. If I could make my way through the neighbor's backyard, I knew I could get to Susan's truck.

I listened for any sound of movement and heard none. I shoved off the house, darted across the patch of grass, and dove over the fence. I landed on my hands, then collapsed my arms into a shoulder roll. Just then, the night erupted in fully automatic gunfire. Grass and dirt sprayed in my face as I rolled. The shooter was somewhere behind the houses to my left. I could tell from the report of the rifle that I was dealing with a third shooter.

I ran for my life across the backyard, bullets spraying the area around me. The night was as black as the darkest Louisiana coffee ever brewed, and I couldn't see where I ran. Suddenly, my hip smashed violently into an immovable object and I hurled headlong over what felt like a cement picnic table. I crashed to the ground with a grunt. I scrambled to my knees and sought refuge behind a nearby tree.

Without looking—and violating everything I'd ever learned about firearms safety—I shoved my pistol around the tree and fired in the direction of the third shooter. Once, twice, three times I fired. It didn't seem to faze the shooter, as he sprayed the area with three-round bursts in response. Bright flashes of orange lit up the area surrounding the gunman with each shot.

I slid to a standing position against the tree, careful to keep it firmly between me and the bad end of the gunfire. My hip ached. I gripped my pistol. The shooter had stopped firing, but I knew he was still out there, just waiting for me to make a sound. I figured he couldn't see me, so as long as I remained silent I should be relatively safe.

Suddenly, the area around me was flooded in brightness. I jerked my head up, realizing someone had turned on the patio lights. I squinted.

A large man in tacky pajama pants pushed the sliding door open and stepped outside. He held a shotgun in his hands, staring wildly about. "What the hell is going on out here?"

"Sir, get inside! There's a gunman—"

Another three-round burst exploded behind me and mowed the man down. I darted around the opposite side of the tree and saw a large boat sitting on a trailer at the back of the yard. It was at least twenty-five yards away. Without making a sound, I sprinted for the boat, my pistol leading the way. After I'd taken a dozen steps, I began firing as I ran. The gunman wasn't expecting it. I moved to my right as I ran, putting the boat between us. He cut loose with another three-round burst, and I saw his exposed head and shoulders in the glow from the patio behind me.

I dove to a prone position, planting my clenched palms on the wet grass. Bullets kicked up grass in my face, but I steadied my hands and took careful aim. I fired once and the shooting stopped. I scrambled to my feet, rushed to his position, nodded. My bullet had ripped through the bridge of his nose, silencing him forever.

Something chirped in my pocket, and I moved behind the boat and put the phone to my ear. I surveyed the area. "Hello?"

"What's going on?" It was Susan. I heard sirens in the background. "We're getting reports of gunfire from Mark McNeal's neighborhood. Tell me it's not you!"

"Mark's dead." I hunkered down behind the boat and pulled the shooter onto his back, then shone the light from the phone in his face. "And so is Daniel Blackley."

"Where are you, exactly?"

I gave her my position. "There are at least two more shooters out there. I'm betting Malcolm Landry and Walter Moore."

"I'll be there in a second. I've got William, Melvin, and Beaver with me. Hang tight and stay on the—"

The phone exploded in my hand. Shards of plastic peppered the side of my face. It was followed shortly by a deep boom from the sniper rifle that had taken out Mark. My left hand burned. Blood oozed into my left eye. I dropped to my face and scurried to the opposite side of the boat. I lay panting, with my gun gripped in my right hand. I dared not peer around the side of the boat. Sirens blared, drew nearer. I knew Susan would come under attack as soon as she arrived.

I shoved my pistol into my waistband, dragged Daniel closer, and pulled the AR-15 from his lifeless hands. I removed the thirty-round magazine and weighed it in my hand—half full. While cursing myself for discarding my load-bearing vest, I felt around on Daniel's belt, until I located a pouch with two more magazines. I snatched them up just as tires screeched in front of the houses.

I pushed off with my legs, running as fast as they could carry me in the direction of the sniper's location. I zigzagged as I ran, letting the patio light guide my path. Gunfire erupted from the street and I heard the boom of the sniper rifle. He had moved!

I ran toward the sound and rounded the corner between two houses, holding the rifle in my right hand, cradling my bloody left hand against my chest. I had almost reached the street when the sniper rifle exploded again and light flashed in front of me. Before I could stop myself, I stepped on something soft that rolled under my feet. I fell forward—the rifle flying from my grasp. I landed on top of the sniper with a grunt.

The sniper came alive beneath me, twisted around and shoved me to the side. I rolled away and pushed myself to my feet. He was on me in a blink and kicked me right in the gut. The force of the kick sent me reeling into the front yard, where a fierce gun battle was taking place. The sniper lunged toward me and streetlights glinted off steel and his ghostly face. It was Walter Moore and he had a crazy look in his eyes.

I moved away from him, calling out, "Walter, it's over! The governor's dead. You can stop now. You don't—"

Walter slashed at me with the long knife. I shoved my arms up in front of my face and felt the sharp blade fillet my left forearm. The burn was intense. Blood poured freely from the gaping wound.

"I got him," someone called from my left. It sounded like Melvin. "Malcolm's down!"

"The bastard got Beaver," Susan bellowed.

Walter cast a concerned glance in their direction, then turned and ran for his rifle.

"Stop!" I stumbled forward, reaching for my waistband—my pistol was gone!

Before I could react, a dark figure flashed by me and knocked me sideways. I righted myself just in time to see Walter turn with the rifle in his hand. Before he could pull the trigger, the figure leapt into the air and came down on him with a thunderous punch to his jaw. Walter's knees buckled and he fell hard to a seated position. Even from behind, there was no mistaking the braided cornrows pulled into twin pigtails behind Susan's head. She shot a knee to Walter's chin and he dumped onto his back, where he lay gasping for air. Without hesitation, Susan lifted a boot high into the air and brought it down on Walter's throat.

I had seen a lot of violence during the course of my law enforcement career, but the sight of Walter's throat being crushed startled even me. Susan stared down at him for a long moment, then turned and rushed to me, steadied me in her arms. "Are you okay?"

My jaw was slack. I stared from her to him, back to her.

"He had a knife in his hands," she said casually. "I didn't have time to draw my gun and shoot him."

CHAPTER 52

Susan watched as the emergency room doctor stitched my arm. They had fixed my hand first, and that took the longest.

"I've had a few of those in my lifetime," Susan said.

I grunted. "I'm sure this is a weekly occurrence for you."

When the doctor was done, I tested the bandage. Nice and snug. I held up my hand. "Doc, will this heal up?"

"We dug out most of the shrapnel from the phone, but some of it will have to stay in place because of the proximity to the nerves." He nodded. "You might set off some metal detectors, but I think you'll regain full use of your hand."

"How'd your debriefing go with Reginald Hoffman?" Susan asked when the doctor had gone.

"Good. He said he'll meet with the district attorney and they'll present the evidence to the grand jury, but he said everything looks good for us."

"He told me the same thing." Susan cocked her head to the side and winced. "He did seem somewhat bothered by the fact I killed Walter Moore with a heel stomp to the throat, so I had to explain to him that when you're justified in using deadly force, it can come in any form."

I shuddered. "I'm still weirded out about that."

"You'll get over it."

I frowned. "So, what was Beaver doing with y'all?"

Susan hung her head, biting her lower lip. "I have to apologize to you. We were wrong about Chloe."

"Wrong? What do you mean?"

"She *was* doing her job last night—interviewing a source. Beaver called her anonymously and told her he had information on the Hays Cain murder investigation. He knew if he identified himself she would never go for it, so he disguised his voice to sound like some old woman."

"Did he have information?"

"Yeah, he did, but it was false. The mayor convinced him that you had killed Hays Cain and Kelly Dykes. He told Beaver there was strong evidence against you and that the sheriff's office was fixing to move in on you." Susan pulled the doctor's stool next to my bed and plopped onto it. "The mayor needed a narrative to feed to the media, so he played Beaver like a fiddle. He knew Beaver was still in love with Chloe, so he made Beaver believe she was in danger with you."

I shook my head, mouth agape. "And she fell for this line of shit?"

"Not at first, but then Beaver took her to the mayor, and he told her the same thing." Susan spun a complete circle in the chair, but stopped herself abruptly. "Oh, and Melvin's bringing Achilles home for you. In fact, they should be there already."

I felt my face light up. "How is he?"

"He looks like you—a little banged up, but handsome as all hell. The vet took good care of him, like I told you she would. She said he's a tough puppy and he pulled through the surgery as well as any she's ever seen."

"I can't wait to see him. It seems like weeks since—"

"Oh, my God! Clint!" I turned to see Chloe standing in the doorway to my hospital room, her hand over her mouth. Tears streamed down her face like a sparkling waterfall. She rushed to my side and threw herself on my chest. "I'm so sorry I doubted you!"

I caught a glimpse of Susan's face and, for a brief moment, thought I detected a hint of jealousy. She stood and nodded. "I'll leave you two to"—she waved her hand over us—"do whatever it is that y'all do."

I wrapped my good arm around Chloe and pulled her close. I stared deep into her eyes, unsure how to feel or what to say. "Well, I doubted you, too, so I guess that makes us even, don't you think?"

Chloe started to explain, but I pushed my finger to her lips. "It's okay. Let's put it behind us."

"But I feel like I need to explain."

"I'd rather not talk about it."

Chloe frowned, but nodded. She stayed with me until I was discharged and then drove me home. I nearly ran up the steps when we arrived, quickly unlocking the door. Achilles pulled himself to his feet and waited for me to open his crate. I dropped to my knees and grabbed him up in my good arm.

"Y'all look like twins," Chloe said, pointing to our matching bandages.

Achilles' bowls were filled with fresh water and food.

"Melvin took care of it," Chloe said.

"I wish he'd cleaned my house while he was at it." I surveyed the damage from the search warrant. Sofa cushions had been sliced to shreds. The stack of mail and paperwork on my table had been strewn about, littering the floor. My vodka bottles had been opened and poured out. "Cops are such assholes!"

Chloe nodded. "But you're my asshole."

I laughed and led her to the bedroom. It was no different. Everything was a mess. Achilles settled in the corner of the room and went to sleep. I dug around until I found clean sheets and Chloe helped me make my bed. I then glanced toward my bathroom. "I need a shower."

Chloe's eyes twinkled. "Need some help?"

I smiled and nodded.

Chloe sauntered over to me, grabbed my hand and led me to the bathroom. Once inside, she pushed the door shut and guided me to the center of the room. She reached under my shirt and placed her cold hands against my stomach, gently slid them upward, lifting my shirt. When her hands reached my chest, she grasped the edge of my shirt and pulled it over my head and tossed it aside. She tucked her blonde hair behind her ears, leaned forward, kissed my chest.

I moaned and wrapped my hands behind her back. She kissed lower and lower on my chest, then reached for my belt.

CHAPTER 53

Sunday, July 6

"Why do you have to work today?" I watched as Chloe snapped her bra in place and then shimmied into her jeans.

"Because I have bills to pay." She searched the floor for her shirt. "Why do I always lose my clothes over here?"

I used my left elbow to push myself to a seated position, then I got up and padded across the floor to the bathroom. I caught Chloe's eyes following me and smiled. When I stepped out of the bathroom, she was dressed.

She frowned. "It sucks that I have to leave."

"I know how it is. You don't get to pick when a story will happen—just like I don't get to pick when someone will die."

"Thanks for understanding." She kissed me and hurried out the door.

I pulled on my boxer briefs and stepped out the back door with Achilles. He moved gingerly around the backyard, as though testing his muscles. When he was done, he limped back into the house, then curled up in the corner of the kitchen. I sat beside him for a long time, scratching his ears and talking to him. Once he fell asleep, I got dressed and surveyed the mess in the kitchen.

"Well," I said, "I guess you're not going to clean yourself."

I started to push my papers into a pile on the floor when a knock sounded at the front door. I tossed the papers on the table and strode across the living room to open the door. It was my father-in-law. "Hey, Nick, how's it going?"

"I'm good. I just wanted to drop by and see how my favorite son-in-law was doing."

"As well as can be expected." I held up my bandaged arm. "This thing won't stop itching and it's driving me crazy. Other than that, everything is perfect. How are you?"

"That's good." Nick walked into the kitchen, bent over and rubbed Achilles between the ears. Achilles barely moved.

"He's been taking it easy."

Nick nodded, taking in the disarray.

"I was just picking up the chaos from the search warrant. Now that I know how it feels to be on the other end of these things, I'll be sure to clean up my mess next time I run a search warrant."

Nick strode into the living room. "Damn, they tore this place apart, didn't they?"

"Yeah," I called over my shoulder. "You should send them a bill for the damage."

I grabbed the pile of papers from the table and walked to the garbage can. I started to drop the pile in the trash, but noticed the check Nick had given me when I first came to town. I snatched it from the pile and let the rest of the trash fall. I started to turn, when the signature at the bottom of the check caught my eye—it was the same signature as that of the notary on the deed to the plantation home. "What the hell?"

"What is it?" Nick asked from behind me.

"You lying bastard!" I spun around, but it was too late—Nick had an old single-action revolver in his hand and it was aimed directly at me. He stretched his thumb forward and cocked it. I held the check up. "You notarized the sale of the plantation house. You told me you knew nothing about it."

Nick nodded, his face stone cold and murderous. "My one regret in this whole ordeal is you thinking Michele betrayed you. That girl never betrayed anyone in her life. She was as honest and loyal as they came."

Sensing something was wrong, Achilles hobbled toward Nick, teeth bared. He issued a throaty growl. "No," I ordered. "Get in the room!"

Achilles hesitated, but continued growling. I gave the command a second time, and he finally obeyed.

I waited until he was in the bedroom and leaned to pull the door closed. The muzzle of Nick's revolver followed me. I lifted my hands, sighing as realization flooded over me. "So, it was your idea to set me up, wasn't it? You blame me and the governor for taking your only child away from you. They're all gone, and I'm the last straw. I was supposed to die in that explosion, but that didn't happen. You killed an innocent man. Now what? Are you going to get your cowardly hands dirty?"

"You took away the last thing that mattered to me, Clint Wolf. For that, you have to die."

"You know, it didn't make sense to me that Malcolm and all would want me dead. But now I get it. All this time you pretended to be grieving with me, but you were plotting against me. You shady bastard!" As I took a step forward, I shook my head. "You don't have the balls to pull—"

The shot was deafening. It felt like I'd been kicked in the stomach by a strong mule. I collapsed. As soon as my knees hit the floor, I heard glass break and a scream. My face twisted in confusion.

Nick didn't flinch. He stepped forward and cocked his revolver, then shoved the burning hot muzzle to my forehead. I smelled burning flesh and glared up at him. "Do it." I took a wheezing breath and straightened my shoulders proudly.

The explosion that followed was farther away than I'd expected. Nick's eyes widened; he hollered in pain. His cries were cut short by a second shot that entered the back of his head and lodged against the front of his cranium, causing a knot to form immediately.

Nick collapsed in front of me, and I sank to the ground beside him, struggling for air. I heard a female's voice screaming commands. It sounded like she was on the phone. My face rocked to its side on the floor and I stared out at the sunlight streaming through the front door. I noticed a broken dish and what looked like cake all over the floor. Something green and white was shoved into a piece of the cake. I squinted. It looked like the number thirty. I suddenly remembered it was my birthday. I grinned as I fought for air. *I made it to thirty.*

Footsteps pounded near, and I glanced up to see a pair of long, tanned legs approaching. I had to fight to get them to come into focus, but I could tell they were muscular.

"Clint!" The woman dropped beside me and pulled my head into her lap. Her dress was red—just like the blood oozing from my stomach.

I tried to talk, but couldn't.

"Clint, can you hear me? It's Susan. Hang on! Keep breathing. An ambulance is en route. Come on...keep breathing!"

I'd heard people who survived near-death experiences say they saw a bright light as they were dying. I smiled to myself because knew I wasn't suffering a near-death experience. I didn't see a bright light—I saw Susan Wilson wearing a dress..

BJ Bourg

BJ Bourg is an award-winning mystery writer and former professional boxer who hails from the swamps of Louisiana. Dubbed the "real deal" by other mystery writers, he has spent his entire adult life solving crimes as a patrol cop, detective sergeant, and chief investigator for a district attorney's office. Not only does he know his way around crime scenes, interrogations, and courtrooms, but he also served as a police sniper commander (earning the title of "Top Shooter" at an FBI sniper school) and a police academy instructor.

BJ is a four-time traditionally-published novelist (his debut novel, JAMES 516, won the 2016 EPIC eBook Award for Best Mystery) and dozens of his articles and stories have been published in national magazines such as Woman's World, Boys' Life, and Writer's Digest. He is a regular contributor to two of the nation's leading law enforcement magazines, Law and Order and Tactical Response, and he has taught at conferences for law enforcement officers, tactical police officers, and writers. Above all else, he is a father and husband, and the highlight of his life is spending time with his beautiful wife and wonderful children.

http://www.bjbourg.com